I0637074

L. M. GOLDER

The Hateful Heavy Heart

First published by L.M. Golder 2025

Copyright © 2025 by L. M. Golder

All rights reserved. No part of this publication may be reproduced, stored, or transmitted in any form or by any means, electronic, mechanical, photocopying, recording, scanning, or otherwise without written permission from the publisher. It is illegal to copy this book, post it to a website, or distribute it by any other means without permission.

This novel is entirely a work of fiction. The names, characters, and incidents portrayed in it are the work of the author's imagination. Any resemblance to actual persons, living or dead, events, or localities is entirely coincidental.

L. M. Golder asserts the moral right to be identified as the author of this work.

First edition

ISBN: 979-8-218-80158-8

Cover art by @algart / instagram
Editing by Britney Waldrop

This book was professionally typeset on Reedsy.
Find out more at reedsy.com

Dedicated to anyone who has ever felt like you aren't worth love. You are worth it. Always.

Contents

Foreword

⁓✦⁓

While this is a romance, please beware of the following content warnings: brief on-page sexual assault, cheating (not done by main characters), mention of abortion, homophobia, depression, anxiety, (lots of) open-door sex, pregnancy, neglect of a parent, death of a side character, and fatphobia. Please read responsibly and keep any potential triggers in mind.

Acknowledgments

I want to thank my husband, my mother, my siblings, and my friends for never giving up on me and for always encouraging me to fulfill my dreams as an author. Thank you to my beta readers, my ARC readers, and my amazing editor for helping put the finishing touches on this book. I couldn't have done this without all the support from these amazing people.

Prologue

14 MONTHS AGO

When he'd first spotted her at the bar, he hadn't imagined he would end the night with her in his bed. Her beauty struck him first. She'd wore a pair of dark denim jeans, a cream-colored chiffon sweater—one with a thinness that made her nipples faintly noticeable in the cool temperature of the pub—and a pair of sandals with several straps. She'd resembled a fairy with her soft, blue eyes, celestial nose, and red lips. Her hair was his favorite thing about her, the dirty blonde waves reaching just past her breasts.

However, it was her words after they'd ordered identical drinks that'd left him speechless.

With the hint of a smile stretching his lips, he'd said to her in his thick Italian accent, "I'm Ruggiero." Then, allowing himself to relax on the stool as they both were handed their Screwdrivers—hers heavy on the vodka, his heavy on the orange juice—he'd asked, "And you?"

She'd taken a small sip, eyeing him over the rim of the glass. He'd felt like he was being studied at underneath a magnifying glass, and thinking of himself as a test subject and her as the scientist only made him want her more. She'd set the glass down and sent him a devious grin. "I'm horny and slightly interested."

1

"No name?" he'd asked.

A roll of her eyes and the scrunch of her nose had made him raise a brow. "I can give you a stripper name." When he didn't reply, she'd added, "Listen, I would give you my name, but if sex with you is bad, I don't want you to attempt tracking me down to try and redeem yourself."

He'd coughed into his fist, stunned by her explanation. "Who said we're going to have sex?" He'd been worried that if he said the wrong thing, she would flee from the little grasp he had on her at that moment.

"I did. I heard Italians have big *salsiccia*." She'd taken another sip, and his cock twitched. It was then that he decided he wanted her, foul-mouthed and all. "Unless you don't live up to expectations."

He should have been insulted, but instead, her words had only dared him on. "I'm not worried about expectations, *bella*. I'm confident in the body I've been given." He leaned a little closer to her, bringing his voice down to a low whisper. "I just wouldn't want to split you in half with my cock."

She'd only smiled, the emotion in her eyes making him dizzy. "Try me."

The light-haired beauty found her way into his home, undressing in the light of his bedroom. Once naked, she climbed on the bed to straddle him reverse cowgirl and lowered herself onto him with a breathy gasp. A couple seconds passed while she adjusted to his size before her back arched and her hands gripped his thighs. Her heat clenched around him, and his eyes never left her as she parted her lips.

He thought she would moan, but instead, she said, "I've had bigger, but you'll have to do."

Going to the bar was a part of her weekly routine. On Thursdays after work, she would freshen up with a few sprays of perfume and a swipe of lipstick before driving to the heart of the city. That was how it had been for the past two months since her boyfriend had broken up with her. It wasn't out of desperation. No, it was out of the need to be satisfied. Sexual frustration only made her more irritated, less tolerable.

It was how she ended up in a stranger's bed tonight, the buzz of her drink still warm in her veins as she exhausted herself on top of a handsome man whose name she'd forgotten. All she remembered was that he seemed nice enough, too nice for her.

His hands were on her hips, keeping her steady. She couldn't see his face as she rode him, but that sat well with her. She never looked at their faces. It made it easier to focus on the task at hand.

The pressure built in her stomach, gradually undoing her. She couldn't deny how good he felt underneath her, inside her.

A breathy moan escaped her as she lowered herself back into him and then lifted herself again, repeating the process in a languid rhythm. His thrusts and the grip of her ass in his hands drew a cry from her.

A low moan parted her mouth as he thrust into her. He met her response with a breathy groan of his own. "Baby," he murmured, and he shifted as he sat up, his chest flush against her back.

His voice was a silvery baritone, laced with an Italian accent. She'd picked him for that very reason. Call her shallow, but she wanted to climax to the sound of him mumbling a string of Italian swears as he was nestled snugly inside of her.

The sensations were overwhelming her, pushing her towards the edge. He ditched the cheeks of her ass for her breasts, cupping them in each hand. As she moved on top of him, he kneaded at them, occasionally pinching a nipple. "A little faster," he encouraged.

Twenty minutes and several deep strokes later, she was working toward her second climax. As he held her body hostage, she quivered around him. She reached behind her and wrapped her arms around his neck, grinding down onto him.

His hand slid from her breast, trailing from her torso to the center of her parted thighs. She suppressed the urge to squeeze her thighs shut as she cried out loudly, the finger between her legs making relaxed circular motions. She knew it was only a matter of minutes until she came hard. He kissed her neck and held her firmly as she ground against his dick, forcing her to come around him.

Ruggiero groaned, his hands finding and kneading her breasts. "Fuck, baby," he breathed. "You're milking me."

She let her breathing return to normal before she lifted herself off him, the feeling of loss hitting her. She didn't once glance back at him as she bent over, retrieving her underwear from the floor.

"You should be a hooker," he told her. She furrowed her brow, but still didn't turn to face him. The humor was carried in his voice; however, the joke wasn't funny. Plus, it made her doubt her first impression of him.

Had her dick comment bothered him that much?

She snatched up her bra and placed the cups over her breasts. Before she was able to secure the garment, his fingers danced on her skin as he clasped the back of her bra. "I'd pay you to have sex with me every night."

Shaking her head in disbelief, she sauntered away from him to find her sweater. Once found, she didn't hesitate to pull it over her head.

"Undressing you felt like unwrapping a gift, especially when it revealed your soaking pussy."

With a sigh, she turned to look at him, her wavy dirty blonde hair brushing her face. He was annoying. Just slightly. "What's your name again?" she questioned, smiling to deliver the blow more softly.

She didn't have any shame in letting it be known she'd forgotten.

He raised an eyebrow, and his tongue flicked out as he wet his lips. He rid himself of the condom and redressed in his pair of boxer briefs.

"We'll have to do this again sometime," he replied. "Except I'd like to cum inside of you."

As casually as she could, she crossed her legs where she stood. If he stopped talking, it would make her departure easier. She grew up believing words had no true effect on her, but they did. They always did.

She gave it another go, taking a seat on the edge of the bed. "What's your name?"

"You can call me daddy." The words poured from the full, soft lips that had pleasured her throughout the night. He could definitely pass for a DILF with his thick brows, hazel eyes, and the five o'clock shadow dusting his face.

She frowned, her fingers playing at the ends of her sweater. "You into that?"

For the umpteenth time, he smiled at her. It was one of those smiles that threatened to make her lightheaded, dizzy even. She could get drunk from it. "I'm not, but I figured I could make a few accommodations if you were." He ran a hand through his dark hair. It was an undercut, she could tell that much, and it seemed that he made it a habit to taper the sides. "Ruggiero."

That was it. That was the name she'd forgotten. He didn't call her out on the fact that it'd slipped her mind. He only waited expectantly for her reply.

"Jace," she told him.

"Isn't that a boy's name?"

She stood up once again, shifting her focus to put her pants on so she could leave. "I'm sure my parents wanted a boy."

He sighed behind her. "Are you still planning on leaving, Jace?"

Her name was leaving his mouth sent shivers down her spine. It was soft, modulated. What would his lips on hers feel like? He'd only kissed her skin. "I am," she confirmed, spotting her pants lying in the corner.

"*Normalmente*, when someone has a one-night stand, they spend the night," he said with a chuckle.

"I might've considered sleeping over. However, you talk too much, and you ask too many questions. I'd leave in the morning regardless." Jace pulled her jeans up, forcing them over her behind. With an impatient sigh, she fastened the waist.

"You want to know why I'm talking so much?"

She turned around and looked at him expectantly. "Why?"

He clasped his hands and set them in his lap. He leaned against the headboard, putting his toned torso on display. Prints of her lipstick adorned his chest. Ruggiero was beautiful and her mind fell into the gutter when her eyes followed the thin trail of hair on his stomach to the waistband of his underwear. "I'm trying to stall your departure," he said simply. "*Sei bellissima.*"

It wasn't her first time being called beautiful, but she disagreed with it when it came to her. She was sexy, perhaps, but that's only because she knew how to work her sex appeal. But she knew she wasn't the prettiest face on the planet, let alone in Memphis, Tennessee.

She'd been in his room for much too long and she wished she had more alcohol that night. It would make it easier to brush over the things he was saying.

Jace was silent as she put her brown gladiator sandals onto her feet. From the corner of her eye, she could see Ruggiero slide his legs into sweatpants. "Do you mind if I walk you to your car?"

She nodded because frankly, she did mind. She was a big girl; she could walk herself out.

"Great." He pulled on a pair of socks and then slipped on a pair of boat shoes. "I would say that I cared, but I don't. It's dark outside and this neighborhood isn't the safest."

"Then why do you live here?"

"Because I can take care of myself." He sauntered toward the white wooden door to his bedroom and held it open for her. With a polite smile, Jace brushed past him and started down the stairs.

She ignored the slight pain between her legs when her thighs brushed together as she rushed down the stairs. He was the biggest she'd had in a while—ever, really. She'd had only one other person who was bigger than him, and she hadn't been able to take him. The pressing reminder of Ruggiero's dick only increased her need to squeeze her thighs together.

The tall brunet followed her outside, where he wordlessly waited as she let herself inside her 2003 Acura. She examined his strong, muscular crossed arms and gave him an appreciative smile through the window as she started her car.

Ruggiero gave her a small wave as she backed out of his driveway. The gesture was cute, and he carried his confidence well, but Ruggiero was simply a one-time thing like everyone else.

Chapter 1

JACE

"Sometimes, you are the most disrespectful person I know," my mom said with a scowl. She picked up her cup and brought the rim to her lips.

I resisted rolling my eyes. Having dinner together was something she insisted we do on Sunday nights every two to three weeks. She said it was her way of staying in touch with her children. There were a million things I could be doing on a Sunday night that would be ten times better than having her sit and ridicule me over takeout.

I responded to her remark with a painfully faked smile. "Like mother, like daughter."

In true Jackson style, he remained silent as my mom and I talked, seeming engrossed with his beef and broccoli.

"No, Jace, you have no filter," she clarified. With her free hand, she combed through her dirty blonde hair, pushing it up and out of her face. While still a very pretty woman, it was clear she had aged, her blue eyes framed with crow's feet. "I'm surprised you haven't said anything tonight that's just downright rude."

I held back a laugh. Nothing was funny except her audacity. "You're my mother. I would never say anything rude to you."

She snorted. "Remember that time when you told me I was trying too hard to look young the night I went on a date with Markus?"

Even Jackson laughed at that one. We could've been twins, only he was a year younger than me.

I failed to hold back my laugh. "That's because you wore that unflattering dress. It was meant for someone about two decades younger than you."

My mom frowned as Jackson shrugged, shoving a forkful of chow mein in his mouth.

"If it helps," I added, "you look pretty hot today." She shook her head, giving me a semi-smile. That was better than her usual scowl.

Our Sundays always followed this pattern. While my mom set the table, either Jackson or I would order the food. Whoever placed the order got to relax while the other picked up the food. No matter when he arrived, he'd make some dirty joke. I would laugh and make one of my own, and then my mom would comment on how ladylike I wasn't. I didn't understand why she liked sounding like a broken record.

Dinner ended around ten o'clock. My mom informed us she had to work early in the morning because she took someone else's shift. It was the earliest dinner had ended in a while, but I wasn't complaining. The quicker I could get back home, the longer I'd get to sleep.

Being a nurse required that I get lots of sleep and on average, I barely slept for five hours.

I bid my goodbyes by telling Jackson he could kiss my ass and giving my mom a hearty hug. My mom pulled me aside, only stopping once we were in the dim lighting of the hallway. "How are you feeling?" she asked.

Not this again.

I hated when she did this, acted like I was some wounded child. "I'm fine, Mom."

"Are you sure? I know how much you loved Garret and I know how much—"

I raised a hand, silencing her before she could say something else stupid. She had a bad habit of trying to instill false sadness in me. "It's been over a year, and it was a mutual decision to break things off. I'm fine," I assured her. Sure, there were days when I missed having someone around, but I was managing.

Most of the time, it seemed like my mom missed Garret more than I did.

"Jace." She sighed. "I know you're my big, strong girl. I just want you to find a nice man and be happy."

I laughed, starting to walk away. "If you mean men who know how to shut me up in the bedroom, then I'm already the happiest woman in the world."

"Jace," she snarled. She grabbed my arm, yanking me back. "I don't mean sleeping around. I mean settling down. Twenty-seven is too old to be constantly spreading your legs for men who don't care about you."

I groaned. I was more than annoyed with her at this point. "And forty-nine is too old to be doing the shit you do to turn on men who are most likely cheating on their wives."

I didn't insult her often, but it was hard to resist Especially when she spent most of the time she claimed was for catching up to ridicule me. Why did she always try to make it sound like I was a whore? I didn't mess with taken men, I never had unprotected sex, and I was single. I was hurting no one.

I snatched my arm away from her and hastily walked to the end of the hallway. If she wanted to act like a child, then so be it. She could act like a child without me being there. I turned the corner, only to be grabbed once again.

10

"That was a low blow, even for you, Jace," Jackson said, his tone low. Guess he didn't want mother dearest to know he'd heard the entire conversation.

"Why were you even listening?" I asked, crossing my arms.

He freed my arm and smirked. "Just in case I had to stop you from scratching her eyes out like when we were in high school."

Jackson knew better than anyone that even though my mom and I were mostly cordial now, we had our fair share of disagreements in the past.

"Whatever." I pushed past him. He didn't follow me. I didn't expect him to. With my hand on the doorknob, I sighed and turned back to him. "Good night. I love you. Don't lie and tell Mom that I'm sorry."

"I love you, too. It's started to rain, so drive safely," Jackson said, lingering in the space between the hallway and the foyer.

I felt bad that I'd be leaving Jackson to wipe my mom's tears away, but the night wasn't supposed to end that way. She didn't need to bring up my ex-boyfriend or what she loved to call my "sloppy sex life." Though I didn't shed any tears, she did hurt my feelings. Just a little bit.

I nodded reassuringly. "Always. Tell mom I love her."

I made sure to close the door firmly behind me. Even in what could be considered a prestigious neighborhood, people had a knack for inviting themselves into your home to "see what you had."

It took me half an hour to make it back home. It didn't usually take that long, but I didn't want to risk dying on the highway on the slick roads.

My apartment was nice and cozy. I hated that I had to use my father's money for the down payment, but I handled all the other expenses afterward. Taking any of my parents' money wasn't something that I wanted to do, especially now that the two were divorced and no longer had joint funds.

As I kicked my shoes off by the door and locked myself in, I toyed with the thought of calling my mother and apologizing. I would have, but I didn't know how to genuine apologize for something I had no remorse for saying. Hell, if I were more sensitive, her constant reminders that I had to look for outside sources to give me gratification would've made me cry, too.

I sauntered through the dimly lit living room. Two out of the four light bulbs had blown out and even with a ladder, I was too short to reach them.

Jackson promised to stop by and replace the bulbs, but Jackson was never good at keeping promises. Knowing this, I hadn't held him to it.

If it were daytime, I would've utilized the beauty of natural light by pulling the shades to the side. But because it wasn't, I settled for walking to the kitchen and using the refrigerator light to aid me in my search for a late-night snack.

Growing up, my pediatrician had always expressed to me that snacking late at night was a factor in weight gain. Considering most of my extra pounds went to my hips, I should've cared. I didn't and I had hoped that at least some of it would sneak its way to my boobs.

I was tired of my little bitty almost-B-but-A-cup-boobs.

I grabbed a handful of cheese crackers from the pantry and shut the fridge door. My bare feet padded against the polished wooden floors as I headed to my bedroom.

Tomorrow I would work again, taking care of old women that reminded me far too much of my mother and my late grandmothers. Of all the women I would aid tomorrow, I couldn't wait to see Cleo, one of my favorite patients.

At seventy-eight years old, she'd be older than my grandparents had they still been alive. Seven years ago, a stroke and a subsequent spinal injury left her paraplegic. Even though I'd cleaned up her piss more times than I could count, I still loved her to death. She never failed to make me laugh.

Cleo was beautiful. Her eyes were the color of the sky during a thunderstorm. Her hands, while small and wrinkled, were soft. Her wavy brown hair, highlighted with silvery grays, framed her gentle face. When I first met her nearly three years ago, her hair was thick. However, with age, her hair had thinned, and some had fallen out. That didn't stop her from asking me to comb it. She said it made her calm enough to sleep.

There was no doubt she'd ask about my mom and me tomorrow. I couldn't help but go on a rant about my mom after every Sunday dinner, but Cleo provoked it. Every time. As if she were my goddamned therapist.

Fortunately, I didn't mind pouring my heart out to her. I'd seen her broken way too many times for her to judge me, not that I thought she ever would.

What would I tell her when she asked what I said to make my mother cry? Even I had qualms about sharing the things I said out of rage. I knew I could be a bitch. I had a full night of promised sleep and potentially sweet dreams ahead of me. I couldn't waste those hours wondering what excuses I'd make for telling off my mom. I'd be surprised if I even made excuses.

In the comfort of my bedroom, I stripped my clothes off. I threw them in the laundry bin, making a mental note to wash the clothes in the basket by the end of the week. I only owned so many clothes, and most of my jeans and scrubs were currently taking refuge inside the basket.

I plugged my phone into the charger and climbed in bed after pulling on a pair of basketball shorts. Once upon a time, they'd belonged to Garret.

Maybe my mom was right. A year or so was a long time to be sleeping around with random people, but I was content. I would settle down eventually, as soon I could find someone who could handle my temper and everything that made me "unlovable," as Garret had called me.

I had my fair share of exes but never had one of them call me unlovable. Never had one of them said that it was because of my choice of words, my small breasts, or that I didn't bother to do *their* laundry. Not until him.

Quite frankly, Garret was a piece of shit. Believe it or not, I didn't even cry when we'd broken up. Over the past year, I learned that his dick wasn't even that great and his character was even worse. Sure, he made me happy for a while, but ultimately, the two of us weren't meant to be together.

I fell asleep with a small smile, thinking that maybe I'd find what I was looking for. Someone who gave me what I wanted in bed, had a heart, and wasn't put off by everything that made me *me*. It seemed hard to come by, but surely it was only a matter of time. It had to be.

Chapter 2

∾⧯⧯∾

JACE

Although being an RN meant the long hours and hands-on work, I loved my job at the nursing home. Patient care was grueling just as much as it was rewarding.

Glendshire was as cute and homely as it could be. The walls were painted in soft pastel colors and adorned by framed floral paintings. Most of the residents were old enough to be my grandparents and I loved them as if they were my own. Especially Cleo.

"Be nicer to the poor woman," Cleo said, frowning. She let out an alarmingly winded laugh, a grin stretching across her face. "She just wishes she had the stamina like you to take so many men."

I grimaced at the words. I handed her bowl of Cinnamon Toast Crunch so she could eat breakfast. Constantly, I urged her to eat something with more nutritional benefits, but Cinnamon Toast Crunch and Froot Loops were Cleo's favorites. Only on Fridays did she like to eat a full breakfast, specifically a platter of pancakes, bacon, and fried eggs. "Mhm. I think she just wishes I cared more."

Cleo eyed me for a few silent moments. "You do care. If you didn't,

15

you wouldn't still be thinking about what she said to you, Jace."

I groaned and put my hands over my face. The crunching sound of Cleo's chewing refused to let me escape into my head. I let out a sigh before putting my calm composure back together. "Cleo, I care that I made her cry. I don't care that she's upset I sleep around."

"All right, all right. If you don't care, it doesn't matter who else does. Remember that."

Truthfully told, when it came to strangers, I didn't care what people thought. But when it came to my own family, I hated to think that I was regarded so poorly. My dad, who I caught up with from time to time, thankfully never commented on my lifestyle. My mom, on the other hand, seemed very interested in what I did in my personal life. It was overwhelming and reminded me why I struggled so hard to get along with her; she never let me breathe.

"I guess you're right," I huffed. "C'mon, let's finish up eating so I can get you to art therapy."

"Oh, yes," she said excitedly, her face brightening with a smile. "I have things I need to talk to Theresa about." With that, she returned to enjoying her bowl of cereal.

I hadn't been to Ale You Need since I moved out of my old apartment nearly six months ago. It wasn't convenient for me to drive there anymore. Gas was simply too expensive. But one Monday night wouldn't hurt.

I missed the bar staff. I missed the familiarity. My visits to the bar had been the only constant thing in my life besides working once I broke up with Garret. That was another reason why I felt little remorse for insulting my mom. There was nothing wrong with sleeping around, though it happened considerably less since I'd moved.

As I walked into the bar and inhaled the sweet aroma, I already felt more at ease. Something was comforting about being in such a nostalgic place. This used to be the pot of gold for my lucky memories. I'd pick people up here and then create rainbows with them in their beds.

I took a seat at one of the bar stools and smiled at the bartender once I recognized who he was. "You're back?" he asked. "It's been a while, *brzydalu*."

Konrad had been calling me 'ugly one' since the day he first served me because he said I was grossly cute. He was very cute himself. He was Polish, had a bit of stubble, a pair of nice, green eyes, and curly dark brown hair. His nose was kind of crooked, but I was pretty sure it was that way because his nose had been broken in the past.

I would've flirted and maybe tried to get a roll in the hay with him if he didn't go on and on about the ex-girlfriend who'd left him for his stepbrother almost two years ago. I knew all about Agueda Rodriguez, her perky tits, and how her hips moved when she danced. Perhaps he'd finally let her go.

Then again it might be hard for me to let go of my ex if I saw them at every family function.

I sent Konrad a small smile and rolled my eyes playfully. "Only for today. This place is about twenty minutes from my new place."

"You still want the screwdriver?" Konrad asked. When I nodded, he got straight to work.

I tapped my fingertips on the counter as I waited, listening to Frankie Valli and the Four Seasons' "Can't Take My Eyes Off of You." It wasn't a common song choice in this bar, but it was one of those oldie-but-goodies.

Konrad returned with my drink the second a handsomely familiar man sat down next to me. I'd gone home with him previously, but he didn't seem to recognize me. I eyed him cautiously over the rim of my glass. The man paid me no attention. Konrad tended to him next, and I watched as he ordered the same drink as me.

Oh, I definitely remembered him.

It had been hard to forget that voice of his as he praised me through a climax. I took another long sip of my drink to give myself a little more courage before turning towards him.

If I had to say, I looked pretty damn good tonight. I'd showered quickly after work and changed into a baby blue sundress and a pair of chunky black sandals. When I'd told Cleo about my plans to go out, she took out her curling iron and spiraled my hair nicely. For the first time in ages, I'd worn a showering cap so I wouldn't ruin Cleo's masterpiece. I did, however, throw my hair into a low ponytail.

I considered approaching him with a cheesy pick-up line like they did in the movies, but that definitely wouldn't get me laid a second time. I decided on a simple, "What brings you out here tonight?"

He didn't turn towards me, but he raised an eyebrow and glanced at me for a hot second as he accepted his drink from Konrad.

Damn Konrad. I didn't think he'd ever seen me fail to woo someone.

"The mix of vodka and orange juice," I said. "Wonderful. Just wonderful. Does it make you feel as reckless as it does me?"

For the second time that night, he ignored me. I held back a scoff. I really didn't appreciate it. I wasn't even trying to fuck anymore. I just wanted to talk to him.

"Hey, you. Haven't we met?" I asked him.

It was then that he finally acknowledged my presence. He gave me a once over, looking at me from head to toe. I hadn't changed dramatically over the past year, besides maybe gaining a few pounds and getting a haircut. I took the moment to check him out, too.

He was still so fucking gorgeous. His hair had grown out, pushed back by his dark sunglasses and tucked neatly behind his ears. His black crew neck accentuated his toned arms. At his low grunt, I returned my eyes to his face. His nose was scrunched up as if he didn't like what he saw. "Maybe you're mistaking me for someone else. I've

18

never seen you before."

I licked my lips and took another sip. He'd never seen me? Bullshit. "Well, I don't think so. I'd never forget someone that told me I should be a hooker."

"It was a compliment," he retorted.

I rolled my eyes. "So, you *do* remember me?"

He scoffed. "Of course, I remember you. It's not every day that someone tells me I have a small cock."

"That was a year ago," I said, shrugging.

"That doesn't make it any better," he said, holding my gaze with defiance.

I stepped off of my stool and leaned toward him, reveling in the darkening of his eyes. I lowered my mouth to his ear and dropped my voice to a whisper. "I lied. Do you know how many times I fingered myself to the thought of you?"

He sent me an amused smile as his arm curled around my waist. His lips brushed my ear, his soft breaths fanning the shell. "I can't tell if you're being truthful or trying to get me to fuck you again."

"I'm being a hundred percent truthful, but if you'd like to dominate me again, I'm all for it."

"If I'm not mistaken, I think it was you who was in control last time," he said.

I shrugged and laid my head on his shoulder. "Take my word for it, you'll be in control next time. Maybe tonight?" I looked at him with hopeful eyes.

He spread his legs and pulled me between them as he slid his other arm around my waist, surrounding me in the smell of amber and musk. "Jason, right? I remember you had a boy's name."

"Roger, right? I know it started with an R."

"My name is Ruggiero," he reminded me, a soft smile on his lips. I fought the urge to run my hand along his jaw and feel his stubble

19

against my palm.

With a cocky smirk, I let my palms rest on his thighs. "And my name is Jace, sweetheart."

"You're adorable, even with your attitude," Ruggiero said.

"Don't act like you don't like it."

"Jace, I won't lie, I want to fuck you, but," he paused, placing a hand on my upper thigh, "I want to take you to dinner first if you could be nice for a second. I don't typically just fuck people without feeding them."

I took a step back. "So, you're turning me down?"

"Let's have dinner at Quintavi's first in a few days and then maybe I'll take you home and give you what you want." His warm palm slid from my thigh as he stood up. Before leading me away from the bar, he placed a twenty-dollar bill on the counter, paying for both of our drinks. "If you want to."

I pretended to think as he walked me toward the doors of the bar, his arm comfortably around my waist. "I might."

"How're you feeling?" he asked. Ruggiero released me and walked ahead to open the door. He then gestured for me to walk forward.

Such a gentleman.

"I'm horny and very interested," I said honestly. I didn't like to bullshit and I wouldn't do it for him.

"*Che bello.* Your car?" he asked. I pointed to my Acura sitting across the street. "Let me know if it ever breaks down. I'll fix it for you."

"Are you a mechanic or something?" He nodded as he slid his arm back around my waist, preparing to cross the street. "So, you're good with your hands?"

The smirk that stretched his lips was taunting. "Very much so. Would you like me to prove it to you?"

After our glasses were empty, we ended up in the backseat of my car, Ruggiero's hands on my inner thighs, spreading my legs apart, the

20

front seats pushed as far up as they could go.

Fuck, I'm glad my windows are tented.

His mouth was on me, sucking and letting his tongue toy with me. He eased two deliciously curled fingers inside of me. I arched into him involuntarily when he added a third, thrusting his fingers rhythmically.

I couldn't help the soft cries that left my mouth when he swirled my clit with his tongue. His fingers pushed deeper and curled again, stroking me inside out.

"Good," he mumbled against me. "Deep breaths."

A fourth finger slid into me. "Oh god," I whispered.

He chuckled deeply. "It's only me, Jace, but I appreciate the nickname."

Ruggiero's tongue covered my clit as he quickened the pace of his fingers. The sudden need to explode grew in the pit of my stomach, overwhelming me to the point of no return. My legs became putty and the rest of my body tensed as I came, closing my eyes and holding his head in place until the sensation passed.

"It looks like I've found a new pastime," he said. He ducked back in between my legs as I caught my breath. After a few seconds, he wiped his mouth with the back of his hand, as if he had just finished a meal. "Napkins?"

I exhaled softly. "Glove compartment."

He reached over the seats, his tall, lean body stretched out. I was dumb for not spending the night a year ago, but I wasn't dumb for telling him his dick was small. It gave him something to remember me by, and that something led threw us in each other's arms tonight.

Ruggiero returned to his knees in front of the seat with a handful of white napkins. "Your car is very resourceful." I watched as he wiped his mouth, and then his hands. With a clean napkin, he cleaned me off before he pulled the hem of my dress down, covering me back up.

"You're single, right?"

I fought the urge to roll my eyes. "Yes, Ruggiero, I'm single. Why else would I just let you do that?"

He put his hands up in defense. "I just wanted to make sure," he said, a smile playing on his face. "I never want to be a homewrecker."

"I love how you made sure after your good deed," I noted, "*and* your dinner invitation." I found my heels on the floor of the car, bending over to put them on.

"What can I say? I'm a gentleman." He joined me on the seat, sliding an arm around me. He tucked the napkins in the pocket of his shirt. "I'll trash those when I get out." After a deep sigh, he said, "I never thought I would run into you again, *bella*."

I sent Ruggiero a soft but genuine smile. "Me neither. But secretly I hoped I'd find someone like you one day, if not you. My mom wants me to settle down and find a nice man. And while I don't know about that first part, you are nice."

"You think I'm a nice man?" he asked.

"Besides saying I should be a hooker and being a little cocky, I think you're very nice," I said, amused at his question.

"*Grazie*. Thank you. That means a lot. Perhaps I'll think the same of you one day." He grinned, his words earning him a playful punch in the arm.

"Hey! I'm not that bad once you get to know me. I'm a sweetheart deep down." He raised an eyebrow. "Okay, maybe not so much, but most find it's part of my charm."

Ruggiero laughed, glancing down at his watch. "Okay, I can believe that."

"What time is it?" I said. As I came down from the high he'd given me, I thought of my early morning shift tomorrow.

"Almost eleven. And I've got to be at work at six."

"Shit. Me too." I'd almost forgotten that I signed up to come in early to help out.

Ruggiero made to get out of my car, placing his hand on the door handle. "So, about dinner, I'm thinking Quintavi's on Wednesday at eight would be nice."

I pretended to think for a moment. "I'll be there on the dot. I've heard that Quintavi's has good food."

"Good." He pushed the door open and got out. I followed suit, climbing out of the backseat. "I don't want to let you leave me this time," he said, opening the driver's door for me.

I lowered myself into the driver's seat and readjusted my seat. "I might still run for the hills. It's only our second time together."

"A guy can only hope. *Buonanotte, bellissima.*"

"Good night, Ruggiero. See you Wednesday." I waited until he'd closed my door and begun walking in the opposite direction to my car to turn my key in the ignition. The engine revved up and I started down the street.

I didn't deserve to have dinner with someone as nice as him. Selfishly, I didn't care. I wanted to see him again and I wasn't making the same mistake twice.

Chapter 3

JACE

The minute I stepped into the break room to eat, my phone rang. I didn't bother to look at the caller ID and answered my phone, my annoyance flaring at being called in the middle of my workday. "Hello?"

"Hey, Jace, it's so nice to hear your voice." I instantly recognized the person I hadn't heard from in over a year.

Nice job, dumb ass, I chastised myself.

"Garret, what the fuck do you want?" I spit out, strutting towards the fridge to get my lunch bag.

"If I'm not mistaken, I'd say that you're a little hangry," he said, chuckling.

Taking a deep breath, I ran a hand through my hair and grabbed my bag. "I'm going to ask you one more time. What the fuck do you want?"

"I—" he hesitated before continuing, "I'm sorry for the things I said to you. I miss you."

I slammed my lunch bag down on the table, unzipping it with

24

irritation. "Where's your fiancée Katherine?" There was more I could say about this Katherine, but I chose to keep my mouth shut.

"She's still around. Doesn't take away the fact that you and I were together for three years," he said, his tone suddenly serious. "I think about what I said to you often and even though—"

"That's enough," I said, cutting him off, unwilling to let this conversation go any further. "What we used to have is in the past and that's where it'll stay."

I hung up the phone, setting it face down on the table. I'd been at work since six and my stomach was aching.

Was he called because he regretted his actions over a year later? I shook my head, finally digging into my leftover pizza. The clocked showed that ten minutes of my break had already passed and I wasted them talking to that prick.

The worst part? The remaining four and a half hours of my shift would give me too much to ruminate on the call.

By the end of my shift, I was overwhelmed, wanting to do nothing more than quiet my mind.

Unlike most of my coworkers, I didn't have any best friends I could vent to or ask for advice, and I couldn't blame anyone but myself for that. There were a few teammates I'd become friends with when I played volleyball during high school, but I stopped answering their calls when I started undergrad, wanting nothing more than a new life.

It was moments like this that I wish I hadn't done that.

I spent the start of my evening watching *The Curious Case of Benjamin Button*, one of my favorite movies, with a bag of kettle corn in an attempt to make myself feel better. When that didn't work, I got dressed and left the house in search of a release.

I didn't like Screw It as much as I'd grown to like Ale You Need, but the place was around the corner from my apartment and the bartenders were friendly enough. It was a small hole-in-the-wall that served a menu of small bites to complement the bar.

As I waited for my drink, I ate my barbecue boneless wings and fries, dipping both in a generous side of ranch. Tonight, I ordered a sex on the beach with a double shot of vodka instead of my usual screwdriver. I wanted something sweet that would perk me up once and for all. I gave the bartender an appreciative nod when she returned with my drink. Wasting no time to bring the glass to my lips, I moaned in delight at its sugary peachy flavor.

In my peripheral vision, I noticed a woman sitting on the stool next to me. I caught a whiff of lavender and hints of menthol as if she'd been smoking. I tried to be subtle as I pushed my basket of food a little farther to the left.

"Sorry," she said, "I don't bite, though."

I turned to get a good look at her. Loose brown curls framed her face, drawing attention to her dark green eyes and her pretty lips. Looking back down at my food, I said, "Sure you don't."

"Not anyone that doesn't ask for it."

"Are you here for a drink or just to talk?" I asked, trying to decide if I was going to take my food and drink elsewhere or entertain the conversation.

"Both." At her admission, I met her gaze again. Before the bartender could walk away, she ordered an old-fashioned and hand the bartender her payment. Her lips curled downward in a frown as her attention returned to me, and she said, "I don't know if I'll have a job after today."

I popped a fry in my mouth. "Tell me about today then."

She didn't hesitate to dive into her job as a bank teller and how she wasn't meeting her quota. "I'm six months in and I'm still struggling with the learning curve." She downed her drink, taking no time to order another.

Orienting myself in the conversation, I ordered another drink, too. "It's nothing that I don't think you'll overcome."

"Thanks," she said with a small smile. She put her hand on top of mine, squeezing lightly. "I'm hoping you're right."

I laughed, feeling lighter with the alcohol coursing through me. "I usually am."

"I didn't ask before. How's your day been?" She scooted closer to me.

"Not great. That's why I'm here, eating and drinking by myself."

What started as listening to each other turned into comforting each other in different ways. The woman kissed me, moving her lips over mine slowly. I kissed her back, gripping her thighs closer to me.

I hadn't anticipated making it into her bed, no matter how nice her breasts and ass were. She pleasured me skillfully with her mouth and her fingers, bringing me to the edge. I gripped the sheets and closed my eyes as the pad of her finger circled my clit and two fingers continued to pump inside of me. "You're so fucking beautiful," she breathed. My mind floated as the firm wetness of her tongue met my skin.

All that existed was the mind-numbing pleasure of her head between my legs. Her tongue applied the just the right pressure, her fingers moving in tandem with the thrusts of my hips. It was so familiar, almost as familiar as Ruggiero's mouth on me. At the thought of them both, my orgasm crested and washed over me.

My breath slowed as my body relaxed, the effects of my drink and orgasm began to wear off. This moment was real. This moment was happening. For the second time tonight, I thought of Ruggiero and our impending date. As guilty as I felt in lieu of my date tomorrow, I couldn't go back and change what just happened.

I was ashamed of myself for yesterday. Sure, Garret's call had unnerved me, but there were other coping mechanisms, and I chose sex. The fact that I had a date hadn't even crossed my mind until I was already in the throes of passion.

Maybe I had a tiny problem with sex. Maybe it was a little pathetic how much I loved having sex. Maybe I needed to lay off a bit. But when I got flustered, I did stupid things. Last night, it was Garret. Tonight, it was my date with Ruggiero. I hadn't even picked out an outfit to wear.

The sound of Cleo's broke through my mangled thoughts. "What's got you so distracted, Jace?"

"Oh, you know, Cleo, just reevaluating my life and thinking of all the things I should have done as opposed to what I actually did."

"Are you alright?" she asked, her eyebrows furrowing. I hated it when she did that. Sometimes, she was very maternal, and it made me feel like shit. My silence answered her question. Cleo reached out and grabbed my arm, pulling me closer toward her bed. "What's the matter?"

I sighed. I wanted to cry. I wanted to cry so badly, and for what? Something I shouldn't even have shame about? "I have a date," I started. "I have a date tonight with the guy I told you about."

"The smoking hot one with the Italian accent? Why's that bad?" she questioned.

I let out a groan. "Because I ended last night with someone other than him. I got drunk and let someone else take me home."

"Since when do you care about what you do?"

"Why are you so inquisitive at this hour of the day?"

She laughed and rolled her eyes at me. "Because your actions last night are distracting you from taking care of what's in the present—cough, cough—me. I'm an old woman who can only move her upper body and run her mouth. I need your help and I need you to focus on me."

I snorted before smiling at her softly. "I forgot how selfless this job required me to be."

28

"Oh, hush," Cleo said, "you like it. And about your date with that boy, I don't want you worrying about it anymore. You'll be fine. Get rid of your guilt. You're a single woman. You can sleep with whoever you want before dates. For the sake of your conscious, just don't do it again and you'll be fine."

Cleo was right. I would be fine.

Cleo was wrong. I wouldn't be fine.

It was a quarter until six and I still didn't know what to wear. I'd contoured my face, added a bit of winged eyeliner and eyeshadow, and even applied my favorite nude lipstick, but I still didn't know what to wear. Was the red too bright? Was black too formal? Was a fitted dress appropriate enough for dinner?

After a long while of contemplation, I ended up going with my favorite black bodycon dress. It was a sleeveless turtleneck design with an open back and I loved it because it wasn't too revealing, but it wasn't too chaste either. The great thing about having smaller breasts was that I could do away with my bra and not worry about straps showing at the back.

I chose a pair of black closed-toe heels That was until I saw myself in the mirror and decided that I wanted some color in the outfit. I had to find something more subtle with less than an hour and a half to do so.

Cream-colored heels should work. They had to work. Obnoxiously enough, I had several pairs of them of heels, thanks to Garret loving to blow money on me. Of course, that was before he gave me the long spiel about how unlovable I was.

I didn't care about that anymore, though. All I cared about was seeing Ruggiero.

I found a matching handbag and all that I had left to do was my hair. My hair was naturally wavy, and I found that it looked better when I practically left it alone.

I had been told before that my hair appeared wind-blown and sexy when I left it alone. I could go for sexy.

With a little less than an hour to spare, I refreshed my makeup and took a bit of time to decide on how I was going to approach my little dilemma. I couldn't decide if I should tell Ruggiero about last night. I didn't think he'd care because I didn't belong to him, but if we were going to be sleeping together, I should be honest about having other partners. It was the right thing to do and if he gave up on me because of it, then so be it. I'd just be fucked.

I took a deep breath. I hoped Cleo was right. I would be fine.

Chapter 4

❧

JACE

Ruggiero was gorgeous. He wore a nicely pressed white button-down with a black bow tie, the sleeves of his shirt rolled halfway up, and a pair of dark dress pants to match. It was rare for me to see a man wearing loafers instead of cowboy boots in this part of town, but here he was.

"Jace, please don't bite me for saying this, but you look beautiful," he said once we sat down. He took a sip of his lemon water, sending me a smile.

I leaned forward on my elbows. "Why would I bite you?"

"Because you're mean as fuck," he answered matter-of-factly.

"Still stuck on what I said about your dick?" I asked, smirking.

He relaxed into his seat before readjusting his tie. "A little. But I proved you wrong and I plan to prove you wrong a second time soon. How's your week been so far?"

"It hasn't been too bad," I said. Besides last night, of course. "How about yours?"

"It hasn't been bad for me, either. We had a busy day at the shop yesterday, but today was fairly slow, so it was a good balance." He seemed as if he were about to say something else, but the waiter arrived.

"Hi," she chirped. "My name is Haley and I'll be your waitress for the night. What can I get for y'all?"

"Go ahead," I said to Ruggiero quietly, permitting him to order for the both of us. God knew that I was too busy thinking of other things to pay attention to the menu in front of me. He didn't know what I liked to eat yet, but I trusted him to choose.

Ruggiero licked his lips as he glanced between the waitress and me. "Can we get two potato soup bread bowls with Caesar salads on the side?"

"Of course, of course," Haley said, taking a second to jot the order down in her notepad. "Will that be all?"

"Actually," Ruggiero started, glancing toward me with a mischievous grin. "Can we also get a bottle of Merlot wine?"

Haley nodded and scribbled a little more. "Alright, you two," she said as she gathered the menus, "I'll be back with your food shortly. The wine will be brought around soon, as well."

Once the waitress was out of earshot, Ruggiero picked the conversation back up. "Did you do anything exciting?"

"Well…" I trailed off, wondering if it was worth it to lie. "Not exactly. I drank too much last night because it wasn't my day in the least and did some things I wish I hadn't."

"Like…"

I lowered my voice before confessing my sins. "I may have let a girl take me back to her place and had some fun with her."

"Ah, okay. What was her name, Jace?" he asked, his eyebrows pulling together in curiosity. I didn't answer him because I hadn't even asked her. "Nice, nice."

I couldn't tell what he was thinking. I hadn't known him long enough to know how to interpret his facial expressions. "Are you upset?"

Ruggiero shrugged. "Maybe I should be, but then you walk in here looking like a dessert and I don't want to throw you in the trash. Besides, it's kind of funny."

I didn't think it was funny at all. I'd stressed myself out to the point of no return over the fear that he would no longer want anything to do with me.

"Did you think that I'd be angry?" he asked. I simply nodded. "Well, I'm not. I just have one question, was her head better than mine?"

"Both were good," I told him honestly. "But I was sober with you, so I think that counts for something."

"I think so, too." With that, he picked up his glass of water and took a sip.

The wine was brought around within a matter of minutes and our food followed quickly after. A comfortable silence fell between us as we dug into our meals.

Ruggiero ate with etiquette, dabbing the corners of his mouth with his napkin when needed. His elbows avoided the surface of the table as if it was lava.

"So, Jace, besides the fact that you're attracted to me, what else can you tell me about yourself?" he asked, dipping his head back down to meet his spoonful of soup.

I wiped my mouth before laying my fork down. Caesar salad wasn't my favorite, but it was tasty. "Well, I'm twenty-seven. I work at Glendshire Woods, the nursing home towards downtown. I love country music—"

"That might be a deal-breaker."

"Really?"

"Potentially," he said, grinning at me. "Let me see what else you have to offer."

I smiled softly at him. "I love listening to country with a dash of

33

bachata, depending on my mood. My favorite color is baby blue. Besides everyone's obvious favorite of potatoes, my favorite dish is a plate of chili cheese fries."

Ruggiero laughed. "So, you love fatty food. That explains the ass."

"Actually," I clarified, "that came from over a decade and a half of playing volleyball."

"I'd love to see you in that uniform one day."

"Maybe," I said. I was eager to learn about him. "Tell me about yourself, Ruggiero."

He shifted in his seat, resting his spoon in the bowl. "Compared to you, I'm sort of an old man. I'm twenty-nine, Italian born and raised, and I've lived in the states for six years. I actually work down the street at Carlisle's Auto Shop."

"I'd love to see you in that uniform one day," I mimicked.

"One day, *bella*. I love Italian music. More specifically, I'm a big fan of Lorenzo Fragola and Marco Mengoni. In terms of American music, my favorite is R&B, specifically the old pining type like Boyz II Men and Ginuwine," he said. "I also favor blue, but specifically cerulean. Unlike you, my favorite food is normal: *lasagne verdi al forno*."

"Sounds fancy,"

"It's also just known as baked spinach lasagna."

"After living in America for six years, you're going to tell me that you don't have a favorite food from here?"

Ruggiero hummed, thinking. "Well, this bread bowl potato soup is pretty delicious."

I rolled my eyes but smiled nonetheless. "You are unbelievable, but I have to agree with you. It's quite delicious."

"Are you ready for wine?" he asked.

"Thought you'd never ask. Only one glass, though. Hangovers aren't my favorite."

I was pleasantly surprised by how our date was going. Ruggiero was a sweetheart and I was... well, I was me. But he didn't make it seem like he was bothered with the way I was.

He handed me my glass and I slipped it into my fingers, bringing it to my lips with a satisfied moan. I loved wine more than I loved vodka and tequila. Maybe that was because wine left me a little more controlled and it made me feel good, but the wine tasted expensive.

"What exact wine is this?" I asked him. I hoped he didn't find me to be too nosy.

"2009 Delectus Knights Valley Merlot."

"How much is it, and will it be on your tab or mine?"

"Just under seventy dollars, but that doesn't matter because it'll be on my tab. What we don't drink will be added to my home collection," he assured me.

I didn't scold him because it wasn't my money being spent. It was his and he could do whatever the fuck he wanted with it.

"I'll make that money back within just a few hours tomorrow. Don't worry so much." He sent me a soft smile. "I'm ready to go home."

Well, fuck. "Oh, okay. Well, it's been nice, I guess."

He laughed—he fucking laughed at me—and ran a hand through his hair. "No, no. This is not a dismissal. I want you to come home with me."

"With the intentions of fucking my brains out?"

"Precisely."

A thought surfaced. "But don't you have to work in the morning?"

He rolled his eyes playfully. "Don't you?"

"Nope. I go in at four in the afternoon on Thursdays."

"I don't go in until eleven tomorrow." He licked his lips before speaking again. "I have a question to ask you. I won't be angry if you say no, I'll just be a little disappointed."

It couldn't have been that bad, right? I nodded. "Go for it."

He licked his lips and clasped his hands together. "What if I trail you home, you pack a little overnight bag, and we ride to my house together? I want you to sleep over."

I didn't hesitate to say yes.

Chapter 5

JACE

As we pulled into his driveway, a wave of familiarity rushed through me. "You still live here?"

He smirked and pushed his truck door open. "Of course I do. The bills are easy to pay."

"If I remember correctly, you told me that this neighborhood wasn't the safest."

He came around the other side to open the door for me. "I still stand by that, but every neighborhood is slightly unsafe," he explained, leading me into the house.

His single-family home hadn't changed much in the past year. It remained warm, cozy, like a blessing in its purest form. Ruggiero was written all over it—calming, sweet, and virile. Only this time, it smelled like cinnamon and apples, a nod to the changing season and the leaves falling outside.

My attraction toward him only grew as he led me up the stairs, my little book bag on his shoulder. My excitement swelled the closer we got to his bedroom. It was hard keeping my thoughts pure and

37

innocent given what we'd be doing in a matter of minutes.

"Why are you looking like that?" he asked, gently setting my book bag down next to his bed. His brown eyes held glints of amusement.

"Like what?"

He laughed lightly as he walked toward me. "Like you're ready to fuck my brains out."

"Because I am, Ruggiero." I met him halfway and wrapped my arms around his waist. "And the fact that you're looking this gorgeous doesn't help. I've been wanting to put your dick in my mouth from the moment I saw you today."

Ruggiero palmed my ass. "I feel honored that you've been keeping me in your thoughts." He gave it a good squeeze, his smile reaching his ears.

"This isn't funny to me, y'know." I moved my hands back to his front, gliding them over his belt loops. As gracefully as I could, I backed him into the wall and unbuckled his belt. I lowered his zipper as I lowered myself to my knees. "Besides, I wasn't only thinking of you," I murmured, dropping his pants and boxers as one. "I was thinking of this, too."

He moaned softly as I brought him into my mouth, sucking on the tip. "I feel like I should be offended." Ruggiero wrapped my hair around his fist, saying, "Let me know if I'm hurting you, baby."

I placed my palms on my thighs, relaxing my jaw and my body, letting him use me as he pleased. He was gentle, careful not to push me to the limit. Head leaned against the wall, he fucked my mouth with shallow strokes.

He pulled back abruptly and quickly drew me to my feet. Quickly grabbing the ends of my dress and sliding it over my head, he stripped me to my underwear. "Someone's eager."

"If I'm not mistaken, I'm sure you're pretty eager, too."

He backed me into the bed and bent down, his fingers sliding up my legs until they reached the hem of my panties. "These are cute, but they're coming off." He let them fall to the ground before standing upright again. "Sit still while I get a condom."

He started to turn, but I grabbed his arm. "Ruggiero, I'm on the pill."

"Jace, but still—"

"Ruggiero, please." He didn't answer me. Instead, he situated himself between my legs, grabbing my waist and tugging me closer. "Wait, take your shirt off. You're going to ruin it."

"*Merda.* You distract me from the simplest of things." He let go of my waist to unfasten his tie and unbutton his shirt. It fell from his shoulders and onto the ground. "Try not to get pregnant, okay? Lay down, please."

I thought of making fun of him for being so polite, but I decided to comply with his request. He slid into me and I held my breath as his length forced me to stretch and accommodate him.

He held my body in place as he moved his hips, spreading me more each time he reentered. He thrust at a pace that was slow and languid, while slowly, so slowly getting faster.

My fingers gripped the sheets as he began stroking deeper and at a faster pace. One of his hands left my waist and went for the hardened bud between my legs, rubbing it with the pad of his thumb.

I doubted my attractiveness as I lay underneath him. I never liked to look at people as I had sex with them, and Ruggiero's eyes were glued to me.

I moaned in protest as he took his fingers away. He shushed me, shifting to raise my foot to rest on his shoulder and thrusting from a different angle.

My teeth dug into my bottom lip at the change in sensation.

"I forgot you weren't a screamer," he said with a smirk.

"I tend to only do that when the sex is good," I lied. I wasn't a screamer but more of a crier, and sex with Ruggiero was proving to be phenomenal.

"I like it better when you don't talk," he grunted, pushing into me deeper.

Of course, he did. Most people liked it better when I didn't talk.

With the way he was fucking me, I didn't know how much more I could handle anyway. His toned chest was glistening with sweat, his brows furrowed in focus.

Fuck, he was hot.

It was hard to stay in the right state of mind when Ruggiero was doing such a damn good job at tiring me out. I could only focus on the small moans and groans we kept offering, the sound of our slick skin meeting with each thrust, and the smell of our cologne and sweat mixing.

I loved it.

I loved it even more so when he slid out of me and instructed me to turn around and support myself on all fours. "Baby, do me a favor and scoot farther onto the bed so I don't fall off."

I sent him a soft smile. "Of course. Wouldn't want my daddy dying."

"Calm yourself." Seconds later, he joined me on the bed, sliding into me once again. "This is my favorite position."

"Yeah?" I asked, pushing back to meet him. I arched my back and lowered my torso, making it easier for the both of us. "You feel so good."

He grabbed my ass with a pleasant hum and began thrusting at an unhurried pace. Each time, he pulled out further, only to push back in slowly, torturing me to the point of no return. "You're so fucking wet."

"Only for you," I moaned.

My words seemed to spur him on as he picked up pace quicker than I could prepare for. I gripped the sheets and buried my face to keep from toppling over. The tension built at my core as he fucked me.

"Breathe, baby, breathe," he murmured.

Only I didn't want to. I was drowning in the most pleasurable way, drowning in the joy of hearing his pleased groans and his skilled strokes. It was overwhelming and I gladly let it consume me.

And then I was being pulled out from underneath the wave, my body shaking as I struggled to hold on. "Come on, baby, let go," he encouraged. And I did.

The wave of pleasure swept me under the current as he continued his deep strokes, and I failed to stop the moan that spilled through my lips. He let go soon after, holding my body firmly against him as a shudder rippled through him as he joined me in the euphoria.

Maybe a condom would have been a good idea after all, but I was damn glad that I was on the pill.

I would be on it a few more years, too, because twenty-seven-year-old Jace Thompson was not ready to be anybody's mother.

A sigh slipped from me as he withdrew himself. "I'm going to sleep like a fucking baby tonight. Thank you, daddy."

I looked back in time to see him furrowing his eyebrows. "I thought you weren't into the whole daddy thing."

"Not so much, but I think it sounds good on you. It's like an in-the-mood thing, kind of like when you call me baby." I turned around so I could fully appreciate the image of him, brushing my hair out of my face. "Why are you stroking your dick?" He smirked, offering me no reply. "I swear, Ruggiero, you may be a nice guy, but you're fucking weird."

"That was strenuous for him and I. Be nice," he said. "A lot of work goes into making you feel good." His stopped touching himself and he reached for my breasts, cupping them in his hands. "Can't believe I didn't touch these tonight, even when you decide to show up to the restaurant with your nipples grazing the fabric of your dress."

I smiled warmly. "Your accent makes even the dumbest phrases sound appealing." I pushed my breasts further into his hands, laughing lightly.

"It's not dumb, it's true." He squeezed them lightly and then ran his thumbs over my nipples.

"Ruggiero, they're sensitive right now."

"I'm upset I neglected them." He bent down and gave both a kiss above the nipple. "Next time." He then grabbed my hand, gently guiding me off the bed. "Come. You're going to get my bed all sticky."

Our shower was quick and straight to the point with Ruggiero tentatively scrubbing me. Once he was also clean, he stepped out and grabbed towels for the both of us. Shortly after, we climbed underneath his comforter and relaxed in his cool sheets.

In a pair of panties and one of Ruggiero's shirts, I cuddled up to him. I leaned closer into him, resting my head on his bare chest. "I think we left the wine in your car."

He laughed softly while reaching over to turn the lamp at his bedside off. "S, I realized it halfway through fucking you."

"You were fucking me while thinking about how you left the wine in the car?" I asked. "That's weird."

"Well, what were you thinking of?"

I hummed. "Mainly you. How you were sweating profusely and how hot it made you look."

"And you call me the weird one." He placed a chaste kiss on my forehead and then sank deeper into the bed. "I'm exhausted." He brought me down with him until my head met the pillow before laying his head on my stomach. "Your body's beautiful. All of you is beautiful."

I ran a hand through his dark hair, loving how soft it was. "Ruggiero, I'm sexy, not beautiful. There's a difference."

"Alright," he mumbled, "you caught me. Your sex appeal is the only reason why I'm attracted to you."

"Isn't it?" I asked him.

He groaned and circled his arms around my waist. "No, but I'm too tired to talk about this. We have plenty of time tomorrow. Sleep tight, *bella*." He closed his eyes and drifted off to sleep.

Chapter 6

RUGGIERO

After not running into Jace for a year, I wanted nothing more than to see her again. I didn't know how she fell into my arms again, but I wasn't mad about it. Not at all. Honestly, I was surprised she even agreed to sleep over last Wednesday.

At first glance, she didn't seem the most approachable person, but her company was more than enjoyable at dinner. Not only was she beautiful, but she was intelligent and had a good heart… despite the things she said sometimes. Part of me was thinking with my cock, but the other part did not care. Talking and bantering with her felt natural.

Which was how I ended up outside of the door to her apartment building, sitting on the step.

I planned to surprise her with a movie night, but now I wondered if I just seemed creepy. A half an hour had passed, and I'd only seen her home once before when I trailed her home after dinner.

I took a deep breath as I saw her car pull into the parking lot. My heart raced. I had no idea how she'd react to this considering I didn't even call first. "You got this," I said to myself.

Jace jumped out of the car, an amused smile on her face. "How long have you been sitting out here?" she asked in her southern lilt, putting her hands on her hips. She looked so cute in her scrubs.

"Mhm." I glanced at my Nixon watch, trying to play it cool. It'd been a long time since I was genuinely interested in someone, and I didn't want to fuck it up. "A little over thirty minutes. Nothing too major."

"You didn't even know anything about my shift," she said. She had a good point. "You could have ended up sitting here for hours."

"But I didn't." I stood up, grabbing the reusable grocery bag I brought as I did so. "You had to come home eventually, and I figured a movie night would be fun."

"Touché." She sent me a tired smile and went for the keypad, putting in the passcode to let us into the building. "Let's go." I held the door open for her before following closely behind.

I sunk into the couch, my muscles loosening. I was so relieved she was okay with it and didn't tell me to leave. "Shut the door, please," she said and then disappeared into the kitchen.

While I waited for her, I laid out a bag of cheese puffs, chocolate, carefully wrapped brownies in plastic wrap, a few snack cakes, and even the wine we didn't finish the last time we were together. I was organizing the snacks on the coffee table when she walked into the living room.

"What is all this?" she asked, her hands returning to her hips.

Those hips felt so good in my hands last week. *She* felt so good in my hands.

Focus, idiot, she asked you a question.

"*È cibo, ovviamente,*" I told her. "I like to feed you."

Jace took the clip out of her hair with a tired sigh. A small smile danced on her lips. "It just looks like you're trying to make me fat, Ruggiero," she said, crossing her arms.

"It'll only give me more to grab on," I said. "You're the only one complaining here."

She rolled her eyes as she made to brush past me. "Yeah, yeah. I need to change out of my uniform."

I stood quickly, grabbing her arm before she got too far, and spun her around to face me. "You look cute in your scrubs," I said. Her skin was so soft under my rough hand. "How was work?"

"It was good," she said, "now, let me go. I smell like antiseptics and sterility."

I snorted. "You smell like Jace. But *sì*, go change." I released her from my grip and shamelessly stared at her ass as she walked away. A few minutes later, I heard the shower turn on.

I guessed I should get comfortable.

I sank back down, occupying myself by scrolling through social media. A football video quickly caught my eye, a compilation of a midfielder's highlights. Once that one was over, I swiped to the next video of football highlights. I was on the fifth video when I started to smell smoke.

I threw my phone down on the couch and trotted into the kitchen. The burning smell was coming from the oven.

I worked fast to find a set of oven mitts and remove the foiled pan. I freed a hand from one of the mitts and peeked underneath the foil. Hunger pains shot through me as I looked at the melted cheese. Hearing her footsteps hurrying into the kitchen, I stepped away from the stove and faced her.

"Look okay?" Jace asked, touching my arm, her hand curling around my wrist, the smell of vanilla and lavender wafting around me. "Thanks for taking that out." She'd changed into a big white t-shirt and a pair of blue running shorts.

"It looks amazing, *bella*." It smelled amazing, too.

She let go and stepped past me, grabbing plates out of the cabinet.

"Great. I'm making you a plate if that's alright with you."

"I am a little hungry," I admitted.

"Alright. I know you like lasagna and your greens."

She didn't hesitate to cut a couple of pieces and put them on the plates, saying, "I used zucchini noodles." Jace handed me my plate and gestured for me to follow her back into the living room.

I sat close to her on the love seat, my leg touching hers. Comfortable, I took a bite. The blended tastes of roasted tomatoes, rich ricotta, and beef burst on my tongue. The zucchini added a twist I wouldn't normally expect.

"How is it?" she asked. She hadn't taken a bite of her food yet.

"It's good. No complaints here."

Her cheeks reddened and she smiled at me. "Good. I'm so glad you like it."

We were quiet as we finished eating. I didn't mind. It was the type of meal that deserved all the attention. She was a great cook and I hoped I'd get to eat more of her cooking.

She set her plate down on the table and leaned back into the couch, rubbing her puffed out belly. She was so fucking cute.

"That thing you're doing with your hands," I said with a gesture, "Is that supposed to be a baby bump?"

She glanced down at her stomach before looking up at me again, smiling wickedly. "It's a food baby." I cocked my head to the side. "I think I'll name her Lazzi, after the lasagna."

"Food baby?"

Jace rolled her eyes, saying. "I am bloated, Ruggiero. It's the product of eating too fast." She took the empty plate from my hands and stood up. "I'll be back."

While Jace was in the kitchen, I searched her wooden TV stand. Inside the middle doors was a VCR/DVD combo player. She had actual VHS tapes, too. "Does this thing work?" I said loudly, grabbing the remote. The shelves of movies and series were impressive. "Like tapes and all?"

She came into the living room, wiping her hands on her shorts. "There isn't anything wrong with VHS tapes, spaghetti head."

What a classic.

"Ow," I said, placing my free hand over my heart. "I almost feel insulted."

"It works," she assured me. "Pick a movie."

I chose *The 40-Year-Old Virgin*. I hadn't seen it in a while. On the couch, Jace snuggled up to me and grabbed the bag of cheese puffs. As the movie began, I wrapped an arm around her waist, pulling her closer to my side.

"How was your day?" I asked her, my voice low.

"It was fine," she replied, her focus remaining on the television. "Now, please, shut up. Watch the movie."

"You're right. I'll hush," I whispered and dragged my eyes back to the screen.

We watched the adult comedy in silence, our fingers brushing every so often. I cherished every touch. I danced my fingers up and down her soft inner thigh. I kept my distance from the hem of her shorts. Her thighs spread some and I put my hand back to her side. I didn't want to give her the wrong idea. My palm curled around her hip, I said, "Just to clarify, I'm not looking for sex tonight."

"Oh," she said, eyes wide, "okay." She pulled her hand out of the bag of cheese puffs, nodding.

I kissed her forehead before grabbing a brownie from the table. "Relax and watch the movie, *bella*."

Chapter 7

JACE

I woke to the sight of Ruggiero's tranquil face. His arm was draped lazily around my waist, holding me close to him. For a moment, I was warm, safe, cherished even.

The intimacy of our position was both mesmerizing and terrifying. It implied we were more than just fucking and more was impossible. I could only offer him a warm body. I wriggled out of Ruggiero's hold and climbed out of bed.

I was searching for a pair of yoga pants when I heard, "*Dio*, you're so beautiful."

I turned to face him, frowning. "It's too early for bullshit," I said. "Are you hungry?"

"Why don't you believe that you're beautiful?" he asked, his brow furrowed.

"Ruggiero, it's early," I repeated. I pulled my pants on hastily. "I don't want to talk about this."

"Okay." He climbed out of my bed and bent down. He kept his eyes on me as he picked up his shirt and pants from the night before and put them on.

"I just—" I paused, shaking my head. "In high school, people didn't like me for my face or my personality. They liked me for my body. That didn't change with adulthood." I dug in my drawers for my old college hoodie. "Being appealing to the eye has never gotten me anywhere and it isn't going to start now."

Ruggiero leaned against the wall and ran a hand through his hair. "You're one of the most beautiful people I've ever met."

I slid on the hoodie, irritation flaring. "I really don't have time for lies. If you want to fuck me, just tell me."

"I do," he admitted, standing up straight. "But not like this. I am not lying to you. I'm not just trying to fuck."

"Why are you here then?" I snapped. He didn't deserve my irritation and yet I couldn't help lashing out.

Shaking his head, he grabbed his keys off of my nightstand. "If you don't know, then maybe I should go," he said, rolling his eyes.

"What, you're really going to tell me that I'm beautiful again, that you like me, and you see something in me? Because if so, that's really funny." I needed to shut up. He wanted each other, but I didn't do well with feelings.

I wanted him to tell me those things. I wanted to believe him when he said I was beautiful, but I knew better.

Ruggiero grimaced. "Jesus, you are really fucking something. Did you know that? You are really something." He eyed me intently. I hated when he stared.

When people stared, they started seeing things that weren't there. They started seeing more than I could give. Someone once told me that if it wasn't for my nasty attitude, I would be wife material. I didn't want to be wife material.

To be a wife meant that I would potentially be someone's mother, and that scared me. I didn't want to have a daughter like me. Maybe a son like Jackson, but not a daughter like me.

"What are you thinking about?" Ruggiero asked, his voice pulling me from my thoughts. "And to your initial question, yes, I am hungry."

Within ten minutes, the two of us were in my kitchen, sitting at the little square table pushed against the wall. I wanted eggs and bacon, but he'd killed my desire to cook. So, instead of a nice warm breakfast, we were munching on cornflakes with a sprinkle of sugar.

Sugar hadn't failed to boost my mood yet.

"How did you sleep?" he asked. His foot brushed against my leg, sending lightning up my body.

"Good," I said. "Do you not work today?"

He swallowed his mouthful. "Not today. Do you?"

"No. Saturdays are days when I recover from work." I remembered what day tomorrow was. "Shit."

He raised an eyebrow at me. "*Sì?*"

"I have dinner with my family tomorrow. And I said that I was going to buy dinner," I explained. I didn't know what to buy. We ate pizza far too often and I was getting tired of Chinese takeout.

Still, Ruggiero seemed perplexed. "Why buy dinner when you seem to cook very well?"

"Cooking dinner will mess up the entire flow. We take turns ordering and paying for food from places we like, but I feel like we've exhausted all our options. I have no idea what to get."

He tilted his head a little, swirling his cereal in the bowl with his spoon. There was no doubt that it was becoming soggy. "Okay. Tell me more about these dinners."

"My mom, my brother Jackson, and I have dinner together every two weeks. Last time around, my mom and I said some shitty things. I made her cry, and I kind of felt like shit." He furrowed his brow but said nothing, so I continued. "We were both in the wrong, but I still apologized."

"Mhm," he said, "so, there is some kindness in your heart."

"Sure, sure," I said, shrugging. My cereal was getting soggier, and it did nothing but lower my appetite.

"Tell me about your brother." He seemed to be done with his cereal. He didn't say it, but he abandoned the cereal floating in the milk, letting it absorb the moisture.

I sighed. "My brother's kind of like me, just a man and younger. He's not a whore or anything, because he's a man and men can't possibly be whores," I said sarcastically. "He's a personal trainer at a gym I forget the name of but loves binging on fast food twice a month. He also likes to tell me that he'll come and replace my light bulbs and never does."

Ruggiero chuckled a little. "The ones in the front room?"

"Yes, oh my God," I laughed, "it makes this place look so dim."

He pushed his bowl far in front of him. He was definitely done with his cereal. "You haven't tried to change them yourself?"

I tried not to grimace. The smirk on Ruggiero's face let me know that I failed. "I'm too short, even with a ladder."

"No one told you to be five foot three, Jace."

"And no one told anyone to make these ceilings tall as fuck," I argued.

"They aren't that tall. It's an apartment unit."

I cut my eyes at him. "Whatever, Ruggiero."

His eyes softened as he looked at me. "I can change your light bulbs, *piccola*. That is if you want me to."

Him? Change my light bulbs? It was such a small gesture and yet I couldn't help but overthink it. What if he offered to wash my laundry? Or worse, what if he offered to stock my refrigerator? Ruggiero was unpredictable.

I shook my head, even though all I wanted to tell him was *'Yes, please change my light bulbs.'*

"Jackson can do it," I mumbled.

"How long have you been asking Jackson to change your light bulbs?"

"Since the end of June."

"That was almost four months ago. So, as I said, I'll change them." Ruggiero pushed his chair out before standing and grabbing his bowl. "Thanks for breakfast," he told me, going to place his bowl in the sink. "I'll see you later."

With that, Ruggiero left me where I sat in the kitchen and exited my apartment.

What the fuck just happened?

I was in the middle of a shower, soap lathered on my body, when there was a knock at my door. I let the knocking continue as I went under the water as I rinsed my body.

With a sigh, I turned off stream and stepped out of the shower. I didn't want to leave the warmth felt oh-so-good, but I wanted the knocking to stop. Besides, it could only be one of four people. I hoped it wasn't the landlord.

I wrapped my red towel around my body before leaving the bathroom, cracking the door so that the mirror could have a chance to defog.

Once I got to the front room, I unlocked the door and yanked it open. "Yes?".

Ruggiero was standing there, a plastic bag in his hand. He was dressed in a pair of khakis and a plain white tee. Always looking so handsome. He gave me a once-over before crossing the threshold, pushing me in with him. Shaking his head, he closed the door behind him. "Where are your clothes?"

I was more than aware of my wet hair and the little beads of water on my skin. I was sure that he was, too. "I was showering, Ruggiero," I deadpanned. "Nice to see you twice in the same day."

"*Sì certo,*" he murmured. He walked around me, his hard body brushing against mine as he did so. "I came to change your lights. Where's your ladder?"

He'd driven all the way here just to change my light bulbs. I couldn't turn him away now. Even if Jackson promised he'd be the one to do it. "Closet to your right," I told him.

He set the bag down on the couch before going into the closet. There, he pulled out the metal ladder my father gave Garret and me. I scowled at the memory.

His eyes darted from the ladder to the coffee table in the middle of the room. I knew that I needed to either finish my shower or get dressed but watching him was entertaining. He was so animated.

He bit his lip before walking toward the coffee table. Placing his hands on the edge, he pushed it to the side as if it were nothing. I loved a strong man.

He paid me little to no attention as he carried the ladder to the middle of the room and opened it. "Don't you have better things to do? I know you feel a draft wearing nothing but that towel."

"No, actually," I said. I made myself comfy on the couch, letting go of my towel and spreading it across the cushions. In my current state, I was very aware of the draft in the room.

He didn't look at me as he grabbed the light bulbs. He tossed the bag to the side and tore the box of bulbs open. He took two out before climbing up the ladder.

I liked watching him. I liked the way his lean body stretched as he reached for the dead bulbs. I crossed my legs, squeezing them as I did so. How the hell was he turning me on when all he was doing was replacing bulbs?

As he climbed down the ladder, my front room was looking brighter already. He glanced at me, his eyes narrowed, and then he put everything back where it needed to be. He even discarded the used bulbs in a grocery bag and stored the rest of the box in the kitchen.

Ruggiero came back into the front room, where he just folded his arms across his chest and stood in front of me. "Are you not going to get dressed? You've been sitting here for a good ten minutes."

I rolled my eyes, keeping my legs crossed. "I thought about it. But then I decided that it would be dumb because all I'd ask for you to do is take my clothes off."

"What if I told you I didn't want to fuck you at the moment?"

"I would respect your decision, of course. But I'm going to get off either way. You can leave or you could watch. I like an audience." I bit my lip, finally acknowledging the pulsing between my legs. I spread further on the couch and let my hand slide down my belly, my thatch of blonde curls, to my clit. "I don't believe in forcing."

His chest rose as he breathed slowly.

"It's your choice, Ruggiero," I told him. "I can't make you do anything you don't want to." My fingers slid from my clit to my pussy. Without hesitation, I let two fingers sink into me.

"You're insatiable." Me? Insatiable? I hadn't gotten off in over a week. No matter how hard I tried, I couldn't emulate his touch. "You need someone who can do more than fuck you," he said, his attention on his task.

"You're right. I need someone who knows how to satisfy me, too." My fingers were sliding in and out of me, and even though he wasn't watching me like I wished he were, his presence alone was enough to egg me on.

"You need someone who can love you, too."

"Well, what are you waiting for?" I taunted. "Fuck me like you love me."

"Yeah?"

"Yes, Ruggiero," I said, nodding, my fingers still moving between my legs.

I couldn't decipher the look on his face. He was never easy to read.

Right now, it was harder than ever. Regardless of what he was thinking, he unbuckled his belt and unzipped his fly. "Okay." Kicking his pants and boxers aside, he moved over me.

I closed my eyes as he grabbed my wrist, my fingers slipping out of me. I also closed my eyes. Eye contact made things too intimate, too personal.

In one fluid movement, he sank deep. I bit my lip, suppressing my moan. He felt so good and yet... I found my mind drifting.

One look at him made me giddy. I saw everything I wanted in him. But I knew that he and I were on two different levels. He was the newest product on the shelf and I was—

"Jace, baby, breathe."

—damaged goods.

I squeezed my eyes shut tighter, my fingers digging into the couch cushions as he thrust faster.

I'm losing my mind.

He was doing everything right, but I didn't like how my skin crawled. I didn't like the way my mind was racing. I hated that I was too scared to open my eyes and look him in the face. I hated how I felt so out of control even though I'd initiated this.

A lack of control was always a bad sign.

I opened my eyes. His brown ones studied my face intently and he smiled at me warmly. In my twenty-seven years of living, only a handful of people had smiled at me while they fucked me.

Including *him*, a person I should've forgotten a long time ago.

Suddenly, I was seventeen. I shut my eyes at the sensation of rough hands gripping my skin. My body wasn't my own. A finger rubbed my clit and the feeling in the pit of my stomach just kept growing and growing. My orgasm hit, pushing me into sensory overload.

The urge to cry rushed over me. I repressed the urge with a pained moan. My body shook and I couldn't tell if it was my climax or panic.

Dopamine flooded my every sense, my pussy clenching around him. I brimmed over with pleasure before I ran dry, numbness spreading throughout my limbs.

Ruggiero followed closely behind me, groaning as he came. "Fuck, Jace, you're perfect," he said breathily, pulling out as he rolled to the cushion next to me.

I fluttered my eyes open. One look at his face and I shot up, grabbing my towel. I didn't give him a glance as I walked away.

He didn't follow me. I was grateful as I closed the bedroom door and locked it behind me. I rummaged through my drawer for clothes to wear. My hands were still shaking.

I sank to the floor, warm tears rolling down my face. I tried to calm myself by taking breaths and counting in my head. *Four, eight, twelve, sixteen.* Why was I still struggling with this? Why did I struggle with Ruggiero?

I knew that Ruggiero was nothing like him and that he'd probably never hurt me. But it felt all too familiar.

Ruggiero isn't here to hurt you, I told myself. *He's not* him.

I heard my name being said softly outside the door. "Jace, I didn't hurt you, did I?"

Of course, he didn't. He didn't do anything wrong. Ruggiero was a good guy, I had to remind myself. I took one last deep breath and wiped my face with the backs of my hands. "No," I called back, "I just got a little overwhelmed. You were good, you felt good."

Whether he believed me or not, he didn't say anything. His footsteps padded away from my door.

As my heartbeat gradually stabilized, I cleaned Ruggiero from my legs before getting dressed in a pair of jeans and my hoodie from earlier.

Not wanting to deal with my hair, I threw it in a messy bun.

When I emerged from my room, he was fully clothed and had

straightened up the front room. I sat next to him, my ears warm as they flushed with blood. His eyes held concern, but he didn't say anything.

He just pulled me to his side.

Chapter 8

JACE

"Jace, maybe you should talk to someone, honey," Cleo suggested. I shook my head. I didn't need to talk to anyone because there wasn't anything wrong with me. I had long ago accepted myself for who I was. I knew I had a few oddities I couldn't change.

The beautiful old woman frowned at me. I could already feel a rebuttal coming. "Look, I'm tired of your stubbornness. Not only is this affecting you, but this is also affecting your relationship with that nice boy."

"We aren't in a relationship," I clarified. "I don't know what we're doing."

She clenched her fists before taking a deep breath. "My cortisol is probably to the damn roof by now. Do you like the boy or not?" I nodded . "Is he aware of that? Because from all the stuff you've been telling me, you're sending him mixed signals. One minute you're giving him all kinds of attention and the next you're pushing him away."

I didn't like it what I was doing to him. But I didn't know how to change it. As much as I wanted him and as much as I wanted him to want me, I didn't know how to accept this desire. I didn't know how to normalize the feeling. I licked my lips, trying to plan out my next words.

"I really like him," I started. "It didn't feel this hard with Garret. I don't know what it is about Ruggiero, but he makes me feel scared. It's like he's too good. And you know me better than anyone else. You know I hate feeling vulnerable. I feel like I'm losing control over my life."

"Why does everything have to be about control with you?"

I laughed humorlessly. "You know why. I let my guard down for one moment and—Cleo, you know. But I won't get hurt if I'm in control."

"You're going to end up losing him. He isn't going to stick around while you try and figure your shit out. I'm always on your side, but I need you to act like an adult for a second. You've been hurt traumatically, but you have to at least try to overcome it, *angyalom*."

Bless her little heart.

I loved Cleo more than almost anything. As much as I loved my mom, Cleo was also motherly figure to me, and she only meant well.

I looked at her, a lump stuck in my throat. I fumbled for a response. All I knew was I needed a stress reliever. I stood up from where I sat on the edge of the bed and grabbed my purse. I'd come back later, maybe. With a forced smile, I told her one thing before walking out: "I need a drink."

Alcohol was on my mind, but instead of caving, I stood in the lobby of the nursing home and helped myself to a cup of water. Water was a cleansing agent, but it wouldn't rid me of the filth I felt.

As much as I fought it, Cleo's words were valid. Nothing was innately wrong with me, but it might help me to speak with someone about my troubles. And as much as I wanted to confide in Ruggiero, I wasn't quite ready for that.

I wasn't ready to speak with anyone about it.

I took a seat in one of the waiting chairs and sipped at the water. I hated that these feelings were resurfacing years later. I was safe, I had control of my life, and I was happy, doing as I pleased. If all that was true, why did panic with Ruggiero?

"Jace, dear, are you alright?" I looked up to see my boss, Mrs. Deen. I rarely saw her, but when I did, her presence never failed to brighten my day.

I nodded and offered a smile. "Fantastic, Mrs. Deen. It's just been a long day."

She frowned, her skepticism bleeding through. "Is there anything I can do for you, dear?"

I hated to swindle her but... "I know I took this shift to replace Gina, but would it hurt too much if I went home?" I asked. "I am feeling a bit sick, in all honesty." It wasn't in all honesty, but I had to play my cards right.

With the suppressed immune systems of the residents, Mrs. Deen was quick to allow me to leave.

I scurried out to my car and climbed in. There were three things on my mind: what I needed to grab for dinner tonight, my lust for alcohol, and my want for sex.

Alcohol and sex were out of the question, as alcohol would just lead to sex and that could cause a rift between Ruggiero and me. I might've been okay with it if the sex were with him, but I hadn't spoken to him since the day before and I didn't feel like texting him. That left me to worry about the latter.

I started home with the thought, ruling out pizza, Chinese food, and seafood. I wasn't in the mood to have the scent of fish wafting around me. Recently, the smell of it had started to make me gag a little.

As I approached a stoplight, my phone began to vibrate in the cupholder. I glanced down to see Ruggiero's name shining brightly on the screen. Shortly before the light could change to green again, I answered the phone, pressing it to my ear. "Hello?"

"Hello, *bella*." His voice, warm and deep, was comforting. "I have something for you. It's a proposition that might help you out tonight."

I grinned. "Food? Like, you have food ideas?"

"I can order some food for you."

"That would be nice. It hasn't been the best day for me. Where were you thinking of ordering from?"

He chuckled into the phone. "Funny coincidence. It's a place called La Famiglia and they serve authentic Italian. Does your family like Italian?"

"They do." As I drove down the street going toward my apartment, I tried to think of the last time we ate pasta as a family. "What's so special about La Famiglia?"

"Mhm, so much. They have some of the best escarole soup I've ever tasted. Their tiramisu is pretty good too."

"Tiramisu? The dessert?"

"*Sì*, Jace, the dessert. Do you want me to just order for you?"

I blushed. "Go ahead. Just make sure there's pasta and other fattening stuff. We like to eat bullshit. I'll have Jackson pick it up around seven."

"I'll call you back after I've placed the order. *Ciao*."

"Thanks, Ruggiero," I said, hanging up. I placed my phone into my purse and steered into the parking lot of my apartment. The place was nice, nothing was broken now that Ruggiero had changed my light bulbs, but I felt like I was outgrowing this place. Already.

With a sigh, I parked my car and dragged myself up the stairs. I kicked my shoes off and threw my purse onto the couch. I was so over the day, mentally and physically.

I was lying on the couch draped in a fuzzy blue blanket when my phone started buzzing in my purse. With a sigh, I reached to grab it. "Hello?"

"*Ciao.* Did I interrupt anything?"

"No," I assured him. "I was just watching a bit of TV."

"What show?"

I considered lying to him. I almost did, but there was no point. In his mind, what could be worse than country music? "*Keeping Up with the Kardashians.*"

A laugh came through the receiver. "You like reality TV?"

"It's a guilty pleasure," I admitted. "Anything else I can do for you?"

"I was just calling to check up on you. You mentioned today hasn't been the best day for you. Everything all right? Was it yesterday?"

I clenched the phone tightly. I should've known he would ask about it eventually. "No, and yes. No, to be honest, not everything is alright. Today has been shit. Yes, it is mostly because of yesterday." I rushed to continue. "But it's not anything you did. Really. It was all me."

"Jace," he said, his tone softening, "you know if you ever need to let your guard down and talk, I'm here, right?"

I stayed quiet for a moment. "I guess."

Ruggiero sighed deeply. "You are a mess, *bella.* But I have always been good at cleaning up. Talk to me."

"I'd rather talk to a fucking rock," I said, hoping he could hear the tease in my tone.

"I'm that bad, *sì?*"

"Sometimes." I nuzzled deeper into the couch. With my free hand, I pressed the mute button on the television remote. "I'm going to nap for a little before I have to go."

"*Ciao,* call me if you need anything."

* * *

It was prom night, and I'd spent a ridiculous amount on my dress, hair, and makeup. I was cute, but for a night I wanted to be beautiful. For a night, I wanted to be seen as more than an object made for pleasure. For a night, I wanted to feel special.

My dress was a blue mermaid cut adorned with silver sequins. I had to admit I felt rather beautiful. My lips were glossed with bright red, my hair in a braided updo.

I felt like a goddess. He told me that I looked like one as I grabbed the plastic cup out of his hand. I took a sip, forcing down the spiked punch.

My prom date, Liam, was a real looker. And I loved to look. He was an offensive lineman on the school's football team with brown hair and blue eyes. He could be a jerk at times, but I let it slide because I could be one as well.

At the end of the night, he took me back to the hotel room he reserved. I wasn't a virgin and I knew most people fucked after prom. I knew that's what he wanted me for.

He pressed me against the wall and as he kissed me, he unzipped the side of my dress. I gave in, arching into him as his lips moved to my neck. "You're so beautiful, Jace."

No one had ever called me beautiful like that.

I let him strip my dress off. I let him undo my hair. I even let him lay me on the bed underneath him. He loosened his tie and raised my arms above my head. He wanted to restrain me. Fear coursed through my veins.

He noticed the change in my mood and gave me a warm smile. "Relax, Jace, trust me. I just want to make you feel good."

Something told me I lost control of the situation at that moment, but I forced myself to relax. I reminded myself that he wanted to make me feel good.

He secured my arms tightly to the bed with his tie and removed the rest of his clothing.

I was changing my mind.

I pulled at my arms, but they wouldn't budge. "Liam, I don't want this anymore."

"Beautiful girl, you're here now." His hands moved to the waistband of my panties and dragged them down to mid-thigh. A hand slid between my legs, and he used the other to keep them apart. I flinched as he touched me. "You're already so wet for me."

* * *

I jolted awake, my heart pounding. My arms were cold with sweat, my cheeks streaked with tears. It was a recurring nightmare, but its frequency had lessened. Or at least I'd thought it had. I inhaled deeply, relieved that I woke up before I experienced the pain, the feeling of his hand around my neck, and the duct tape on my mouth.

Chapter 9

❧

JACE

"J ace," my mom started, "are you alright?"

I picked at my food and did my best to keep a calm composure. Everything was bothering me. I wouldn't tell her I was irritated with myself and with my past and with the fact that I couldn't bring myself to be vulnerable with a man I knew wouldn't hurt me.

I nodded but stayed silent. From across the table, Jackson was eyeing me, but he didn't say anything. His sad-ass half-smile told me he was worried.

My mom licked her lips and pushed her hair out of her face, turning her attention back to the food Ruggiero ordered. "Well, this—" she paused to look at the label, "—penne alla vodka was good. Dessert anyone?"

"Yeah," I said, nodding eagerly. The tiramisu looked delicious. "I'll take some."

"Yeah, me too," Jackson said. "Soo, Jacey, how's work?"

"Work… is work. Cleo's doing fine." I sighed as my mom slid a plate of the dessert toward me. "What about you?"

I looked up to see Jackson gave me the same uneasy smile. Yeah, he was worried. "Work's been great, actually. I have a new client. He's a heavier dude, but he wants to tone up, so we've got a plan to replace a bit of that body fat with muscle."

"That's good of you," my mom said.

"Yeah," Jackson agreed. "I also hooked him up with one of my nutritionist buddies."

We fell into another silence, save for the occasional small talk that Jackson and my mom attempted I laughed a bit. I tried to be animated with them.

Dinner didn't feel the same tonight.

"Jace, you've been awfully quiet," my mom stated. Of course, she had to bring attention to the elephant in the room. "I almost miss hearing you two say crude jokes and toss indirect insults at me."

I laughed lightly. "The insults are never indirect."

"You know what I mean." She reached across the table and placed her hand over mine. "I know we don't always get along, but you're my daughter and I care about you. You don't look well tonight. Are you feeling sick?"

I avoided her eye contact. "No, I'm in good health."

"How are you mentally?"

"I am mentally sane," I assured her.

"And emotionally?"

"Mom," Jackson said. "I just don't think tonight is her night."

I laughed shakily. "It's not. I swear to God it's not." I laughed again before standing up. "Excuse me, please."

I hurriedly walked to the restroom. Nothing had been going my way today and that terrible dream had just been the icing on the cake. Once in the bathroom, I locked the door. I turned the faucet on cold and then wiped my face with my cold, wet hands.

"Get it together, Jace," I willed myself. "That was almost a decade ago."

I stood in front of the mirror. I looked like a mess. My hair was in an unruly bun, and my eyes looked so tired. I usually didn't mind my face without makeup, but right now, I looked like I simply didn't give a fuck about myself.

There was a soft knock at the door. "Jace, are you okay?" It was my brother, bless his heart. He reminded me of my dad—never took a lot seriously, very tough on the outside, but a big softie on the inside.

"I'm fine, thank you."

"Long day?" I heard him shift against the door, leaning his body into it.

"Mhm. Very long," I answered. "I'm just ready for the day to be over."

"I'm sure tomorrow will be ten times better, big sis."

"I sure hope you're right."

As I heard his footsteps fading, I took the time to use the restroom and wash my hands. While doing so, I stole another look at myself. I really looked like shit. I pulled the elastic band from my hair to redo my messy bun. It made me look slightly better.

Back in the front room, Jackson and my mom were still eating their dessert. I grabbed my jacket, slung my purse on my shoulder, and pushed my chair in.

"You turning in for the night, Jace?" my mom asked. I nodded. "Well, come give your mama a hug before you go."

I hugged her tightly, told her I loved her, and patted Jackson on the back before letting myself out of the house.

My drive home was the most peaceful part of my day. The town was quiet, the moon full and lovely, and Sam Hunt's debut album was keeping me company. Halfway through the ride, my phone rang.

"Hello?" I answered tiredly.

"*Ciao*. How are you?" Ruggiero's voice was soft and warm,

comforting even.

I sighed into the receiver. "I've been better. How about yourself?"

"Not too bad. How was dinner? Everything work out?"

"Yes, thank you. Do you work tomorrow?" It was a long shot, but the only chances one could miss were the ones they didn't take.

"Yes, around eleven. Don't you?"

"I do, but I'm going to take a sick day. Will you come over tonight?"

"Hmm," he started, "the intention of this call was only to check up on you and wish you a good night, but yes, I'll come over."

"Thank you."

I hung up, arriving at my apartment. As I waited for Ruggiero, I straightened up a bit and then hopping in the shower.

I bathed quickly, washing my body with my favorite soap. Out of the shower, I moisturized and dressed in a Batman shirt and a pair of panties. My day had been long. Showering and taking care of my body was a way to rejuvenate.

Just as I finished putting on a pair of socks, I heard Ruggiero knocking. I opened the door to see him standing there already in his pajamas—a pair of grey sweatpants and a white t-shirt—and an overnight bag. He looked absolutely ravishing, but I was a good girl and kept my eyes on his face. "Hey. Don't you look rather delicious," I said, stepping out of the way so he could walk in.

"Evening. How are you?"

I closed the door behind him and led him to my room. "I'm… living. I'm decent. You?"

"I'm well." He set his bag down before bringing me in for a hug, squeezing me tightly. His hugs warmed me like hot chocolate. "I promise, tomorrow will be better."

I wanted to believe him, but doubt remained in the back of my mind. "Okay."

Ruggiero pressed a small kiss to my forehead and released me. He took a step to the side and removed his shoes. I couldn't tear my eyes away from him as he shimmied out of his grey sweatpants and removed his shirt.

How did I end up getting so lucky?

"You know," he started, closing the space between us, "I'm real. Completely tangible." He grabbed one of my hands, placing it on his chest. "You can touch me."

"I know," I told him. He let go of my hand and I trailed it from his chest, up to his neck, and his face. He was too good for me.

He wrapped an arm around my waist, pulling me even closer to him. My heart was beating rapidly against my chest. He kissed my forehead again, then my nose, and then my lips softly. *"Nei tuoi occhi c'è il cielo."*

"What?" I asked, my voice a whisper.

"I said heaven is in your eyes."

"It sounds better in Italian," I said, letting my hand fall away from his face.

Ruggiero laughed softly. "I agree. It is the language of love, *cara mia.*" He kept his arm around my waist. "Let's go to bed."

That night, I didn't dream of Liam. I didn't dream of him tying me to the bed. No, I dreamed of Ruggiero, holding my hand, rubbing a much larger and rounder version of my belly. He pressed small kisses to my rounded belly, repeatedly telling me he loved me. I didn't know which dream scared me more.

Chapter 10

꧁꧂

JACE

The next morning, I woke up to the smell of ham. Did Ruggiero cook for me? And did he go to the store? The only pork I had in my fridge was bacon. With a large yawn, I stretched my body and opened my eyes.

I rolled on my side, rays of sunlight painting my face. Squinting, I shielded myself from the beaming light with my hand as I stepped out of bed. Ruggiero had opened my curtains and neatly tied them to frame the window. Looking out over the parking lot and dumpster, the view was a little crappy, but it was a beautiful day outside. A good start to a hopefully good day.

I bent over in a quick stretch before I went into the bathroom to complete my morning routine. Once my bladder was emptied and breath was fresh, I washed my face to get the sleep out of my eyes.

Alright, time for food now.

I found Ruggiero in the kitchen, dressed in a tank top and his work pants, and I couldn't resist breaking into a smile. His dark hair was wet, curled around his ears. I laughed to myself. He'd definitely showered

71

while I slept and used my shampoo. Crossing my arms, I said, "I didn't know you liked to play husband."

"Not playing husband," he said, shaking his head. "I like to feed you, Jace, and want to ensure your day starts well."

"Aren't you a sweetheart?" I put my arms around him and my heart fluttered as his arms circled my waist.

"Opposites attract. I'm a sweetheart and you're my little *diavola*." He pressed a kiss to my forehead and then released me. "I don't want the food to burn."

I stood there, watching him. A swarm of butterflies erupted in my stomach as he slid my floral oven mitt onto his hand and opened the oven.

At his sweet gestures, pieces of my dream flooded me.

"Hey," I said while Ruggiero grabbed the food from the oven. "Last time we had sex, did you use a condom?"

He raised a brow at me. "We never use condoms." Ruggiero set the food on top of the stove and then turned toward me. "You're on birth control, remember?" He frowned. "Why? I'm not sleeping with anyone else if that's what you were wondering."

Well, duh.

We hadn't said it out loud yet, but I was pretty sure we were exclusive when it came to sex. At least I hoped so.

"No, no, I just… it's nothing," I mumbled.

"Did you miss your period?" he asked, his brown eyes wide with concern.

"No, I should get it by the end of the month." I sighed and ran a hand through my hair. "Don't worry about it. It's nothing. I just had a dream."

His voice was warm and encouraging. "Tell me about your dream, *bella*."

"I was pregnant and you were kissing my stomach," I told him slowly.

"It was... weird."

Ruggiero shook his head and laughed. "It's just a dream, *cara mia*."

"Yeah," I said, nodding. "You're right."

"But hey, if it's symbolic for the future, Italians make good family men," he said, winking at me.

I hope it's not symbolic. I can't handle that.

I played off my worry, rolling my eyes. "Yeah, yeah, Ruggiero. You're crazy." Curious, I inched closer to him, to see what it was he was making. "What is that?"

"Pizza rústica," he said matter-of-factly.

"Come again."

"Pizza. Rústica."

"Which is?"

"It's called Italian Easter ham pie." He gave me a soft smile, pressing a kiss to my forehead. "Don't be so skeptical. It's good."

His kiss made my heart skip a beat, but I hid my feelings behind my furrowed brows. "Mhm, okay. I'll try anything once."

Ruggiero's face broke out into a grin and he placed a couple of pieces on each plate. He gestured for me to sit and I silently complied. He placed the plates on the table, grabbing two forks and returning to the table. "Now, are you going to eat or am I going to have to feed you?"

"Well, I can't eat if you have both of the forks, silly." I was attempting to keep my composure, but truth be told, I had butterflies in my stomach. It had been a while since someone cooked for me, and it scared me how much I felt for him.

He seemed almost perfect.

"My apologies, Jace." He offered me the utensil and I thanked him with a nod. "Alright, now, I want to see you take a bite," Ruggiero said, watching me intently.

I broke eye contact and focused on my food, though it was hard to pretend like he wasn't still staring. The food looked good. If anything, it looked like a very thick quiche. I sectioned off a piece. Closing my mouth around the fork, I hummed appreciatively.

"You like?"

I let silence pass for a few moments as I finished chewing. "Of course, Ruggiero. Rarely do I just outright not like something. However, some of the meals my dad used to make were ... not good."

He chuckled. "Throw out some examples."

"Well, for starters, he sure knows how to ruin some meatloaf. And don't get me started on all the different casseroles he attempted."

"None of them were good?"

"*None* of them were good. Not even one." I laughed before eating another bite. "But this," I started, using my hand to cover my mouth, "this is good as fuck."

He laughed along with me. "Well, I pray I get the chance to cook for you again."

Ruggiero and I continued to talk over breakfast, sharing little anecdotes about our lives between chewing. I learned about his childhood in Italy, how he was an only child and while it was lonely, he learned to pick up hobbies to occupy himself, like cooking and helping his father, who had also been a mechanic. I told him about my awkward high school years and the time a weirdo asked Jackson and I if we were dating, after mentioning that we looked alike. Ruggiero was so easy to talk to. I'd been smiling more since we started seeing each other.

He wiped his face with his napkin and stood up. "I've got to head out for work. The longer I'm here, the less likely it is I'll go."

"And why is that?" I poked.

"Oh, Jace, I think you know. I could sit here staring at you all day if given the chance. You look too sinful in that Batman shirt and those panties." He winked at me, grabbing his plate and making his way to the sink.

I followed in his actions. Once my plate was in the sink, I got close to him, breathing in his inviting scent. I didn't know what kind of cologne he used, but it made him smell delicious.

"Or…" I caressed his arm and gave him with a warm smile. I ghosted my fingers over the front of his crotch. "I'm sure we can squeeze in a little unholiness to send you off."

He smirked, letting his hand trail under my shirt and then between my legs. His fingers petting my warmth softly. "Or, my little *diavola*, I can return later with the promise to get you off. How's that sound?"

I stood on my tiptoes, letting his hand fall away to press a kiss to his lips. "Okay." I turned around, purposely letting my butt graze his front as I walked away. "But I want it so good that my toes curl."

His voice followed closely behind me. "As always. Your wish is my command."

I stopped at the door to let him out. "What a gentleman you are," I teased, unlocking it.

"Of course, *bella*." Ruggiero smiled at me. "Do a little spin for me, will you?"

Laughing lightly, I spun. There was something nice about being admired this way. So openly. I only looked half-decent and had yet to shower for the day. It sounded cliche, but with Ruggiero, I felt like the most attractive woman in the world. "Like that?"

"Yes, like that. And I'll grab my bag when I come back. One more time before I go," he said. He pulled me into his arms and kissed me gently. After a few seconds, he stepped away. "Have a good day, Jace. I'll see you later."

"You too, Ruggiero." With a lazy smile, I shut the door behind him. I couldn't wait to see him later. As much as I didn't want to admit it, it was nice for someone to be truly interested in me.

Chapter 11

❧⟡❧

RUGGIERO

I slammed the car door shut and leaned against the steering wheel with a sigh. I'd left my bag over at Jace's house this morning, but I was tempted to go home anyway. My uniform was filthy, and I probably reeked of motor oil. I sniffed my shirt, a varnish-like scent burning my nose. Never mind. I definitely smelled like motor oil.

I took my shirt off and threw it in the passenger seat. As much as I didn't want to go to her smelling like petroleum, I wouldn't ruin her night. I had no idea what we were to each other, but she expected me to come back. I just hoped she was okay with me breaking my promise to have sex.

To liven my mood, I played music from my phone, choosing a curated R&B playlist. Humming to Justin Timberlake's "Suit & Tie," I started my truck and headed in the direction of Jace's apartment. Timberlake wasn't my all-time favorite artist, but I liked his music. It was ironic. I wanted to be on my suit and tie shit and I was dirty as fuck. My tank top was still pretty clean, so that was good.

If I didn't know any better, I'd think the song was about her. I couldn't help it; I was an ass man and hers was pretty damn nice.

I thought back to the second time we had sex. She'd called me daddy. I looked forward to the next moment she called me by the name. It wouldn't be tonight; my antidepressants coupled with the stressful day I had wouldn't allow it. I'd never been the type to fuck just to relieve stress and I wasn't going to start now, especially with her. She deserved more than that. Still, I hoped she'd call me daddy again soon.

A few songs later, I pulled into the parking lot. I called her as I shut off the engine. She answered in two rings. "Hello, Ruggiero."

"Hi, Jace," I said, smiling. "I'm here."

"What are you waiting for then?" She laughed. "Come inside."

"Alright, I'm coming." I hung up and got out of the truck, leaving my uniform shirt. As exhausted as I was, my heart galloped with excitement as I approached the building.

The door to the building swung open. Jace stood there in an oversized Dollywood t-shirt and a pair of house shoes, beautiful as always. Her smile was radiant. She waved me towards her. "Why're you walking so slow, Mr. de Fiore?" she half-shouted. "I'm barely wearing any clothes and I'm sure my neighbors wouldn't appreciate it."

With a smirk, I shook my head, jogging to the entrance. Once inside, I grimaced as she looked me over. "Sorry about the mess," I said, gesturing to my dirtied pants. "Long day at the shop."

"Ruggiero, I don't care about that. I know where you work." She grabbed my hand and led me to her apartment. "Do you know how many times I've had to touch literal shit at work?"

I avoided making a face. *Honestly? No. I don't want to either.*

"Alright, but I'm not tracking grime across your carpet." I took my boots off before heading inside. Setting them down next to the door, I pulled her in for a hug. I breathed in her scent, reveling in her. "It's nice to see you, *bella*."

She wrapped her arms around my waist, hugging me tightly. "It's nice to see you too." She let go and found a seat on the couch. "Feel free to join me."

I was still hesitant about touching her furniture. Usually, when I got off of work, I went home and took a hot shower.

Stripping from these muddied clothes was always an option. Without a second thought, I unfastened my pants, pushing them off. I folded the pants and sat them on top of my boots. Satisfied, I walked to the couch.

She laughed. "You didn't have to do all of that."

"I know I didn't, but I did it anyway." I sat next to her and kissed her cheek. Slinging an arm around her, I relaxed in front of the TV. A woman with long black hair was on the screen, her face annoyed as she fussed.

Is this the Kardashian show she likes?

I smiled at the thought. I didn't care much for reality TV, but I'd watch whatever she wanted. Remembering my promise, I looked at her, pulling her a little closer. "Jace."

She met my eyes, placing a hand on my thigh.

"I just wanted to apologize, *cara mia*. We were supposed to have such a good session that your toes curled."

Rolling her eyes, she grinned. "It's okay, Ruggiero. You're a working man. You're allowed to be tired."

"Thank you," I said. I truly appreciated her words.

Jace leaned against me. "No problem." She turned her attention back to the show. Her thumb caressed my thigh, sending tingles along my skin.

I wanted to reach out and caress her face, but I stopped myself. *What are we doing? What are we to each other? Am I being too affectionate?*

I ran my free hand through my hair. I was sitting in my boxers, watching this show about rich women, and I had no idea what we were doing. It'd been a long time since I'd dated anyone, but it felt like that's what we were doing.

I won't ask. I'm going to ask. I don't want to ask. It won't hurt to ask. Just have to rip off the band aid.

My curiosity got the best of me. "Jace, what are we doing here?"

"We're having a good time," she said. She didn't take her eyes from the screen. "Tell me about work."

I hid my hurt behind a masked smile. "Work was fine." I put my hand on top of hers, lacing our fingers. "I think we're having more than a good time."

"Yeah, hanging out and having sex with you has been nice." She took her hand away, placing it on her lap.

Ouch. Glad she's frank, I guess.

"Okay, let me ask a different question." She paused the show and turned to me, giving me her full attention. I didn't miss the hint of annoyance on her face. "Why did your last relationship end? I know that sometimes you're a little hard to get through to, but you're not awful. You're pretty nice when you want to be. I don't have to tell you this because you know, but sex with you is amazing, too. So, forgive me, but I am curious."

"Assuming I even have a previous relationship to tell you about, let's just say it ended for various reasons," she told me, her aggravation clear. "Arguments, mutual dissatisfaction, mutual loss of interest, adultery."

I nodded. Didn't seem like it was mutual. By her pained gaze, she didn't think it was mutual, either. "Do you think that we could ever—"

"Why did your last relationship end?" she asked.

I shifted in my seat. I didn't love telling people about Martina, but I'd disclose since I was asking her to. "I was twenty-three. She was twice my age and felt like she was stealing my chance away from a conventional relationship." She especially felt that way when she was diagnosed with stage four ovarian cancer a year in.

"Hmm. Did you love her?" Her hand returned to my thigh. "Is that the reason why you moved here?"

"Yes and no," I admitted. "Yes, I did love her. I hadn't cared about her age, but the age difference bothered her. The insecurity about it made it hard for her to fully commit."

Was that why Jace didn't want to do anything more than "have fun"? Because of her *insecurities?*

I took a deep breath, nervous, and raked my hand through my hair again. "I didn't move here because of her, though. Italy was starting to suffocate me, and I was ready for new scenery. And at the time, it was very opportunistic for skilled manual laborers." I paused, mulling over my next words. "I regret very little. If things hadn't taken a left turn, I would have never met you, *bella*."

Jace snatched her hand away and stood up from the couch. "Why don't you go take a shower and I'll finish up dinner? I'm sure you're hungry."

Good going, Ruggiero. She shut down—again.

I looked up at her, ignoring the burning sensation in my chest. "Will you be joining me?"

She crossed her arms. "The food will burn."

"Okay," I said. I wouldn't argue with her. I pressed a kiss to her forehead before finding my way to the shower.

I turned the water on and stepped underneath the spray to wet my hair. I stretched forward, bracing my hands on the shower tiles as the stream massaged my skin. The water pelting my muscles only did so much to relax me.

This woman was giving me so many mixed signals. If we were just having a good time, why had she asked me to come over last night?

I grabbed the washrag I used this morning and squirted some of her lavender-scented body wash on it. I lathered the soap on my body, paying special attention to the grease on my hands.

Did I not make it clear from the start that I wasn't interested in just fucking? I didn't typically ask someone to dinner if I only wanted to have fun, nor surprise them with a movie night.

But she never said she wanted more, idiot.

So, why did it feel like she wanted more? Why else would she share details about her dream? Why else was it important for me to know she dreamed she was having *my* baby?

I scrubbed my skin vigorously. I was probably the one overthinking, reading too much into everything. I could step away and leave her alone, or I could enjoy it for what it was. Either way, she wanted me. And she was clearly hiding something. Whatever it was, it frightened her. Was that why she was hesitant to go any further?

I rinsed off, got out of the shower, and dried my body. After hanging my towel back on the rack, I headed to her room to get more clothes out of my bag and caught a whiff of the food she made. It was mouthwatering. I dressed quickly in a t-shirt and a pair of pajama pants.

As I walked to the kitchen, I decided it was settled. I wasn't ready to let her go yet, so I'd just have to learn how to have fun. Her delicious cooking only strengthened my resolve.

Chapter 12

꧁꧂

JACE

Ruggiero and I had hung out since our unavoidable "what are we" conversation. That didn't stop me from thinking about the flicker of hurt on his face when I brushed off his question days later. But I'd rather that than hurt him in the end. I wouldn't be able to give him more. No matter how much my heart yearned for a companion, I didn't do well with more.

We were fuck buddies and we had a great time together. It didn't matter that I felt special around him, cherished even. It couldn't happen. Remaining fuck buddies would keep things from becoming complicated. I refused to entertain anything else.

"Hello? You still in the real world, Jacey?" Jackson waved his hand in front of my face.

I looked away from the window. "Yeah, Jackson, I'm right here. It's hard to miss you wearing that yellow jersey."

Since I'd been spending so much time with Ruggiero when I wasn't at work, I'd decided to hang out with my brother for a change. While having dinner at my mom's every couple of weeks wasn't bad, I liked hanging out with just Jackson, like when we were kids.

"Whatever you say." Jackson leaned back in his seat and sipped his protein shake. "You just seem far away."

I shook my head. "I just have a lot on my mind." I didn't have many friends and I was glad to have Jackson around.

"Alright, so tell me about it. What's got you so wound up?"

"I met a guy," I blurted out. His eyes widened and I narrowed mine. "Don't act like that. I meet guys all the time."

"Yeah, right, sis. You don't meet guys that you stress over." Jackson paused as the waitress returned with our pizza. Thanking her, he turned his attention back to me. "Who's the guy? Why are you so stressed? Do I need to talk to him?"

I slid a few pieces onto my place and patting his hand with my free one. "Relax, Jackson. He's a nice guy. He hasn't done anything wrong."

"Okay, so what's the problem?" He eyed me as he grabbed a piece of pizza off of the tray.

"We've been seeing each other for a bit, but I think he wants to date me. And I don't know, I'm just so tired of dating guys. I'm tired of relationships." I took a swig of my beer. "Even worse, the dreams are coming back."

I trusted Jackson with almost everything. Aside from Cleo, he was the only one who knew about what happened my senior year, the year that changed my life. He knew about my dreams far too well. After it happened, I had nightmares until I started college. Now, the dreams occurred episodically with no rhyme or reason.

He winced. "Shit, Jace. I'm sorry." He raked a hand through his hair. "Did you ever decide to talk to someone about it?"

I looked down at the wooden tabletop. I picked at my pizza toppings, using my other hand to run a finger over the different names people had etched into the table. "You know I don't like talking about it."

Jackson scoffed. "And here we are talking about it. I'm still so fucking angry I never got to kick his ass."

I rolled my eyes and plucked off more toppings. "We're only talking about it because of the dreams."

"That's the point, sis. If you don't want to talk to *me* about it—"

"Then I need to talk to someone about it. Blah blah blah." He'd said it so many times over the past decade that he sounded like a broken record. "It's fine. The dreams will go away like they always do."

At least I hoped they would.

He cocked his head. "So, what about this guy you met?"

I sighed heavily, meeting his gaze again. "After Garret, I'm not sure I want to be with anyone. Why keep getting in relationships when they never work?"

And why ruin this thing with Ruggiero by involving too many emotions? Things between us didn't need to change. I didn't want them to change and risk him disappearing once he started learning more about me.

"Jacey, you just haven't found anyone that works for you..." His lips stretched into a boyish grin. "Unless you did."

Jackson had unwavering hope that I would stop attracting the wrong men and find true love. His hope felt like a fever dream.

"Maybe I have, maybe I haven't," I mumbled. "It doesn't matter."

"It does matter. You didn't deserve for Garret to cheat on you and you definitely didn't deserve what happened back in high school." He frowned, reaching forward to grab my hand. "Look, I don't know this guy. He might not even stick around. But not everyone is going to treat you like they did."

How could I trust that? I'd spent the entire year or so sticking to one-night stands to carefully avoid commitment, and somehow I'd wrapped myself up in Ruggiero. Why did I agree to dinner that night?

Because you like him. Duh.

"I guess." I finished off my drink, ready to change the subject. "As I told him, we can just enjoy things, and he's okay with that."

"Alright, fair. So, stop stressing. You've got no reason to." He picked up his shake and took a long, dramatic sip. "Promise you'll at least consider talking to someone."

"I promise," I groaned.

"Good." His hand covered his mouth as he chewed. Jackson was only annoying because he cared. The guy hadn't even hesitated to say yes when I invited him out for lunch today. "That's a step, at least."

"I think so, too," I said, smiling. "What's new in your life?"

"I've been talking to this girl. We've gone out for drinks a few times and she's super sweet." He sat up in his seat and drank more of his shake.

"That's it?" I raised a brow.

He pulled his phone out of his pocket and grinned at whatever was on the screen. "If you're going to be tight-lipped about your someone, I will, too." Jackson laid his phone face-down on the table and grabbed the canister of parmesan cheese. "Are we gonna eat our pizza or what?"

"Yeah, we'll eat our pizza," I said. "No point in letting it get cold."

Lunch continued with light, superficial conversation. We steered away from talking about the rough things in life and instead shared our favorite parts of our jobs.

We'd both chosen careers where we could be a service to others. I told him about my love of interacting with our temporary and permanent residents, offering them a sense of companionship in addition to helping them with their health. In turn, Jackson told me of his love of improving people's health through exercise, helping them achieve the body and mental peace they want. I didn't exercise as often as I wanted but what the experts said was true; exercise boosted emotional well-being.

When we finished eating, we wrapped each other in hugs before heading to our cars. I waved, telling him I'd see him next week at dinner.

I drove home with his words fresh on my mind. They reminded me too much of my talks with Cleo. I was used to Cleo nagging at me, but Jackson usually steered clear of it unless necessary. I didn't know why I'd thought I could get away with casually mentioning the dreams without him saying something about getting help. I couldn't even be upset with him because I knew he loved me.

Sun in my eyes, I took my sunglasses out of the overhead compartment and slid them on. It was a nice fall afternoon. It was one of my off days this week and I was proud of myself for getting out of the house instead of laying in bed, letting my dreams consume me. I was self-aware enough to know that wallowing away in my covers wouldn't do me any good.

I wasn't sure what I ate that was sprinkled in positivity, but I had the urge to continue making myself proud. As the wind caressed me through the open window and blew flyaways of hair around my face, I mentally planned out the rest of my day.

Once home, I kicked my shoes off and plopped down on my couch. I grabbed my laptop from the coffee table, deciding it was time to look into "talking to someone." Cleo and Jackson might've had a point. I wasn't excited about getting my brain and feelings analyzed, but... how long was I going to be held hostage to my past? How long was I going to be kept restless because of the nightmares? Every time I thought about the incident, my skin crawled with fear and disgust. I was pretty good at pushing it down so I could enjoy the nice things in life, but sometimes I struggled. Lately, that struggle had been more difficult.

I googled psychology websites to see what I could find. Some of them looked reputable. Others looked suspicious, like I'd end up with a bunch of spam calls if I put my information into one of their forms. Taking a deep breath, I settled on a site for a company called *Walk to Tranquility.* The name wasn't super flattering, but the page didn't seem like it would give my laptop a virus.

I explored the website, appreciating that it allowed me to choose filters to narrow down the services. It was user-friendly and showed me results for Memphis. My discomfort eased as I navigated it, but it didn't dissipate entirely. The more specific my results became, the more real what I was doing became.

Profile pictures of psychiatrists and mental health counselors filled the screen. Almost all of them smiled in their portraits; some of them looked as if they were forcing it, but most looked as genuine as they could. I clicked on profile after profile, reading their bios. I scanned each of them with growing disappointment until I came across one that stopped me in my tracks.

Hi, I'm Joanna, a psychiatric NP with WTT. Before I tell you about the things I specialize in, I want to share some things about myself. I am a Honduran-American cis-female who grew up in Midtown. I am the middle child out of five and if I haven't seen it all, I've seen a whole lot. I treat many different issues, but I specialize in sexual abuse because I have firsthand experience with it and I understand how hard it can be to overcome. I would like to help you overcome those experiences in your life if you are open to it. Please do not hesitate to call me at the number provided or to send me an email for an initial consultation.

My cursor hovered over her email. She seemed… nice. Nice enough for me to give her a try, at least.

I frequently lectured the residents I cared for at Glendshire about how important it was to try new things, such as testing a new medication recommended by their doctor or attending community events to socialize. I'd even given residents warm hand-offs to our behavioral health team after they scored high on their depression and anxiety screenings.

I could do this. I could be brave.

I copy-and-pasted her email, holding my breath as I typed out a message to the nurse practitioner before I could back out of it. I didn't want the help, but… it might be good for me.

I exhaled once the message was sent, feeling both satisfied and horrified. It wasn't like a text message where I could just unsend it, especially when the email moved from my 'outbound' folder to my 'sent.'

I slapped my laptop shut and thrust it aside on the coffee table. Now that I was done with that stressful task, I didn't want to think about therapy or psychiatry for the remainder of the day. Instead, I'd pursue my next plan: distracting myself until nighttime.

I pulled my phone out and dialed Ruggiero's number. What better distraction than the man that had been occupying my brain? I put the phone on speaker and listened to it ring. As he'd done again and again without fail, he answered.

"Hello, *bella*." His voice was warm and soothed my body like hot tea.

"Hi, Ruggiero." I stood and stepped around the coffee table. "Would you like to come watch a movie with me?"

"I don't have time for a movie, but I can watch a little TV when I get off of work."

I wondered what else he was doing after work, but I wouldn't ask. It wasn't my business. "TV is fine," I said cheerily, sauntering to the kitchen. "See you later then?"

"Yes, *bella*, I'll see you later. I'll call once I'm headed your way. Until then, I'd better get back."

"Okay, yeah, go do your job. Talk to you soon." I hung up, feeling giddy.

Even though I would continue keeping him at arm's length when it came to my heart, he'd already come to know my body so well in the month since we reunited. It was tempting to let him in. His presence was exciting and comforting, and that's all I'd allow it to be.

When he worked a day shift, he didn't get off until it was nearly evening... which meant I had hours before I'd be spending time with a human.

I decided I would bake. I didn't bake as much as I used to, but I did enjoy it. I thought back to the night he surprised me after work, all smiles as he sat on the step. Once inside, he'd pulled out a myriad of desserts in the middle of my living room. He likely wouldn't be around for dinner, so I'd make him something sweet to satisfy his sweet tooth.

Nothing seemed better to me than a classic batch of chocolate chip cookies. Cooking and baking were relaxing. Mixing the ingredients and kneading the dough would keep my mind occupied and the final result would warm his stomach.

Chapter 13

֍

RUGGIERO

"Fuck, Ruggiero." Jace's voice came out in a breathy moan, her needy hands on the back of my head, pressing me to her.

My fingers dug into her waist as I thrust my tongue inside her, keeping her steady against the back of the couch as her knees weakened. My cock was hard in my pants. I wanted nothing more than to sink into her, but if I let myself, I'd never make my plans. I had no doubt. I loved her taste. Her sweet noises. Her hands gripping my hair.

It was already too much being on my knees, face buried between her legs as she moaned and cried for me, saying my name in that voice I'd grown to cherish so much. I could do this for the rest of the evening if I hadn't committed to poker night with the guys.

I couldn't help my arrogant grin as I took in her low, heavy eyes and the teeth biting into her bottom lip. I maintained eye-contact I traced the wet seam of her lips with a finger. I loved the pleasure in the flutter of her eyes, her harsh pulls on my hair. "You should invite me over for TV more often." I licked my lips as I dragged my finger up to her clit, my touch light as I circled it.

"Not if you're going to tease me like this," she gritted out. "I wouldn't have called you if—"

I shut her up as I pushed my fingers into her, her complaints dissolving into moans. "Jace, I've fucked you enough to know you enjoy the teasing, no matter how much you pretend you don't." Her pussy clenched around me as I fucked her harder with my hand. I put my mouth to her clit, my gaze still fixed to her beautifully tortured face as I swirled my tongue around the small bud.

Jace was gorgeous as she lost herself to the onslaught of pleasure, even more so when she came around my fingers. I gave her a few moments and then I withdrew my hand. Standing up, I wrapped an arm around Jace to steady her as she caught her breath.

I sucked my fingers, cleaning them of her arousal before asking, "Was that good for you?"

Jace turned towards me with rosy cheeks and a smile. "Silly question, Ruggiero," she said, pulling the hem of her dress back over her hips. "It's always good."

"Where's that aggression from a few moments ago?" I asked teasingly.

She closed the distance between us and moved my hand away from my face, guiding it towards her body to mirror my other hand on her waist. She looked up at me, her blue eyes brighter than they were when I'd first arrived. "You may have changed that."

"You came hard, you mean to say," I said. "Let's be honest here."

"Fine. I wish you didn't have to go. How's that for being honest?"

My heart squeezed but only for a second. She didn't want to admit it, but she liked me, at least in some capacity. I wouldn't press the topic, though.

My eyes flicked to my watch as I said, "I don't bail on my commitments, *bella*." Poker night started in fifteen minutes, and I had a thirty-minute drive to Jamie's if traffic was light. I kissed her forehead, grabbing my keys off the side table. "Text me, okay? We can make plans that way."

"Okay," she said softly.

I turned away from her and left her apartment. If I stayed for a minute longer, I might miss my plans altogether.

"It's about time, pretty boy," no one other than Lucky shouted as I walked through the door to Jamie's house. "Who's the lucky someone?"

I wasn't surprised to find him sitting on the arm of the couch, dressed in a plaid shirt, dark jeans, and his favorite pair of cowboy boots. All he needed was a Stetson to sit on top of his shoulder-length blonde hair.

I met Lucky three years ago when I'd started at Carlisle's. We hit it off immediately. Although Lucky grew up right here in Memphis, our childhoods were similar in how our parents constantly expected more. I'd been amazed that I could find someone like me overseas.

"Fuck off, Lucky." I dropped the pack of beer I bought on the way to Jamie's house onto the table. I grabbed a bottle and used the bottle opener on my key chain to pop the lid off. "Are the others waiting out back?"

"Yeah, they are," he said. He stood up and draped his arm over my shoulders. "Let's go."

True to Lucky's word, Jamie and Chris were outside, both of them with a drink in their hand. Like Lucky, I'd met them at the shop, though neither of them worked there anymore. Jamie was studying for the bar exam and was a paralegal at an attorney's office downtown. He dressed like it, too, always in business casual, even on a night out.

And Chris… honestly, I didn't know what Chris did. If someone were to take one glance at him, they'd probably think he was some sort of influencer.

He was the first to notice me. "What the hell took so long?" He looked down at his Tudor watch.

"I had things to do," I said.

"Well, I'm glad to see you." Chris paused to take a swig of his beer. "Thought you wouldn't show for a minute."

"Seriously," Jamie agreed. "I'm trying to think of the last time you were late and I'm drawing blanks."

I wouldn't tell them that instead of just going home and getting ready, I'd made an extra stop to see a lovely woman with the prettiest blue eyes, who made the softest and yummiest chocolate chip cookies. A woman who I could tell, underneath her hard layers, had a good heart and was keeping it guarded for a reason. A reason I would find out with time.

I trusted the three of them with the world, but I wasn't ready to talk about her. Not when I had no idea what was going on myself.

"Alright, let's lay off it." Lucky took his arm from around me and sat down in a lawn chair. "I'm ready to get this game started."

The rest of us pulled up chairs around the patio table.

Aside from reading leisurely and working my ass off at the shop— and now spending time with Jace—I loved playing cards. I started with *briscola* with the kids outside and then I was taught *scopa* by my father. When I moved to the States and met these guys, I started playing a whole lot of poker. We aimed to get together one to two times a month to play. It was our sacred time and the guys were right to give me shit.

I was never late, not in the three years since we'd started this routine.

Lucky grabbed the deck of cards from the center of the table to shuffle them. "How much are we putting in?"

Jamie straightened the collar of his polo. "Depends." He took a slow sip of what looked like a glass of whiskey. "High or low stakes?"

I remained silent, letting them make the choice.

Chris ran a hand through his cropped brown hair. "Mel and I've already budgeted for the month, so I've got the money to spare." He dug in his pocket for his wallet and slammed it on the table as if to make a point. "My vote is high stakes."

Chris and Mel were high school sweethearts. Though I'd witnessed healthy communication between the two, it was clear who called the shots and it wasn't my dear friend Christopher. I couldn't blame him.

Jace and I weren't together—and might not ever be—but she nearly had me wrapped around her finger. Especially considering how well she fed me.

"Alright, a hundred-dollar buy-in. That cool with everyone?" Lucky's eyes scanned the table and he made sure to meet all of our gazes. "If you're going to object, do it now. Otherwise, put your money on the table." As Lucky took his wallet out, Jamie and I followed suit.

Once our money was swapped with chips, Lucky dealt and we jumped into the game. I surveyed my cards with a groan. My cards weren't the best but I'd make it work. Playing poker was natural to me. Even during the shitty things I'd experienced in life, I could always find joy in playing any card game. Add in the friends I'd made and I was content.

As close as we were, we played poker brutally. Our conversations remained light, but we gave each other no leeway. I had no remorse when I chose to call on Lucky's bet, and I grinned shamelessly as Jamie passed the pot.

"You're kind of fucking me up, pretty boy," Lucky grunted.

"I'm sorry you're shit at this." I laughed. "I'll be right back." I stood, heading to the kitchen for more beer.

"He's not wrong," I heard Chris say before I was out of earshot.

I grabbed a cold beer and cracked it open. Leaning against the counter, I took a deep breath. I needed this time tonight. Lately, I was so wound up, emotionally and sexually.

The therapist I used to see would have told me to make sure I was interested in Jace for the right reasons, that I wasn't acting on a savior complex. I had think about it on my way over. Truth was, I didn't know what Jace was going through and I hadn't gone out of my way to help her. When she shut down, I didn't question it. I let her have her space.

Twenty-year-old me would have begged her to know what was wrong. He'd go above and beyond to fix whatever was bothering her, despite the problem having nothing to do with him. I took a long swig. I was glad twenty-year-old me didn't meet Jace. She would've eaten him up.

I checked my phone as I walked back outside. It had buzzed a few times since I'd arrived. My dad had messaged me a couple times, as well as Jace. Jace's text opened with a photo. Handmade gnocchi decorated a wooden cutting board, each dumpling unique, hints of flour still remaining on the surface. Underneath, she'd typed, *Tried my hand at a classic earlier.*

My stomach grumbled. I quickly responded, telling her how good it looked, and put my phone away. I needed to get back to the game before one of the guys came searching for me. Then they'd really be on my ass.

Our night wrapped up late after playing a few games of poker. I loved spending time with my friends, but I couldn't wait to get into bed. My head hurt from all the beer I'd drank and considering I'd worked a full shift today, I was bone-tired.

The affectionate man he was, Chris spread his arms wide and pulled all of us into a hug. "I should probably get home, fellas."

Chris gave us a final pat on the back and nearly sprinted to the door. A short time later, his headlights flashed through the window.

"I'm with Chris," I said, unable to hold back my yawn. "It's been great, but I'm exhausted."

"Alright, get out, all of you." Jamie threw his arms up dramatically, his lazy smile tell-tale of his fatigue. "I understand no one wants to hang out with me anymore."

I gave them both a nod. "Good night, Jamie, Lucky." I collected my empty bottles and threw them away before heading out the door.

On the drive home, I thought of my parents and my father's unanswered text messages. He was still in Italy and he'd learned how to use a cell phone so he could check up on me every few days. Especially since I'd left and never gone back.

My mother hadn't forgiven me, but he had. Her coldness didn't surprise me. There were a great number of things my mother hadn't forgiven me for. For a while, our relationship, or lack thereof, had been a frequent topic when I was in therapy.

I shook my head. There was no need to think of my mother and the ever-present disappointment on her face. Instead, I shifted my thoughts to my father and his relentless acceptance of me. I would make sure I responded to his message tomorrow if not tonight.

He had likely asked how I was doing and what was new. I would tell him, omitting Jace for the time being. We weren't really at the stage for me to make my family aware of her and we might not ever be. And more than anything, my father wanted me to settle down and start a family. I wouldn't excite him over something that may never come to fruition.

You're going to be thirty next year, he told me a few weeks ago on the phone. *I want you to be able to enjoy the benefits of love before you're too old and regretful.*

I didn't need the reminder of how old I was, but I understood what he meant. Before we broke up, Martina had told me the same thing. She wanted me to enjoy life, adulthood, and eventually parenthood.

I wanted those things, too. One day. I wasn't in a rush. While I'd never suffered any physical abuse, I wouldn't want any child to experience the childhood I'd had. Parenting was a hard job to tackle only once I knew I was ready for it. While my father wanted me to settle down, he also wanted me to be happy.

Se sono rose, fioriranno, he always said. *If they are roses, they will bloom.* It was a proverb that meant time would tell.

My thoughts drifted to Jace as the phrase rattled through my mind. I was drawn to her like a magnet, helpless to her appeal. Whatever we were—whatever we were meant to be—would become known with time. I would just have to trust that time would tell.

Chapter 14

RUGGIERO

I glanced at the clock and tore my gloves off, ditching them on the worktable when I passed it. It was noon and I was hungry.

I strolled into the break room, looking forward to the time to myself. I'd brought a turkey sandwich and a fantasy book I was in the middle of reading. It followed a fae prince that was drawn to a half-fae woman. She was unaware of her true origins and the intricacies of how the fae and humans collided; the prince felt it was his responsibility to show her. I was a third of the way in and the two had just discovered that things in the kingdom were wayward.

I pulled my lunchbox from the fridge and sat down at the table. Once I had my sandwich in one hand and the book in the other, I dove back into the story. Within a few minutes, I was swept into the fae kingdom and the secret corridor the two found to use as a safe space against listening ears.

"So, tell me about the girl or the boy who's caught your attention."

Damn it, Lucky.

He always picked the worst moments to interrupt me.

I dog-eared the page and shut the book. "There isn't anyone," I told him, doing my best to sound convincing.

"You can't waltz in here like you usually do and think I'm going to let you escape into your stories as usual." He threw his lunch bag on the table. "I wasn't going to put you on blast last night, but I know there's someone." He shrugged and slid into the chair across from me. "So, tell me about them."

Because this was Lucky fucking Fry, I knew he wouldn't let up. Not until I revealed something. "I almost hate that we're friends," I muttered.

He smirked. "Sucks because we are. Where did you meet them?" he asked, taking a large bite of his sub sandwich.

"Both times, I met her at Ale You Need. Seems almost cliche, but we both ordered screwdrivers." Accepting that I would spend the duration of my break talking instead of reading, I put the book away in my lunch box. My friend was insufferable, but I loved him. "She's a nurse."

He grunted, slouching in the chair. "Not giving me a lot of details, pretty boy."

I furrowed my brow. "That's the point."

"What's her name?"

I ignored him, refusing to give him an answer. To punctuate my point, I ate my turkey sandwich like it was the best thing in the world.

"I should've known it wouldn't be this easy."

I laid the remaining half of my sandwich down carefully and met his eyes. "Don't tell the others."

"How come?" he asked, frowning.

I leaned back in the chair with a sigh. "It's just casual. There's no need to make it a big deal."

He was my best friend and if anyone was going to confront me about my tardiness last night, I would rather it be him. He was the only one that knew I hadn't truly dated in over six years and that I was careful with my company. Occasionally, I took someone home from the bar but they rarely stuck.

"Okay, so if that's true, next time we play poker, don't be late. You know we take that time seriously. I mean, I'd understand if she were someone special to you, but—"

"Lucky," I groaned. "It's casual. You got me, okay? I like her, yes, but we are keeping things casual. Given that, I'd like to keep things quiet for the moment."

"Okay, okay," he said, putting his hands up in a show of surrender. "I'll back off."

My friend was nosy and insufferable, but I expected nothing less than his surrender.

I wiped my hands with a napkin as I finished the last of my food. "Thanks. I promise I'll inform you if it becomes anything more."

"That sounds alright to me. How's your dad?"

"He's good. I talked to him today. Their anniversary is coming up and I sent them a gift."

"What does Ruggiero give the humble father who wants nothing and the mother who has everything?" he mused. "Honestly, my parents' anniversary is around the corner, too. I need some ideas."

"For starters, I don't buy them separate gifts. I haven't done that in years. I try to give them an experience," I explained. "For one of their first dates many decades ago, they went to an opera house in Trieste. I bought them tickets to an upcoming performance there. I didn't spoil the surprise, but I did tell my father to expect mail."

Lucky furrowed his brow. "Didn't you buy them admission to a wine tasting last year?"

I smiled warmly. "I did."

"Geeze, Louise. Your parents are spoiled. This didn't help me with my parents' gifts at all."

If I was spoiling anyone, it was my father. My mother hadn't done much for me besides ridicule me and make me hate myself for who I was. The internalized hate lessened over the years, but it never completely disappeared. But I wouldn't get into all of that with Lucky.

My phone buzzed in my pocket. I ignored it, clasping my hands together on the table. "Well, what do you get for the mother that's never satisfied and the father that's often absent?"

He shrugged, pulling out a bag of chips. "I've got a month or so to figure it out. You and I will figure something out."

"I don't doubt it," I said. My phone buzzed again. Tempted, I slid my phone out of my back pocket. The screen showed a new message from Jace.

Do you celebrate Halloween?

Sometimes.

I smiled as I read her message. I didn't make it a point to celebrate the holiday, but I'd gone to a few parties and bar-crawled with the guys in the past.

Her reply came quickly.

I know this is early, but my brother's best friend is throwing a party at the end of October. Do you want to come with me?

"That her texting you, pretty boy?" Lucky asked.

A cocky smirk spread across his face. "It's her," I confirmed.

I'll come.

Great. You're welcome to bring some friends too.

101

"You can wipe that grimy smile off your face. It wasn't a hard guess, Lucky. We just talked about her." I ran my hand down my face with a sigh, standing to grab coffee. I had a long day ahead of me and I needed the caffeine.

"No need to look beat."

I rounded the corner to the coffee maker. "She invited me to a Halloween party. Well, us, in a sense."

His smile grew. "*Us?* One minute she's a secret and the next I get to meet her?"

"Only you," I said, my voice firm. "Like I said earlier, I want to keep this quiet."

"As you wish, pretty boy. My lips are sealed," he promised, pretending to zip his lips up, lock them, and throw the key. "So what will our costumes be?"

"We'll figure something out," I muttered. The coffee slowly started dripping into the pot. I leaned against the counter, crossing my arms. It would be a long few weeks leading up to the party.

"I have the perfect idea," he sang.

As he started explaining his plan, I decided I was going to need more than one cup of coffee today to deal with my best friend.

Chapter 15

❧

RUGGIERO

"Remind me why I'm supposed to hold this glass all night."

Lucky wanted me to wear an outfit that wasn't too different from what I usually wore: a black shirt and a pair of blue jeans. He'd added a silver chain, a silver bracelet, one hoop earring, and a whiskey glass to my usual get-up.

Lucky's costume was a far cry from his style. He wore a long-sleeved plaid button-down and a pair of ridiculous glasses that made his eyes look like they were on the outside of a fishbowl. "It's a vital part of the costume, pretty boy. Julian *always* has a cup."

"And you're supposed to be?"

"I'm supposed to be Bubbles." He narrowed his eyes in annoyance and shook his head. "Geez, dude, you really need to watch *Trailer Park Boys*. I'm getting tired of you not understanding the references."

I rolled my eyes. "I'm so sorry, your highness, that I don't decide to watch television when I go home."

Lucky gave an exasperated sigh. "It's been three years, pretty boy. Three. Years."

103

It was true. He told me about the show shortly after we met, as it was one of his favorites. But with my ever-growing list of books I wanted to read, I didn't have the time to commit to a new television series. It was bad enough I'd been sucked into watching Jace's comfort show whenever she had it on.

"Sorry, Lucky." I gazed in the full-length mirror in his living room, emitting a deep sigh. "This is worse than I imagined. I look like a beefcake."

"How on Earth did I get stuck with you?" He met me at the mirror, draping an arm around my shoulders as he undoubtedly checked himself out. "The beefcake persona is what you're going for here. Let's lower your standards for your appearance just for one night, okay? It's a costume."

"Yes, I know it's a costume. I'm glad because you look fucking stupid." I laughed, shoving him playfully.

He shoved me back and I tightened my grip around my glass to keep from dropping it. "Y'know, considering how high maintenance you are, it's a wonder how you've managed to find someone who's actually interested in you."

"Ouch, Lucky," I said and feigned a hiss. I wouldn't tell him that I didn't know how interested she was. So far, she'd made it known that she mainly liked my body. "Kind of funny that you're talking shit. When's the last time someone has been into you?"

"Do me a favor and shut the fuck up, pretty boy. The problem isn't people being interested in me; it's me being interested in people." He slid his wallet into his pocket before sitting on the couch to put his shoes on.

"Ah," I said, setting the cup on the side table, "I forgot that you can dish it, but you can't take it. What about the last girl you were talking to? The one that dumped you?"

Lucky stood, shoving his keys in his pocket. "Who's driving to this shindig? Me or you?"

I smiled. "How about you drive in the event she wants to take me home? No need to leave you stranded at some stranger's house."

"And what if I choose to bring someone home? Do you plan to cockblock the whole ride back?"

"Oh, but you are hardly interested in people. That's the problem, remember?"

"I'm not as picky when it comes to sex. You know that." He looked at himself one last time in the mirror. "Grab your keys *and* the glass so we can get out of here."

I obliged, swiftly walking to the front door and pulling it open. "After you, handsome," I said, gesturing to him with the glass.

"Fuck you."

Once we were checked for firearms and given wristbands, we were let into the party. Her brother's friend lived not too far from Mud Island, which I'd been told was a rather wealthy part of the city.

I didn't know how I'd find Jace in the sea of strangers. The large house wasn't yet full, but I could tell it would be soon. The foyer was already bustling with people in various costumes illuminated by the dim lighting as they danced to EDM, some masked and others with impressive makeup morphing their features from man to monster.

The more daring of us, Lucky walked further into the house and I followed in stride. "I wonder what this guy, or his parents, does for a living," Lucky said. "I've only been to this side of town a handful of times."

"Your guess is as good as mine," I said. "This guy is her brother's friend and we're her guests."

"Where is your girl, by the way?"

I shrugged. "Again, your guess is as good as mine." I pulled out my phone and shot Jace a text to inform her that Lucky and I were there.

Excitement raced through my veins at the thought of her. I hadn't seen her since last week when I'd almost been tempted to ditch all of my plans. I didn't know what her costume was, just as she didn't know mine, but I knew whatever she'd chosen would be on par with her usual effortless yet sultry appeal. She had a way of making even scrubs look sexy. Hell, she had a way of making everything sexy.

"Well, pretty boy," Lucky said, turning on his heel to face me "Until we find her, let's find the alcohol. Thirsty isn't the word to describe how I feel."

Together, we moved through the nameless faces and dancing bodies until we found an expansive kitchen, an island and high-top chairs in its center. Unlike the foyer and the halls, the kitchen was brightly lit and, to my enjoyment, the EDM was softer. The marbled counter was lined with spirits and the island full of finger foods and bags of chips. Near the sink were rows of paper plates and plastic cups. The few guests that occupied the kitchen busied themselves with pouring drinks and grabbing food.

Lucky threw me a smile and patted my shoulder. "I'm going to go join those scary-looking masked people. I just know that guy has some good vodka."

I nodded and leaned against the wall, the empty glass in one hand and my phone in the other. As if on cue, my phone vibrated with a notification.

Oops. Jackson and I just got here. Where are you? I'll come find you!

All good, cara mia. In the kitchen.

Okay, awesome (: Here we come.

I didn't alert Lucky of her impending arrival. Instead, I slipped my phone back into my pocket and pushed off the wall. I was tired of my glass being empty and right now, in a home I wasn't familiar with surrounded by people I didn't know, I wanted nothing more than the smooth burn of whiskey sliding down my throat. In a few short steps, I joined Lucky at the marbled counters.

He cared little for my presence, his head thrown back as he downed a red cup of what smelled like cheap tequila. He lowered the cup with a grin, using the back of his hand to wipe the remnants from his mouth. "Fuck, that's some good liquor. Top shelf, I'd bet."

"Any good whiskey over here? Rum? I feel like this Julian character didn't walk around with an empty glass."

"You're right, pretty boy. He walks around with a rum and coke," he clarified, placing his cup in an open spot on the counter top. His hands moved across the counter, eyes skimming the labels. "You want to stay in character, or do you want whiskey instead?"

I envisioned the bouncer putting the neon blue wristband on Jace's left arm as he did Lucky and me after patting her down for weapons. Something twisted in my gut at the thought of the bouncer's hands on her, even if that was part of his job. There was no need for anyone else to touch her. By now, she was probably almost to the kitchen. My skin pricked with need at the thought of being in the same room with her again, and I was unable to stop the events of our last meeting from flooding my brain.

Nothing will happen tonight. Look at all the people around.

We were here to enjoy the party, nothing more nothing less. No matter how good she might look tonight, she deserved to be taken in comfort, not in the shadows of some party with EDM music as the soundtrack.

I held my glass towards Lucky and bottle of dark liquor he held. "I'm sure."

"Hold it steady," he said, filling the glass with whiskey. "Needing some liquid courage tonight?"

"More like a distraction. I have a feeling it's going to be a long night."

"And why's that?" He picked up the bottle of tequila again to refill his cup.

Before I could answer, I heard her honeyed voice calling out to me. "Ruggiero," she sang, "I'm here."

I wasn't prepared for what I saw when I turned around. I took her in, rendered speechless. I didn't know what this one-piece suit was called, but I fucking loved it.

Chapter 16

JACE

Slowly, Ruggiero turned to face me as he lifted a glass to his lips. The blonde-haired man next to him followed suit, his mouth stretching into a grin. The stranger's eyes were obscured by a pair of thick glasses, but I was certain he was staring at me and Jackson.

Arm still looped with Jackson's, I walked towards them, my gaze fixed on Ruggiero. His costume was familiar, the ensemble something I'd seen before but couldn't place where. Wherever it was from, it looked damn good on him. His black shirt was form-fitting, drawing my eyes to his muscular arms and those hands I appreciated so much.

"Let me guess," Jackson said as we stopped in front of them. "*Trailer Park Boys?*"

Of course, Jackson would know where the outfit was from.

The man's smile grew even wider. "And Ruggiero here thought people wouldn't get the reference." He set down his red cup and extended his hand. "I'm Lucky."

Jackson grabbed his hand, shaking it with a matching grin. "Jackson.

I fucking love that show."

Ruggiero hadn't said anything yet, despite my calling for his attention, and I desperately wanted to hear his voice.

"Very glad to meet someone with taste." Once done greeting Jackson, Lucky faced me. "And you are?"

"I'm Jace, nice to meet you," I said, barely giving Lucky a glance as I bypassed his handshake and moved closer to hug Ruggiero.

I missed him so much.

I threw my arms around his waist and buried my face in his chest. His free arm slipped around me without hesitation, enveloping me in his warmth.

Why didn't we hug more?

Maybe because you *don't hug often.*

I thought back to the two of us on my couch, watching that raunchy comedy. He denied any advances and at first it'd hurt, but then he'd pulled me in close, settling his hand comfortably on my hip. He was tender that night, even more so the next day when I panicked during sex. His tenderness was alarming and comforting all at the same time.

This is nothing more than sex and hanging out, I reminded myself. *Nothing more. It* can't *be anything more.*

Clearing my throat, I loosened my arms and put a respectable amount of space between us. I opened my mouth to speak, but any thought of what I was about to say vanished as I met the desire Ruggiero's eyes. I stepped further away, hoping more space would stop whatever the fuck was going on.

As if sensing my bafflement, Ruggiero snaked an arm around my waist once again, his smile charismatic as he looked down at me. "It's nice to see you, *bella*." With his other hand occupied by a glass, he nodded towards my brother. "You must be the infamous Jackson. It's a pleasure to meet you. I'd shake your hand, but—"

"My dear sister jumped you before you could do that. I've heard

110

very little about you, but you get brownie points for the costume."
Jackson smiled boyishly at the men, his eyes cutting to Ruggiero's arm
around me for a split second. "It's nice to meet you, Julian with the
Italian accent."

"Forgive me, but what exactly are you meant to be tonight?"
Ruggiero asked, his brows furrowed as he observed my brother's
costume.

Mentally shaking off my uninvited nervousness, I grinned and
joined the conversation again. "Ever seen *The Witcher*? He's Geralt
of Rivia, except Jackson's hair isn't white and he isn't buff like the
character."

Judging by Ruggiero's expression, he still had no idea what the
costume was, but he said nothing further about it. Instead, he turned
to me, one eyebrow raised. He dipped his head down, his lips brushing
my ear, and said, "Can we get out of here?"

I ignored the warm electricity running down my spine and answered
him with a nod before returning my attention to Ruggiero and my
guests. "Lucky, it was a pleasure meeting you. Jackson, be nice to
Lucky. Okay? Okay." I patted Jackson on the shoulder and attempted
to smile sweetly at Lucky. "We'll leave you fellas to your night."

I shook Ruggiero's arm from around me, gesturing for him to follow
me. I wanted to talk to him, to touch him, to let go in his arms in
private. I didn't have to turn around to know that he was trailing
behind me; I could feel his presence, his warmth close by. He hadn't
said anything about my outfit yet, but knowing him, he was likely
staring at my ass. To be fair, I didn't take much care in concealing it
and the tail was surely drawing his attention.

My apparel tonight was on par with a nickname Ruggiero had let
slip only twice—*diavola*, or devil. I dug out an old pair of black knee-
high boots and complemented them with a red devil headband, black
bodysuit, and sheer red tights I found at a store near my house. Simple

enough for a quick costume, sexy enough for me to feel empowered once again.

The last few times Ruggiero and I were together, I let my guard down, allowing myself to be swept away by his good humor and sweet gestures. Tonight, I'd remind myself once more that my aversion to romance and the boundaries I built were my armor, my sexual prowess was my shield.

He remained silent as I led him to a room. I knew Spencer's house well enough. He was a close friend of Jackson's and I'd been to some of his parties before. His large home had many discreet places for people to connect on borrowed time, such as the spare bedroom I took Ruggiero to upstairs.

It was only when I shut the door and locked it that he spoke.

"What on God's earth are you wearing?" he asked, licking his lips. He set the glass down on the dresser and ran his hands through his hair, looking up and down my body as he awaited my answer.

Grinning, I stepped forward, touching his chest. "Something fit for a devil." I moved my hands to his shoulders. "A sexy one, I'd say."

He grunted, breathing me in. One of his hands tangled itself in my hair, gently tilting my head upward. I tried not to focus on the awe and the desire in his darkening brown eyes. "You are looking very sexy. Can't tell if I like the horns or the tail more."

"It's okay to like both." I tried a smile, hoping it met my eyes.

He did such a marvelous job at unnerving me in the best ways. He was throwing me off course—I was the one that snuck *him* into a private place—and I both admired and hated him for it. His hand stayed raveled in my hair, pulling just hard enough that it brought more excitement than pain.

"Good, *diavola*, because I like all of it." He forced me back into the door and trailed kisses along my neck, starting the sensitive skin behind my ear, leisurely making his way down the column of my neck.

I let myself relax, flattening my palms on the door behind me to keep myself steady. I ignored the urge to shut my eyes as warmth flooded through me. His eyes flicked to mine momentarily before he dipped his head lower, placing warm, open-mouthed kisses that lingered dangerously close to the neckline of my bodysuit.

With a stifled moan, I arched into him, curling my fists. He found the curve of my hip just as jello threatened to replace the bones in my legs.

"You had to know what would happen if you wore this, *bella*. It was not in my plans to be walking around whoever's house with a hard cock." His lips made their way back up until they met the shell of my ear. "Was that your plan?"

This was part of my plan, but not like this. I was supposed to be the one in charge. I should've flipped us around, pinned him against the door, and asserted my dominance. But I didn't. I wanted to let go with him and enjoy it.

Giving up control was part of regaining it too, right? It had to be.

At least, I hoped so, because he was jumbling my brain right now, all of my expectations flying out the window.

He exhaled, straightening his back, his grip loosening on my hair. "Jace, baby, you with me?"

"Hmm?" I met his searching gaze.

"It seems like your mind is wandering. I can stop—"

I cut him off, wanting the worry in his eyes to go away. "No, no, Ruggiero. I—" I paused before I blurted the truth, that I was overthinking and I didn't want to get too close. I chose a white lie instead. "I don't want you to stop."

"I don't have to," he said, briefly licking his lips, running a hand over his chin. "But if you want me to continue, you'll have to tell me what you want me to do."

I was unable to hold back my smile. It was like he'd read my mind about the roles we were meant to be playing tonight and the mess that was my brain became less cluttered as the reins were given back to me.

"I think I can make that happen for you, handsome," I said, feeling more sure of my next directives. I leaned forward, placing my hand on top of his where it rested on my hip. "Will you do me a favor?"

"Tell me and it's yours. Whatever you want."

He couldn't mean that, but I'd breach that topic later to avoid killing the mood. My hand left his to drag down the front of his pants where I fondled the zipper with a finger. "I want you naked."

He smirked but moved his hands to his belt. "I thought I came here for a Halloween party and now, what? Am I giving you a strip tease, *diavola?*"

"You can still enjoy the party," I assured him, moving away from the door, no longer wanting to be caged in the tight spot. "Now or after, your choice."

I didn't give him another look as I strolled toward the queen bed, but I could feel his eyes on me. It was quiet for a few breaths and then came the soft hum of his belt being removed. I ran my fingers over the silky comforter, smiling to myself at the rustling of his jeans pushing down his legs.

He listened so well.

"Am I meant to take off my socks, too?"

I turned around to smirk at the ridiculous man. He was completely naked save for the jewelry he wore, his growing erection hard to miss, and, as he alluded to, his socks. I was unable to hold back a laugh. His socks were calf-length, the fabric a dark green until it got to the feet, where they became checkered with red.

"Do you usually fuck me with socks on? I don't pay attention to that," I said, biting back another laugh.

"Beats me," he said with a shrug before bending over, pulling the socks off one by one. "Well, now that I think about it, I fuck you half-clothed a lot, so probably." With a pause, he sat on the end of the bed, his strong back towards me. "I think I should put them back on. It's helpful for grip."

I tried to muffle my giggles with my hands as he covered his feet once again with the checkered socks. His fretting over whether to keep his socks on was adorably amusing. Or maybe it was the vodka I'd pre-gamed with that was tickling me so.

He stood again and walking toward me with a smirk. "If I didn't know any better, I'd think you were laughing at *me*. Doesn't really feel good to take all my clothes off and get laughed at."

I grabbed one of the decorative star-shaped pillows and tossed it at him. "Oh, shut up. You know I'm not laughing at you." He caught the pillow with ease, disbelief in his eyes. "Well, I am, but not at your dick."

He stared at me for a moment, his brow furrowing as he shielded his dick with the pillow. "I'm doing my best to believe you didn't lead me to this room and have me strip down to my birthday suit just to laugh at me."

"You're right, I'm sorry. We should get back on track." No doubt, he could file this moment in his brain as yet another time that I insulted his manhood. I sat, idly running my palm over the comforter again, hoping he could tell I was still interested. "It's only fair that I'm naked, too. Will you undress me?"

Ruggiero remained silent as he threw the pillow on the floor and bent down on one knee. My breath hitched with the warmth of his grip on the outside of my boot as he unzipped it. Gently, he pulled the boot off, kissed my exposed ankle, and moved to the other one.

I braced myself with my arms, digging my fingers into the bed as his warm palms skated over my legs. Hands massaging my calves, he looked up at me, his brown eyes void of amusement and dark with need. A hand slid to my inner thigh sent a shiver down my spine and a hot pulsing straight to my core.

I'm in deep, deep trouble.

Even though I was the one with the reins, I didn't think he'd show me an ounce of mercy once we began.

Chapter 17

RUGGIERO

Those big blue eyes gave me their full attention as I massaged her legs. Party or not, I wanted to take my time. I homed in on the small cues of her arousal. Her chest heaving steadily, her pupils darkening. And my favorite—her small hands gripping the sheets.

It was hard not to palm myself as I watched her reactions. I hadn't even gotten to the spot I yearned for yet.

She's going to be the death of me.

As much as I hated to admit it, her laughter—something that I didn't hear often enough—had only made me harder. I wanted to fuck the amusement out of her until all that could leave her mouth was unintelligible moans.

My hand climbed up her skin, fingers dancing near the opening of her one-piece. I smiled, watching her breath hitch—again. I was a fan of the easy access her outfit gave me and I didn't hesitate to pop the button to reveal the wet gusset of her panties behind her tights. Unwilling to ruin her costume, I tucked away the urge to rip through

117

the sheer fabric.

"Take these off," I said. "Please."

Her eyes didn't leave mine as she lifted her hips. She used a hand to roll down the waistband and finish removing her tights. "Just set them to the side."

I took over, happy to finish the job. The reveal of her soft skin underneath the tights was a gift in itself. I removed her panties next, refusing to linger on the task any longer. My gift was unwrapped and I wanted to indulge in it.

"I'd like you to leave the rest on," I said, and licked my lips in admiration. I tossed her tights somewhere on the bed, eager to hear what she wanted next.

"I'll grant you your wish. Here's mine." She spread her legs slowly, opening herself up to me like a blossoming flower. "Let me feel your tongue, please."

Fuck, yes.

I flattened my palm against her thigh, digging my fingers into the flesh just so, as I leaned forward, giving her wet lips a slow, upward lick. My cock responded in kind with a twitch. I dropped my hand to my cock and squeezed the base, willing myself to hold back. To avoid fucking my hand, I put all of my focus into eating her pussy, savoring the taste that was uniquely hers.

I kept a keen eye on her body, on the arch of her back, the hard peaks of her nipples pushing against the one piece. Jace struggled to keep her eyes open as I sunk my tongue deep inside of her. Her cheeks were flushed, a sheen of sweat on her neck.

"Oh, fuck, you're so good," she breathed, her chest heaving faster.

I groaned against her wetness, lowering myself to both knees as I speared her rhythmically with my tongue. Her taste was indescribably earthy and sweet—it was her. Smoothing a hand down my length, I sucked her lips into my mouth, loving the way she squirmed against the bed.

One of her hands pushed against my head as she managed to say, "Ruggiero, you're going to make me cum."

I pulled away, shamelessly licking her taste from my lips. "Would that be such a bad thing?"

"Yeah, because I didn't tell you to do that." She kicked a foot at me playfully and dragged the one-piece over her head. I wasn't surprised to see that my naughty girl wasn't wearing a bra underneath. "I'll cum when I say so."

I held off a scoff. *Like hell she will.*

Unfortunately for Jace, in the few weeks that we'd spent together, I'd come to know her body well. In each of our trysts, I took more notes on her favored places of my lips, my tongue, my hands, my cock—on and in her. The mental map I was constructing was far from complete, but I'd covered enough ground that I was confident in my ability to draw pleasure from her.

I'd let her find that one out on her own. My plan was to continue to enjoy this and try not to cum too quickly myself. Which, if the tight grip I held around the base of my cock said anything, was pretty fucking hard.

"Of course, *bella*. What next? Do I keep eating or...?" I trailed off, meeting her gaze. Her horns remained, but her eyes were heavy, cheeks flushed.

Truth be told, I didn't care what she wanted me to do as long as it involved my hands on her. I could kiss her red-painted lips again until the lipstick smeared, I could make her cum against my hand, or I could fuck her senseless. No matter what, I'd be happy.

The little devil was mine for the night—or at least until we finished with each other and decided to get back to the party.

Jace batted her eyelashes before turning over and crawling slowly towards the middle of the bed. Once she reached it, she stretched out like a cat, her bare ass high in the air. She looked back at me and winked. "You're done eating. I'm ready for you to fuck me."

Thank fuck. My dick is so hard it could break off.

Glad the games were over, I climbed on the bed after her, planting a loving kiss on her wet center. I was more than eager to have her around me as I sat up on my knees, lining myself up with her. I grabbed a handful of ass and eased her back on the tip.

It had been a couple of weeks since I was inside her and it would be a struggle not to lose control. Since the first night I'd had her, losing control was all I wanted to do.

"No more teasing," she grunted, pushing towards me until she swallowed more of my length. "Fuck me now and fuck me hard, Ruggiero."

"Do you ever like it soft?" I asked.

I didn't wait for her response as I pulled out without haste, thrusting into the hilt. I groaned at how well she fit around me, how perfect it felt being buried in her. For a moment, I closed my eyes to the sound of her approving moans as I stroked, imagining I had the privilege of filling her up like this for the rest of my days.

With steady rolls of my hips, I poured my desire into the task she'd given me.

"Oh, fuck," she cried, "you feel so good."

I snapped my eyes back open to take her in. Sliding the hand on her ass to her hip and smoothing the other down her arched back, I thrust faster, eager to witness her falling apart around me.

Fuck, she was gorgeous.

There were many things I wanted to say, so many things she wouldn't want to hear. And still, there were things she had to know.

"*Dio*, you look so beautiful like this. You're taking me so well," I said, gripping her hair just enough to give me some yield. "I'm so proud of you."

Between a broken moan, she managed to say, "Thank you." And then in true Jace fashion, she bit out her demand, "Now, make me cum."

I grinned, sliding out and flipping her over without hesitation. I lowered my head between her legs, covering her with my mouth, swirling my tongue around that small nub. Her whining underneath me made me groan and shot a pulsing heat through my cock. Determined to be tucked inside her when I came, I kept a tight grip on my cock and used the other hand to pump two fingers inside of her. Thighs spread wide, back arching against the bed, she clenched around my fingers.

She was close and I took advantage of the opportunity to lift myself and sink back inside her. With a few hard thrusts of my hips, she cinched around me, her eyes fluttering shut in pleasure as she let go. My orgasm ripped a moan from me, an explosion of ecstasy coursing through my limbs as I filled her with my release.

"That good for you?" I asked. Reluctantly, I pulled out of her, pressing a kiss to one of her round cheeks before climbing off the bed. I wanted to lie down with her, holding her as we talked under the covers, but the music outside of the room was a clear reminder that we were at a party, this was a guest room, and we couldn't hide away all night.

"It was good," she mumbled. "Always good."

As I walked to my pile of clothes, I kept my eyes on her. She lay in this stranger's bed, tired and freshly fucked with my cum leaking out of her. Cum that would no doubt stain the comforter as consequence of our actions.

Until Jace, I usually leaned toward using condoms with partners, but I had to admit I liked knowing that she was continuously marked by me, and doing it felt pretty fucking good.

"While I'm very much enjoying the view, we can't stay in here," I told her, pulling my jeans on. "You have to get up."

She propped herself up on her elbows, smiling at me lazily. "No need to kill the vibe, sir."

"Not trying to, *cara mia*, but Lucky and your brother might be wondering where we are."

"My brother doesn't care about where I am right now. We drove separately because we both had bad intentions." Her gaze followed my hands as I dressed myself. Somehow, through all of our roughhousing, her devil headband remained, only slightly crooked. "This isn't why I invited you, but I have been wanting you."

"Me too," I admitted. Once my shoes were on, I checked my phone. I groaned, muttering a "fuck" as I looked at the screen.

I had two missed calls and three texts from Lucky.

Where you at pretty boy

Still need a ride?

Soooo I've been wooed by a pretty lady and I'm leaving, hope you're good

Well, fuck. Why had I left my car at Lucky's again? I should've thought about this more. Then again, I thought his idea of taking someone home was just a jest, but clearly, it wasn't.

I shoved my phone in my pocket, returning my attention to Jace. She'd finally gotten out of bed, but her movements were delayed as she yanked her tights up her legs, as if she were forcing herself to do so.

"Do you want to help or are you going to just stare at me like a creep?" she asked, cocking her head.

I smirked. "Don't think that's a good idea. I'd be too tempted to keep you naked. Besides, we are on borrowed time. I have plenty of future chances to help you out."

She furrowed her brows. "You mean, helping me out with activities of daily living or helping me with your dick?"

"Both, if you'd like," I said, giving her my best smile.

She shook her head and shimmied back into her one-piece. I should have asked her what it was actually called, but I didn't really care. It didn't matter. What mattered was that it fit her well and hugged her in all the right places. I would continue to admire how she looked in her costume, but in the meantime, I needed a ride home.

I toyed with the chain around my neck as I mustered up the courage to ask for more of her kindness. Especially since this felt a little humiliating to me. "I hate to ask, but Lucky left me. Could you drive me to my truck later when you're ready to go? It's at Lucky's. If not, I'll—"

Jace laughed heartily. "Relax. I'd love to drive you to your truck."

"Thank you, Jace."

"No need to thank me. You do a lot for me as is, and we aren't even dating," she said.

I answered with a smile, unsure of what else to say. The words were spoken in good nature, and while they were true, I hated the reminder. Just like I hated how I had to hold myself back from asking her to take me home with her.

I wanted nothing more than to go to her place and do this all over again, and I believed she'd be game for it, but I couldn't. Now that my lust was sated, my head swam with thoughts once again. My heart wanted her and I had to protect it.

Once we were both decent, we left the room, almost as we'd found it. The guy's house was still lively with people, but all I could focus on was her. I wasn't dumb enough to believe I was in love—not yet when there was still so much to learn about her—but I was infatuated, allured.

I wasn't sure what she'd say if she knew that. She'd probably brush it off like she did when I'd asked what we were, when I'd nudged the question of being something more than… this. Every time we met up, we teetered along with the work of attaching strings. My heart needed to get on board with my brain before I fell off the deep end.

So, later that night when we were settled in the privacy of her car en route to my friend's home to retrieve my truck, and she asked me if I wanted to go back to her place, I told her no.

I had to.

Chapter 18

JACE

"Fuck me," I groaned after leaving a resident's room.

My stomach grumbled as I trudged to the kitchen, my legs tired as they carried me. I'd partied hard during Halloween weekend and now that I had a clear mind, my attention was brought to the bodily changes I'd been experiencing and ignoring.

It was the second of November and I still hadn't gotten my period. Sometimes, it was late when I was stressed, but most of the time, it was pretty regular. I searched my brain for some excuses for why it could be nearly a week late, but they all led to two possibilities: I had an endocrine disorder or I was pregnant. Or both. Or neither, hopefully?

Unfortunately, having an endocrine disorder was a low possibility because the last time I'd been to my primary care doctor, all of my labs were normal. Well, I could've developed something rapidly over the past few months, but... I doubted that.

Though I'd snag a pregnancy test after work to prove it, I knew the truth in my heart.

Ruggiero and I had been having sex without protection for a little over a month. I could say we'd tried to be more careful and used the pull-out method, but no. Almost every time he came, he was tucked inside of me, firmly holding me against his body so I couldn't move, just the way I liked it.

Fuck me.

With the suspicions clouding my head, I'd been flustered all day. Even Cleo noticed something was wrong when I'd responded to her banter with forced smiles and hums. So, instead of taking my break when I should have, I saved the last thirty minutes of my shift to finally sit down.

I leaned back in the metal chair, propping my feet up on the chair across from me, as I stared at my Tupperware bowl of chili topped with a hearty scoop of sour cream. My mind was reeling so much that I didn't even want to eat, despite how much my stomach protested.

Could I even eat?

I'd had my period in September, so I could be anywhere from two to six weeks pregnant. I held a hand to my mouth, a low simmer of bile swirling at the pit of my stomach.

Oh, I am such an idiot. What am I supposed to do?

If I were pregnant, it would still be early enough that I could choose a path other than parenthood. It wouldn't be the first time; I'd done it nearly a decade ago. I could choose to live my life as I was now— carelessly and freely.

For a brief moment, I let myself picture a little boy or girl, with my long hair, Ruggiero's hazel eyes, and his nose. Or maybe with his soft thick brown hair, my eyes, and my nose. Or a mix of it all.

My heart squeezed and I shook my head. I didn't need to think about that. Nothing was even confirmed. I forced myself to eat the chili. In the event it was true—and I was confident that it was—then I had to eat, or I'd grow weak.

And then there was Ruggiero, who I couldn't get out of my mind. Despite my insistence that we just fuck around, I craved to know what he would think. Would he want me to have an abortion? Or would he prefer to help me raise them? Or maybe, maybe he would just give me money.

With a frustrated groan, I took another bite of my food. If I weren't so upset, I'd be able to enjoy the fruits of my culinary skills. Instead, eating felt like a chore.

The whole day had felt like a chore, which sucked because I loved my job most of the time.

I managed to force my thoughts aside and finish my meal. Once I was all packed up and said my goodbyes to colleagues, I hauled ass to the pharmacy. I didn't want to guess any longer. I needed to know.

After some searching, my eyes landed on a test that had exactly what I was looking for. Quick results with early detection. It was a little pricey, and it probably showed on my face when the pharmacy tech rang me out, but now the stupid little box was in my purse as I finished the short drive home. In t-minus ten minutes, I'd have my answer.

Unfortunately for me, t-minus ten minutes happened too fast. One minute, I was driving with the windows rolled down, the autumn breeze in my hair. The next, I was pacing my living room as I waited for the test results.

You know the results, stupid!

When I was starting to get lightheaded, the timer finally went off. I rushed into the bathroom and before I could turn back, I looked at the tests.

Both screens displayed a pair of heavy parallel lines, confirming my suspicions.

The reveal was a little anticlimactic; neither a rush of excitement nor disappointment coursed through me. But only because I'd been expecting it. All I felt was the cold kiss of acceptance.

Ruggiero strolled into my apartment looking calm and collected, his hands in his pockets as he found a spot—his spot—on the couch. Even though it was the last thing I wanted to do, calling him felt like the right thing to do. Like the safe thing to do.

"Do you want anything to drink?" I asked as I closed the door and locked it.

"I'll take a glass of water," he said with a smile. "Thank you, *bella*."

In the kitchen, I poured two glasses of water.

Back in the living room, Ruggiero was waiting for me, patiently. His eyes held nothing but curiosity. There was no doubt he was thinking of why I called him with such urgency. "Thank you, again."

"You're welcome," I responded and sat down next to him. I slowly drank a sip of water and after swallowing it, I had to spit the words out or else I might never say them. I didn't look at him, keeping him only in my peripheral vision as I said, "Ruggiero, I'm pregnant."

He stopped drinking his water. In fact, it seemed like everything stopped. Not a single sound ensued and after four long seconds—I counted—he took in a deep breath. Then, he released it. Ruggiero set the glass down on the coffee table. He raised his hand to my cheek and gently cupped it as he turned my face towards him. "Jace, I am speechless."

His eyes held an emotion I couldn't name.

"Is that a good or a bad speechless?" I whispered. I'd never heard my heartbeat so loudly before.

"It's a great speechless," he said softly. "I am so happy. But the words to describe it, I don't know in English. I'm sorry, but yes, it's a good speechless, I promise." He kissed my forehead with careful tenderness. "How do you feel about it?"

"I don't know," I said. "I mean, just look at me. I'm not the mom type."

He obeyed my words, giving me all of his attention, his eyes searching what seemed like every flaw on my face. The pressure of his gaze was too much, so I closed my eyes.

"What am I supposed to be seeing, other than a gorgeous, intelligent woman? Maybe a little mean and stubborn sometimes, but I don't see anything to be unsure of." He took my glass from me, and I heard him set it on the table. Then his hands took hold of mine. Ruggiero pressed a kiss to my forehead, then to my neck, and whispered, "I am supportive of whatever you want."

By his tone, I knew that he meant what he was telling me. I knew that there was truth to his words. Even after how I'd been holding him at arm's length, careful not to give him too much of myself.

"I want the baby, I think. I want to keep them," I said quickly, allowing myself to look at him again, "but I just fear that I am not meant to have one."

Now that part of the truth had been said, I couldn't take it back.

He raised his head to look at me. He freed a hand and moved strands of my hair behind my ear. "Why do you think that? Do you remember your dream? I think that this might be meant to be, Jace. I think that there's no reason to think that it's not."

"You're kind—"

"No, I'm not just being kind. I mean it. If not meant for you, who is the baby meant for?" I looked down, feeling bashful. "I don't think this is a mistake. Do you want the baby? More importantly, are you comfortable with your baby having me as a father?"

I gave a nervous laugh. "I—" I breathed deeply. "I have to tell you something else."

He nodded slowly. "I'm listening."

"When I was seventeen, I was raped on prom night. When it happened, it was a moment of vulnerability, and I was taken advantage of."

Ruggiero's face was hard to read. That made me nervous, and so I kept talking, anything to deafen the noise of silence.

"Ever since then, I've been obsessed with control. My logic was if I never allowed someone else to control me that way, I would never have to experience something like that again." I took another sip. "I now see the holes in my logic and really, whatever logic I was using was driven by trauma. It was more so a defense mechanism than a coping mechanism but being hyper sexual was a means to reclaim the control I lost that night. I know it sounds silly, but—"

"No, it sounds perfectly reasonable to me. You experienced something that was very traumatizing, and it took a toll on you mentally and emotionally. What you feel and how you felt is valid. I just can't say how healthy it is." His hands squeezed mine.

I smiled a little, grateful that he was receiving this news so well. I didn't see a hint of judgment in his eyes.

"Yeah, well, some weeks later, I found out I was pregnant. Already having a plan for myself, and a college acceptance to fulfill the plan, I gave up being a mom. I think of it now and then, but this is forcing me to confront those memories. I've already had the chance to be a mom and I gave it up." I pulled my hands away, placing them in my lap and shaking my head. "How awful is it that I want to endure this pregnancy, but I rejected it all those years ago?"

He didn't try to grab my hands again, just flattened his against his thighs. "I think you're allowed the choice. You don't have to feel guilty for putting yourself first all those years ago. And if you want, I want to have this baby with you. I like you, Jace, and this is a result of *our* actions because we can't keep our hands off each other." He smiled. "So, I'll ask again. Are you comfortable with me being their father?"

"Yes," I said. I didn't doubt it. We weren't in love, but Ruggiero was kind and grounded. And his response to all of this… it wasn't what I'd expected but I was happy with that. He accepted me. "Are you comfortable with your baby having me as a mother? Bitchy Jace?"

"As comfortable as I can get." His expression was serious. "And you're only bitchy because you don't want to let people in. You can let me in."

"You mean that?" I whispered, almost moved to tears.

"Yes, I mean it. And if you want, we can be nothing more than co-parents. I know you aren't looking for anything serious and we can choose to be cordial."

I blew out a breath and grabbed his hand firmly in mine. "I like you, too," I said with a shaky laugh. "I, um, I consulted a psychiatrist."

"I'm proud of you. I was in therapy for a few years. I'm currently seeing a psychiatrist." His thumb rubbed the back of my hand and the rest of the tension in my body melted away.

The only thing I wanted to do next was throw my arms around him in a hug. Whatever we became, whether co-parents or something more one day, I was glad this journey would be with him.

Chapter 19

❧❧❧

JACE

Ruggiero and I were in my bed, and I had my head on Ruggiero's bare chest, enjoying his warmth. His arm was lazily wrapped around me as he stroked my hair. After we ate dinner together, he gave in to my silent requests and stayed. Now that we had talked about the near future, things between us felt light and easy for the first time in a while.

"Jace," he cooed, giving my hair a light tug.

Smiling, I tilted my head up at him. "Yes?"

"You're not as bad as you think you are," he told me. With the view he was offering, it was almost like peering up at Mount Rushmore. Not as big, of course, but his protruding features were more noticeable than usual. And those eyelashes, God. They were so long. "You're like a feline."

"A cat?" I asked. Did he just say that?

He laughed and I could feel his chest vibrate. "Yes, a cat. But like my nonna's cat Siena, who's very feisty and always ready to claw someone's eyes out. But around my nonna, she's very cuddly and sweet."

I scoffed, sitting up. I placed my palms on either side of his chest, holding myself up. "You compared me to a cat named Siena?"

He nodded, one hand in my hair still stroking my hair. "You're cuter, though." His fingers dropped from my hair to the outside of my camisole, where he gave my breast a light squeeze. "More human, too."

I rolled my eyes, amused that he was having to look up at me. He wasn't a foot taller than me, but he was tall enough. A whole eight inches enough. "You're silly," I said. I stroked his bare chin, his skin smooth against my hand. "Where'd your stubble go?"

"It'll grow back," he assured me. "I was starting to look like a grizzly bear, though."

I laughed lightly. "No, you were still cute, Ruggiero. Speaking of which… do you have a nickname? Your name is long."

He pulled his eyebrows together, first seeming confused and then feigning a look of hurt. I scoffed. Faker. "I'll have you know I have a very respectable name. It means 'Famous Warrior' in Italian."

"Look," I started, patting his chest, "that's fantastic. But it's still entirely too long. Can't I just call you like…Roger?"

"Roo-jare-oh… Rah-jer…" he tested it out, putting the names together by phonetic pronunciation. "Absolutely not. They sound nothing alike." He tapped his jaw. "Call me—"

"Egotistical," I finished for him.

"No," he disagreed, "I am handsome, and I know it. I am only confident, not egotistical. But before you rudely interrupted, I was going to say call me Adamo."

My brow furrowed. "Where the hell did that come from?"

He just smiled at me. "It's what my mother calls me. It's my second name."

"Say it again," I instructed, shifting so that I was more comfortably.

I sat up all the way, straddling his waist, the hand he had on my waist falling to my thigh.

"Adamo," he said. "You try it."

"Ah-dahm-oh," I repeated.

He shook his head, grinning up at me, showing me his beautiful pearly whites. "You're putting too much emphasis on the 'd.'"

"Whatever." I ran my hands along his chest idly, feeling his breath hitch now and then. I slowly dragged my palms from his shoulders, down his ribs, and then to his stomach, where the little trail of hair was stemming out from underneath his boxers. "Ruggiero Adamo de Fiore, hmm?" With a smile, I brought my hands back up to his shoulders. "Interesting name."

"Do you have a middle name?" he asked. The palm on my bare thigh was hot with his desire. He dragged it over where my underwear sat on my hip, and let it slip under my cami.

"Louisa."

"You don't look like a Louisa." He traced invisible shapes on my stomach. Everywhere he touched was inflamed. "But I suppose I don't look like an Adamo either."

"Nope," I mumbled. I let my fingers dance at the waistband of his boxers. I wanted to enjoy the conversation with him, but I also wanted to stick my hand in his boxers. So I did and as I let my hand move through the tuft of dark hair, I ignored his staring. I stopped finally when I reached his shaft, stroking him softly. "Keep talking."

"It's kind of hard to focus with your hand down my pants, baby," he muttered.

I waved him off and then returned a hand to his waistband, lifting myself slightly so that I could pull his boxers down further. His hand fell from my body as I straddled his thighs, my hand returning to his shaft. I smiled at the feel of him hardening. "Try."

"Well, for starters." His dick twitched in my grip and he released a

134

sigh, and I tightened my grip to accommodate him. "You look beautiful, as always."

"If you want me to blow you, all you have to do is ask," I teased. "But thank you. You look beautiful, too."

I paused to spit in my palm and returned to close it around him before moving it up and down. He was warm and hard, and I couldn't ignore the pulse.

"You know," he breathed, "that if you just used your mouth, the spitting wouldn't be necessary."

I squeezed at the base lightly. "Oh, hush, you liked it."

"*Sì. Mi sto godendo,*" he mumbled.

"Huh?" I said, letting my thumb run over the tip.

"Yes," he breathed, "I'm in ecstasy."

"Good," I said. I let go of him and positioned myself between his legs. I allowed myself to get comfortable as I took him in my hand again, sliding it up and down and then putting him in my mouth. He responded with a low moan.

Something was arousing about pleasuring Ruggiero, especially considering he was vocal. I liked knowing that I could make him come undone with just my mouth and my hands. There was also the fact that he looked utterly delectable when he allowed himself to give in to the pleasure.

Ruggiero pushed his hands into my hair, a groan leaving his mouth. "Fuck, you feel so good," he said, his hips bucking forward.

I slid him out of my mouth and dragged my tongue along the underside of his shaft, using my other hand to fondle his balls. I guided him back inside my mouth, swirling my tongue around the tip.

"*Oddio,*" he mumbled, his hands pushing my head down further, starting to fuck my mouth gently. "So, so good."

Ruggiero was close, I knew. We'd been doing this long enough for me to know what he was like moments leading up to his climax—the tightening of his grip, the more frequent groans, the light pulsing of his dick. And then warm salty yet sweet liquid streamed into my mouth. I waited until he was finished and swallowed.

"That was… surprisingly pleasant," I said, sitting up on my knees and resting my butt on the heels of my feet. "What did you eat today?"

He'd returned his hands to his sides, breathing softly. He looked gorgeous and spent. "I had a fruit salad along with my tuna sandwich for lunch."

I smiled at him, genuinely. "It's like you knew I'd be sucking you off today."

Finally, he sat up, propping himself up with his elbows. "I promise you I wasn't expecting it, but I can't say that I'm upset it happened."

"Sure," I said, shrugging it off. I glanced at the clock to see that it was 11:37 pm and climbed off the bed. "I'm going to go brush my teeth, sweetheart, and you should work on trying to fall asleep."

He lifted his hips slightly, sliding his boxers back up. "Jace, you don't want anything from me?"

I shook my head and ran a hand through my tousled hair. "That was exclusively for you. Don't feel selfish, I enjoyed it, I promise." I started down the hallway.

In the bathroom, I brushed my teeth and washed my face for the night. Just as I was returning the cloth to its home, Ruggiero walked into the bathroom.

His body pushed me against the counter as his hands came around and rubbed at my sides. I swiveled in his hands and placed my hands on either side of him, pulling him down to me. Ruggiero kissed my forehead and then the tip of my nose before he finally reached my lips.

"We need to go to bed," I whispered, but I was enjoying the feeling of his body against mine.

"We will, baby," he assured me. "Turn around, please."

I did as he asked, pushing my front against the counter once again.

"Bend over." Again, I complied.

His hands dropped to my panties and he began to slide them down my legs. Though I told him I didn't want anything from him, if he was willing to give me a little pleasure, I wasn't going to turn him away.

"Jace," he sang softly, "Fuck, you're so gorgeous." The pad of his finger on my clit was warm, hot. I sighed contently against the counter. He then pushed two fingers inside of me, moving them in and out.

I closed my eyes, enjoying the way he stroked me.

"Baby, can I fuck you?"

"Yes," I breathed. "Please."

He pulled his fingers from me but replaced them with his dick's prodding head. He pushed in slowly, stopping momentarily once his full length was inside. "Does that feel okay?"

I nodded, pushing my backside against him to take more. "Always," I told him. "You going to move or what?"

"Always so impatient," he mumbled. To my pleasure, he moved out and then back in, his strokes slow and measured. I gripped either side of the counter hard.

"Can you put some pep in your step?" I asked him, clenching around him. I didn't mean for it to come out as harshly as it did, but he knew what he was doing. I was against the bathroom counter, for starters. "Give it to me harder, Ruggiero."

"Always so polite," he said sarcastically. But he complied with my requests, gripping me by my waist and thrusting into me with more speed and force. He felt all but amazing, and it made me angry that my body was too close to the sink for me to touch myself. "Work with me," he said before pushing up my right leg and placing it on the counter. The slight change in position made him feel all the better and I could no longer keep in my moans.

The top of my head was pressed against the mirror and the sensation was making me lose my mind. I hated that I couldn't put my hands into his hair or hold onto him. One of his hands left my waist and played with my clit. I cried out thankfully.

"I thought...you weren't...a screamer," he managed to get out as he thrust.

"Shut up," I bit back. "Oh my god, oh my god." I felt like he was turning me inside out. His dick was tormenting sweetly, and his fingers massaged at the apex of my thighs.

"Say my name," he urged.

"Ruggier-*oh*," I moaned. I shut my eyes, my orgasm washing over me. It was good, it felt so good. My body quivered around Ruggiero, but he held me up, still riding me out through my climax. He came shortly after, his dick twitching as filled me with his warmth.

After a few moments of breathing, he helped me off of the counter, and in the mirror, I saw my flushed cheeks. I turned around to look at him, feeling full. I clenched my legs together and in response, I could feel his release bringing moisture to my thighs.

"So much for sleeping, *sì?*" he asked me before pressing a soft kiss to my forehead. "I'll run us a bath."

"Good," I replied. "But don't you dare to lay a finger on me except to help me wash my back. I want to be clean so I can sleep."

"Of course, Jace. Your wish is my command." He pressed a shy kiss to my lips before turning in the direction of the bath.

I stood with my back to the counter, watching as he plugged the bottom of the tub. I felt several pounds lighter knowing that my pain could be trusted with Ruggiero. He didn't make me feel any less than human about it. And I felt content knowing that he knew how much I appreciated him.

Chapter 20

❧❧❧

JACE

I walked into the nursing home the next day with a bounce in my step, still thinking about the kiss Ruggiero and I shared this morning when he said goodbye. It wasn't the forehead kiss he usually gave me. No, it was his warm, wet mouth covering mine, that smooth tongue sliding against mine. Flames had lit in my belly, but when I leaned into him, he held me in place by my hips parted our lips.

"You need to get ready for work," he'd whispered. I could tell he was hesitant to leave, that he wanted to go further, but he was responsible and put space between us. "I'll call you later."

I'd said nothing more but offered him a small smile, hiding my disappointment. He'd slipped out the door with a grin.

Over two hours later, I couldn't shake how the kiss made me feel—like I wasn't unlovable as Garret had said. Why was I depriving myself of this, of him? I'd told myself it was because I was tired of dating, but no, I was tired of the people I'd been dating. No matter how much time we spent together, I wasn't getting tired of Ruggiero.

I only wanted more of him.

I just had to accept it, given we were already having a baby together. How long could I resist him and the wonderful things he made me feel? And at what cost? I was depriving myself of something that, while scary, seemed like it could be healthy.

Once I put my belongings at my desk, I continued to ponder as I made my way to Cleo's room. In the three years that she had known me, the only person I'd been with exclusively was Garret. I now knew she didn't liked him much, but she only ever wanted me to be happy, so she never mentioned it until after we were over. Since then, she'd been very supportive of my endeavors, including my many one-night stands.

I knocked on the door before letting myself in, a tray of food and water in hand. She was sitting upright in the bed wearing a purple gown, her hand curled around the remote. I glanced toward the television to see that she was watching reruns of *The Golden Girls*.

"Good morning, darling," she said with a smile.

"Good morning, my beautiful Cleo," I returned, setting the tray down on the nightstand.

Cleo furrowed her brow and grimaced. "Why the hell are you being so sweet today? Do you want something from me?"

"Oh, hush," I said. "Besides great hugs and good advice, what can you give me?"

She nodded. "Oh, right. I guess no more of those for you."

I laughed as I opened the drawer near the sink to retrieve her pill packs. "Well, good thing I don't need those today. I have good news for you."

Cleo waited expectantly as I brought over her medication.

"You're supposed to ask what it is."

"I figured you'd tell me, but okay. What's the news?" she asked.

I was unable to hold back my smile as I placed the pills in her hand.

"I'm pregnant," I blurted. "Ruggiero knows and he's excited."

Cleo coughed into a tissue before popping the pills in her mouth. She quickly grabbed her cup of water and washed the medicine down. "Jesus, girl, you almost got those pills stuck in my windpipe." Then she grabbed my arm and pulled me close with a smile. "I'm incredibly excited for you, but why don't you take a seat so we can chat?"

I crossed my arms. "Only if you're going to start eating your breakfast. Sure, it isn't your favorite cereal but it is fresh and warm."

She glanced over at the plate of bacon, eggs, and toast before carefully placing the tray in her lap. "I could always ask you to warm up my cereal, but sure, I'll accept your bargain."

Satisfied only once she'd eaten a few bites, I sat down next to her on the bed. "What would you like us to chat about? The news I shared?"

"I don't know what else it would be about besides the man you're seeing, but it's all tied together. I wanted to give you some motherly wisdom," she said. "I already know you're going to be an amazing mother. You have the right heart for it. *But* you also have the habit of beating yourself up for a lot of things, which will make parenthood hard."

I placed a hand on her arm with a smile. "Thanks, Cleo. It means a lot that you think I'll be a good mom. I'm excited, but I'm more so a little terrified."

"There's nothing to be afraid of. You'll still be you, a perfect mix of cutthroat and caring as you are now. Honestly, you're not unlike who I was when I was your age, and though my children and I aren't the closest, they turned out fine."

Cleo had two children. I'd met them a few times and I wasn't too fond of them. The story was that they brought her to Glendshire because they were unable to care for her any longer. The truth was that they could have, but they didn't want to. They said that because she was a burden, they could not live successful lives.

Her daughter, Dorina, was a twenty-nine-year-old event planner. She'd made a name for herself in Nashville organizing parties and weddings. Her beau, Gavril Cazacu, was now a considerably wealthy man because of his grandfather's recent death four years ago. Dorina had been helping her mother, but after tying the knot with Gavril, she was persuaded to "let go of the dead weight."

Her son, Kelemen, ran a chain of nightclubs in Tallahassee. He was also becoming known for his architecture in Florida, having designed a few houses on the shore. Kelemen, while he assured us, "I love my mom, I do," at check-in, he also expressed that, "I just don't have enough time or resources for her upkeep. I feel like she's holding me back." Even though he'd previously been taking frequent flights to the Tallahassee for a while to manage his nightclubs, he boarded a plane to permanently move to the coastal state an hour after dropping Cleo off.

Because of their selfishness, she opted for keeping her house unoccupied rather than giving it up to her children.

"You're right," I said with a sigh. "Your kids have done some amazing things and it's all because they had you."

Cleo patted my shoulder. "Thank you, *angyalom*. In my nearly eighty years of living, I've come to accept that I did the best I could raising my children. There's not much I can do about it now. I call them when I can and we talk when they answer the phone, whether that be once every few days or few weeks." Her smile was endearing as her hand fell away and she paused to take a sip of water. "I'm glad I have you."

Her words wrapped around my heart like a warm hug. If she wasn't eating, I'd hug her. "I am so lucky to have you, Cleo."

"Just promise me one thing."

"Anything," I said.

"Just like myself and your mother, you *will* make mistakes, but I want you to promise me that you won't ever be too good to apologize to your children when you're in the wrong," she said. "Children, no matter how young, deserve respect, too, and I think that's what many parents forget sometimes.

"At times, I might have been too hard on Dorina and Keleman, but as a single mother, I had to care for them, teach them, and provide for them all at the same time. I made many, many mistakes, such as not being home enough when their father and I divorced. My main focus was being able to put food on the table, or not always having the emotional capacity myself to support their emotional health. I fear I never apologized enough to them."

I laid a supportive hand on her arm. We talked about her kids sometimes, but never this deeply. "I promise to apologize to my children when I'm wrong."

I meant it. I knew that months of screaming matches between my mom and me would've been avoided, if only she would have apologized. She was getting better at it, slowly but surely, but when I was growing up, it wasn't really a thing.

"Then you'll be an amazing mother," she said with a wink. "Now, run along, my darling. I'm going to finish my breakfast *and* my marathon."

I stood up and spun around to face her. "I had more rounds to make anyway. You're not the only one who enjoys seeing this resting bitch face," I said. "Now, set your breakfast to the side for a moment, please. I'm going to check your vitals before I go."

In the evening, I curled up on the couch. Words and sounds emitted from the TV and yet I processed very few of them.

The astoundment of being pregnant still hadn't worn off. There was a human growing inside of me. The talk with Cleo had been reassuring, but it didn't take away my fears completely.

Thankfully, I'd been proactive and scheduled with the psychiatrist I'd reached out to. My first appointment was tomorrow, and I would receive a psychiatric evaluation. I had a morbid excitement to know what I was causing my nightmares.

I didn't want an excuse for the way I was, but rather an explanation. When I was in school, I read several essays about how divorce could be a form childhood trauma and could have possibly had an effect on how someone's brain developed.

There was a psychological explanation for most things. There were a handful of patients at the nursing home that suffered from anxiety, others that had personality disorders or mood disorders with severe symptoms. I was no stranger to these things, but as far as I knew, I didn't have any significant family mental health history.

Unfortunately for me, though, I'd been through more than enough for a twenty-seven-year-old. I wouldn't wish the things I'd experienced on anyone, nor the trauma that came from them. Each day, I put on a face of strength and courage, but there'd always been a hollowness inside me. I wouldn't be surprised if depressive states had been ebbing and floating throughout my life.

Maybe meeting with Joanna would be rewarding. How different could she be from other healthcare providers? Worst case, I didn't like her and I switched to someone else. Regardless, I knew this would help me be a better mom.

Given I already wasn't paying attention to the show I was watching, I took my phone out and dialed Ruggiero's number. We should probably talk about co-parenting, or at least how we wanted things to go regarding the baby's growth.

Chapter 21

꧁ ꧂

RUGGIERO

Recently, Jace and I'd decided we needed to spend more time together. If we were to co-parent, becoming more familiar with each other outside of the bedroom was important. Thus, we planned to hang out at least one or two times a week without any sexual intentions.

To ensure we were both on our best behavior, we'd picked somewhere simple and public—a park. I considered myself a fairly adventurous guy, but I couldn't see us getting handsy where children ran around.

I arrived about an hour or so early to have some time to myself to think. I was going to be a father. The thought had been pressing in my mind like a chant since she told me on Monday. It might've been because I hadn't told the news to anyone else yet, but I was just starting to believe it.

I was going to be a father.

It was something I'd always wanted, though passively. When I left Italy six years ago, my mother said it was silly to wish for parenthood given my sexuality. I'd hoped living in America would change that, or at least give me a more realistic chance at meeting someone who didn't mind my sexuality nor think it would prevent me from being a good father. And though I would've been on board if Jace wanted to get rid of the baby, I was happy she decided to keep them and allow me to help her raise them.

Except she didn't know that I enjoyed a man's company just as much as I did a woman's. She'd told me that she'd kissed a woman and more, but that didn't translate to an acceptance for men like me. Because it didn't change my attraction to her, I hadn't thought I needed to tell her, but if we were going to raise this baby together, it would come up on its own eventually.

Then came the matter of my background, which wasn't as pristine as most thought.

I forced myself to take a deep breath as reason after reason of why I wasn't deserving of this fate surfaced in my mind. I glanced at my watch. A little more than thirty minutes remained until her arrival.

In an attempt to clear my mind, I settled comfortably on the park bench, opened the novel I'd been reading, and blocked out the rest of the world. The fae kingdom, though vibrant and bustling with the royal court, was in peril to an extent that the prince and the halfling woman hadn't anticipated. The kingdom and its encompassing regions had been part of a decades-long scheme fashioned by the king himself. To their surprise—and my own—the king had several trusted members of the court helping him along.

A squeezing hand on my shoulder jolted me.

I folded the corner of my page and slammed the book shut. Jace was standing in front of me, her eyes scanning my face inquisitively and the corner of her mouth pulled upward in a smirk. Her face looked soft and clean and a little rosy, like she'd washed it before coming here.

"Hey. Seems like you've been here for a while," she said, the hand on my shoulder falling away. Her wavy hair was down, drawing my eyes to her black cashmere sweater, its v-neck exposing her smooth skin and a bit of cleavage. The hem of her blue jean skirt rode up some as she sat down and crossed her black knee-high boots at the ankles.

I kept my tone polite, or at least tried to, as I met her gaze. "I have, *bella*. It's nice outside."

She hated me. She had to. Why else would she come dressed like this on what was meant to be an innocent excursion?

"It is a nice day, especially for November." She smiled at me, her warm hand coming to rest on my knee. "What're you reading?"

"Just something I picked up from the library," I said. "You look beautiful."

"Thanks," she mumbled.

"Of course." I nodded, setting the book down next to me, and put my hand on top of hers. A faint blush spread across her cheeks. "I'm happy to see you today."

"I'm happy to see you, too. Do you want to sit on this bench a while longer? I've had a pretty busy day and would love an excuse to be off of my feet for a moment."

I laughed. "We can sit here as long as you'd like. I don't have anywhere else to be today."

I'd been more affection since Monday, pleased to know that, despite her aversion to a relationship, she enjoyed spending time with me and returned my romantic feelings. Still, I was unsure how to proceed. How affectionate should I be in public? We didn't spend much time together outside our homes, where all we seemed to do was display our attractions. Then again, her hand was on my knee and could easily move higher.

"Great. I love that." Jace wriggled until she relaxed on the bench, surprising me as she rested her head on my shoulder. "My shift was a tiring one and when it was over, I did some cleaning until I could think straight again."

Feeling more comfortable to make a move, I lifted my hand from hers, letting it rest on the expanse of her thigh between her skirt and boot. Just some days ago, I was tracing this bit of skin with my tongue. *Focus, idiot.*

"Anything new happen to you this week?" I asked.

"Well, I had my first psych appointment Wednesday afternoon. It went well and she referred me to a therapist. Said something about how medication works better in tandem with therapy, especially given my current work circumstances." Her hand rubbed my knee over my pants. "I haven't scheduled with the therapist yet, but I will."

I nuzzled my chin in her hair. "This is great. I'm so proud of you," I said, squeezing her thigh softly. "It's true that they work better together. I can attest to that."

She straightened her posture and looked at me. I'd never seen her eyes so full of admiration. "I'm happy you're here with me. You're just so… fuck, how do I say it? You're so reassuring."

Her words sent blood rushing to my ears. I reveled in each moment that she bared her thoughts to me. "That's a huge compliment coming from you."

"It's the truth. I've broken down in front of you, more than once, and you still treat me the same. And saying you're proud of me—" she paused, her eyes sparkling with budding tears. "You don't know how much that means to me."

I kept my hand on her thigh and leaned in to cradle her face with my other. "I'm not a perfect guy, and I have my moments, too. Though I love teasing you, I won't ever treat you differently for having emotions. It's only human."

A tear fell as she blinked, but she didn't pull away. "Thank you for letting me be human."

I brushed it away with my thumb. "Always."

Though her eyes were still glassy, her small smile returned. "How'd you learn to be such a good person? No one becomes this understanding without some bullshit in their past."

I grimaced. I avoided putting space between our faces—our lips— but I dropped my hand to my lap. "Sure you want to know all of that?"

Her hand on my knee drifted higher. "I wouldn't have asked if I wasn't."

Where did I even begin? I'd had all I needed as a child—except for the love of my mother. She fed me, she clothed me, but she didn't seem to love me. I had long accepted it, but I didn't really want to get into it with Jace. There were lighter things I could go with, like what sports I played.

"Okay, well, I played rugby growing up."

"I can see you playing rugby. You're a good size for it," she said.

"Well, yeah. It was either that or keep getting in trouble for fighting."

Rugby gave me the physicality of fighting that I yearned for. The pain. The grit.

Jace grinned, shaking her head. "No way *you* used to get into fights. You're such a nice guy."

"Being a nice guy didn't mean was I wasn't a fighter, *bella*," I said. "I don't fight anymore, but it can be very addicting. I joined the rugby team because it was the closest I could get to doing it without upsetting my parents."

Her blue eyes remained wide with shock. "I'm trying to think of a reason why you'd be getting into fights."

I laughed. My parents used to say the same. "I had a bad temper, and I fought for stupid, petty reasons. But as you can see, I've since mellowed out." Little used to be better than the adrenaline that came from the skin-on-skin contact, the bursting impacts of fists, and the metallic taste of blood in my mouth.

"Did you have a come-to-Jesus moment or something?" she asked.

"Sort of, I guess. Almost ten years ago, I wound up arrested after fighting in a bar," I said. My stomach tensed as I realized I was getting painfully close to another truth.

Jace stood and extended a hand towards me. "I think we should walk as you tell me the story."

I grabbed my book and nodded, taking her hand as I joined her on the sidewalk. "The arrest resulted in a ten-month sentence in the town's jail and a fine of a thousand euros. It put a bit of a wrench in my plans to go to university."

"How so?" she asked. I didn't know where we were walking to, but I followed her nonetheless.

"After my sixteenth birthday, I enrolled at the University of Udine for their three-year program in foreign languages and literature. The arrest happened when I was in my final year at the university. I wasn't playing rugby anymore and I hadn't stopped fighting, but I did a good job at keeping it separate from my university life before the arrest. It allowed me to have my own cash so that I didn't have to rely on my parents so much." I glanced toward her to find any evidence of judgment in her gaze, but there was none. Her features held genuine curiosity. "I went to the bar with a guy I was seeing to celebrate his birthday. Halfway through the night, a man started flirting with him and then harassing him with slurs once rejected. Once he started grabbing and groping at him, I intervened."

"Sounds like that idiot got what he deserved," she said.

"Yeah, but I got charged with aggravated assault. I didn't care. I couldn't stand by and watch that. Between me and him, I appeared more masculine. Though he didn't dress femininely, he was soft and quiet. I knew that's why they were picking on him."

"Were you two serious?"

"We were, though it was many, many years ago. We were together for a little under a year. He visited me for a bit while I was in jail, but shortly after we broke it off." Talking about my distant relationship with Andrea no longer affected me, but I feared what she thought. I also didn't want to spend too much time on the subject.

She halted in her steps, giving me her full attention. "You spent those ten months without him?"

I nodded. "Most of them, yes." I forced myself to look at her once again and study her expression. She only eyed eat me with interest and passion, her blue eyes exploring my face now that she had the chance. "It was an amicable breakup. Besides, I was plenty occupied there. I continued studying English and took a few history courses. My father also visited me."

Jace furrowed her brow, frowning. "Your mom didn't visit?"

I shook my head. "No. Once she found out that I'd been arrested and the story behind it, she wanted little to do with me. She called me a," I paused, wincing, "she called me a disgrace."

"Oh, Ruggiero," she murmured, stepping closer to me. She brought her hands up to cradle my face, pulling it closer to her own. "I hope you know you're far from a disgrace. You already know I like women. I'd be a hypocrite if I judged you."

My heart squeezed. I hoped she wasn't just saying what I wanted to hear. "Are you sure you don't mind, *bella*?" I asked, relaxing in her hold.

"I'm sure." And then she kissed me, right there in the open, for anyone to see.

Chapter 22

JACE

Ruggiero seemed more than surprised that I kissed him on the way to the restaurant I led him to. I hadn't meant to. Not that soon, at least. I wanted us to have dinner together, chat, and end the night on a good note. But hearing about the past decade of his life moved me to comfort him as he'd done for me, and kissing him felt right.

I didn't care who saw. I wanted Ruggiero, badly. I was tired of resisting. Before I went home today, I would make sure he knew.

"So, how do you like the pizza? Is it better back home?" I asked and then took a sip of my soda.

He wiped his face with a napkin. "It's pretty good. I never ate much pizza in Udine, but surely you know that nothing is better than the real thing."

"Guess you're saying this pizza is fake."

He smirked. "No. Just saying that I wouldn't call it authentic."

"You make me a pizza. Maybe it'll be authentic then."

"It just might be, *bella*. If you're nice, I think we can work out a deal."

I smiled, humored by his teasing. "I think you can agree that I'm pretty nice. Remember, I told you, deep down inside, it was there."

"There are so many things that are nice about you. But yes, you're pretty nice when you aren't talking shit." He ran a hand through his hair and leaned back in his chair. "You're also very nice when you're lying on your back with your legs spread."

"Ruggiero, we are in a pizzeria," I scolded. I wouldn't tell him, but his words elicited their expected response.

"That doesn't negate the statement, *bella*. I know I'm not supposed to be this forward today, but you just look so damn beautiful," he said.

I gave him my best amused smile, glad he couldn't see me squeezing my thighs together beneath the table. "The outfit's sexy, I'd agree."

His eyes trailed a path down my face to my breasts. "Not just the outfit. You know that."

For a quick moment, I wondered if I should match his energy or pivot the conversation to something more innocent. When wasn't I game for a challenge?

I gently shoved my plate to the side. "I bet you're wishing you could undress me."

Ruggiero shook his head. "I'm not. I'd rather watch you undress yourself." Sometimes, it's better to watch."

"You're right. I do like watching you undress."

"Fuck," he mumbled, running a hand down his face. "This is how we have one on the way now."

"Then stop looking at me with those fuck-me eyes." At the rate we were going, we'd probably end up with more on the way.

I loved being full of him just as much as he loved filling me up.

He didn't stop looking at me. Instead, he leaned forward and brushed my hair behind my ear. "Can I ask you something and you be open-minded?"

I nodded, my eyes flickering to and from his lips. I wanted to kiss him again and again and again.

"I want to try soft bondage," he murmured.

I flinched at the thought of being tied down before quickly straightening up. When I told him about my assault, I didn't divulge how my wrists were bound to the headboard. "I don't… I don't want to be tied down."

Ruggiero smiled softly. "I don't want to tie you down."

A few seconds passed until I realized what he was saying. "You want me to tie *you* down?"

He nodded and pressed a kiss to my cheek. "I do. I know you like control," he said. "I'd like to relinquish mine to you."

"Oh my." His declaration ignited a new feeling within me. I was surprised to find that I was turned on by the idea of having full dominance over his pleasure.

"Would you like that?" he asked, his eyes imploring mine.

"I think so. I might need a little guidance," I admitted. I squirmed in my seat. "You know we're supposed to be getting to know each other more and touching each other less, right?"

Ruggiero laughed. "We aren't touching each other. We're only talking, Jace. I think discussing kinks counts as getting to know each other. We don't have much time to think about this stuff when we're already doing it."

"Sure, let's say it counts. Give me another kinky wish of yours," I said, finally digging into my second slice of pizza.

"I like being edged," he said. "Now tell me some of yours, *bella*."

"Hmm." I thought back to some of my sexual encounters with Ruggiero and others. I had a habit of asking people not to pull out. "I think I might have a breeding kink, though I never expected my birth control to fail."

"No one expects that. Did you miss a pill?"

I thought back to the last couple of weeks. "Maybe."

"Hmm. Hard to know the strength of my seed because I tend to favor condoms with partners."

"Wow, you're just like me, huh?" I asked through a laugh. "I don't know why I assumed you were primarily celibate before me."

He scoffed. "That's funny. I was pretty open to sleeping with you the first time we met, wasn't I? I'm sorry you thought me to be a well-mannered man all of the time. I do have needs and while I have hands, nothing is better than the real thing."

"Well, for what it's worth, I'm happy you were so eager to jump in the bed with me," I said, seemingly unable to stop smiling. "I ended up in a great spot."

Ruggiero raised his eyebrows. "Am I included in that great spot?"

"You're a really big part of it," I expressed. "You take me out of my comfort zone and always have. Yet... I feel safe with you."

"I feel safe with you, too. It's been a long time since I..." he trailed off for a moment. "Since I felt so comfortable with someone else. You're honest and upfront and you've never judged me."

"I could never judge you the way you've been so tender to me. You don't pity me for my past, you just accept me as I am. That means the world to me. That's why I wanted to ask you..." My words dwindled as I watched the curiosity spark in his eyes.

He wiggled his eyebrows. "You wanted to ask me what, *bella?*"

I hope I don't look stupid. I hope he doesn't laugh at me.

My heart fluttered with increasing beats. Though afraid of his unlikely rejection, I put on a brave face as I asked, "Will you be my boyfriend?"

Ruggiero's eyes softened, the humor in them disappearing. "That is a question I wasn't expecting."

"Oh, well, it's something I wanted to ask. I like you, I like being around you, I like *this*," I said. Looking for a distraction from the palpitations in my chest, I tapped my foot. "I don't want to deny this anymore. The last guy I dated cheated on me. He and the woman, Katherine, are getting married soon. It—it broke my heart. He told me that I was unlovable."

His lips curved in a frown. "That's really shitty, Jace. I'm sorry. I can't imagine doing that to you."

"No worries." I smiled. "My reason for sharing this is because you make me feel like that's not true. Even though we aren't in love, you make me feel lovable, like I'm okay just the way I am."

His hand landed on my knee, halting the bouncing of my leg. "*Mia cara*, you are very lovable and I would love to be your boyfriend."

I took a deep breath, relieved. My heart slowed to its normal rhythm and my shoulders relaxed.

Wow. This went a lot better than I thought it would.

The amusement in his gaze returned. "Did you think I'd say no?"

"I don't know. You'd have had the right to. I haven't been the easiest person to get along with and I haven't been very open with you."

Ruggiero shrugged. "You've been pretty open to me," he said. "And I understand where you're coming from. It's always hard to trust after you've been hurt."

"Still. I was giving you too many mixed signals because I kept telling myself I didn't deserve you."

He leaned forward, the hand on my knee sliding to my thigh. "What changed your mind?"

"Well, I've been doing some thinking. You're an adult. You're pursuing me. You seem to believe I deserve you." I laid my hand on top of his. "So, I wanted to give you the option."

"Glad we're on the same page. I've been dying to make you mine." His hand slid from my thigh as he stood. "I'm going to grab a box for our leftovers. Be right back."

I watched him walk away, momentarily appreciating his ass—round, muscular, and extremely grabbable—and then I finally let myself enjoy the shock and pleasure of what just happened.

He'd said yes.

Ruggiero de Fiore was my boyfriend, which meant he was all mine.

Ever the gentleman, he walked me to my car as we ended our time together. My heart begged me to ask him to come home with me, but I wouldn't. He wasn't just someone I fucked anymore.

"To feed both of my babies, I'm sending you home with the rest of this pizza," Ruggiero said, holding the door open as I climbed into the car.

His words threatened to turn me to mush.

"How generous of you, Ruggiero." I took the box from his hands and put it in the passenger seat. "We give our thanks in advance."

Ruggiero smiled toothily. He leaned over me, hands on the top of the car. "You thank me enough, *cara mia*. It's you that I should be thanking. I had a really good time tonight."

"I did, too," I agreed, meaning it from the heart.

Sex with Ruggiero was nice, but the days where all we did was talk were quickly becoming my favorites.

He patted the roof of the car. "Good night, *bella*."

"Good night, Ruggiero. See you later."

I released a satisfied sigh once the door shut. This was the best night that I'd had in a while. It reminded me that intimacy didn't only happen in the bedroom. It happened when I cooked for him and felt satisfied that his belly was full. It happened when we laid in bed and cuddled. It happened when we curled up on the couch together and watched movies.

Our time together tonight had been laden with intimacy. Besides a bit of filthy small talk over dinner, we'd remained innocent. His touches on my skin still burned hot and I still melted under his gaze, especially on that bench when his fingers had kept rubbing circles on my thigh. The temptation to ask him to take me in my car had been strong, but I wouldn't have changed tonight for anything.

Once home, I snuggled into the bed and fell asleep with one handsome mechanic on my mind.

Chapter 23

⚜

RUGGIERO

The next couple of weeks seemed to pass in a blur of joy and adoration. Jace had finally let her guard down, allowing me to praise and compliment her freely. I hadn't been this happy in a long while. Jace was a breath of fresh air in my otherwise monotonous life.

Her decision to be with me had been her own. I was grateful she invited me into her life. I let her into mine with open arms. Together, we would raise this baby as a family of our own.

More often than not, I slept at her place with a promise that we'd continue dedicating time to getting to know each other. But for me, I didn't know if our sleeping arrangements were enough. I wanted her at home with me, in my bed.

One thing I did know was that there was no longer a chance that I might fall in love with her. I was already falling, plummeting headfirst. I knew for certain I loved her when we'd gone to our first ultrasound appointment and I witnessed the unbridled joy on her face when we saw the unrefined image that was our baby.

"They're real," she'd whispered, eyes brimming with tears as she squeezed my hand.

I wouldn't say those three words, though. Not yet. Something deep inside me told me that I might scare her away if I confessed my love so soon. For now, I would enjoy what she was willing to give me.

To have someone to love and call my own for the first time in six years nearly rivaled euphoria. Lust brought us together, but it was love guiding my heart. It was the satisfied need to pamper and care for someone. It was the desire for her to devour and consume me whole. It was the fact that being with Jace just felt right.

Even now, as she lounged on the couch next to me shoving chips into her mouth while watching her show, all I could think of was that I loved her. Greasy fingers and all.

"You're staring, Rue," she said, giving me a side glance. "Is there something on my face?"

"No." I shook my head. "You're just beautiful."

She grinned, biting back a laugh. "You're so sappy."

"Says the one who has adopted a nickname for me," I said, brushing a crumb from her lip. "My nicknames for you don't count because I've been calling you them since day one."

"A, Rue is cute. B, you've just proven that you've *always* been sappy." Jace uncrossed her legs, her small baby bump making its cameo.

"What can I say, *cara mia*? I'm kind of a Casanova."

"I can't argue with that." Jace kissed me on the cheek before standing. "When I come back, I'd like to talk to you about something."

"Of course."

Jace returned with twin glasses of water and a smile. She'd been smiling widely more often, especially since starting therapy last week, and I loved it. It was beautiful and it revealed a small gap between her two front teeth.

"So, what's on your mind, *cara mia*?" I asked, giving her my attention.

160

She handed me one of the glasses and placed a hand on my knee. "Well, Thanksgiving is next week. I have the day off, but I wanted to spend it at the nursing home with a patient of mine. I'm not sure what you do during the holiday, but I wanted to know if you'd come with me."

My heart warmed at her invitation.

"Sometimes, I spend it with one of my friends' families, but I would love celebrating it with you," I said. "Who's this lucky patient?"

"Her name is Cleo. Her children aren't in the state and I wanted to make sure she still had a lovely day." The hand on my knee squeezed softly. "Without her, I don't know that I would've had the courage to let you into my life."

"Ahh. So, this Cleo knows about me?"

She looked down, suddenly interested in the surface of her water. "She's known about you since day one."

"Which day one?" I asked. I had to know.

Slowly, she lifted her head back up. Her cheeks burned red. "I told her about the night you asked me on a date."

I cradled her jaw with a hand, pulling her eyes toward mine. "No need to be embarrassed, *bella*. It just means you've liked me more than you've been letting on."

She discarded her glass on the table, then she wrapped her arms around my torso, enveloping my senses with the soft vanilla of her hair. "Yes, I have. I'm sorry it took me so long to say so."

I pressed a kiss to her forehead. "Don't be. I've enjoyed the chase. Besides, I don't mind taking things slow. It just means you're sure about me."

She laughed breathily. "I'm very sure about you, Rue. Surer than I've been about anything for a while."

Needing her closer, I dragged her into my lap. "You don't know how happy that makes me."

161

Her passion for using my body didn't bother me anymore. Now, I knew it wasn't the only thing she liked about me, but rather a bonus.

"I can feel how happy it's making you," she said. "It's pretty hard to miss."

"Mhm," I hummed, nuzzling into her neck. My hands kneaded her thighs. "I'm guessing no pun intended."

Unhurried, clumsy hands fumbled at my belt. "Correct. That's more your speed."

"And undoing my pants is yours?" I teased, lowering my voice. Before she could finish, I coaxed her down until her back hit the cushions.

"Correct," she repeated. As if to prove her point, she spread her legs and smoothed her hands under my shirt. One of those curious hands traveled downward, underneath the waistband of my boxers.

The coolness of her palm shocked me, my abdomen clenching involuntarily. My hips bucked forward. "I'm trying to be modest," I grunted.

She grinned. "Have you noticed my breasts have grown a little?"

I was quiet, feigning ignorance. Her breasts had gotten bigger over the past few weeks. "I think I would have to see them. I also tend to prefer looking at your face rather than your breasts. May I see them?"

She bent slightly to pull her shirt off, revealing those full, pointed breasts.

My breathing slowed some. "*Oddio*, I apologize. They're always nice, but they look very, very nice today. They look a little tender, too."

"They are," she said with a pout. "They're a little sensitive, too."

"Maybe they will feel better if I suck on them a little?" I offered.

At her nod, I took one nipple into my mouth, sucking gently. She gasped as I bit her nipple briefly and sucked it again.

"Is this okay?"

162

She gave me another nod.

Pleased, I took her other nipple into my mouth, repeating the motions. Her skin was smooth and sweet. "Jace, I want to give you more babies."

"And I thought I was the one with the breeding kink."

Or maybe since the day you let me cum in you, filling you up is all I've wanted to do.

"Maybe it's both of us." Knowing I didn't want to go slow, I hoisted her in my arms. "The bed will be better for your back."

I carried Jace to the bed and laid her down. Her gaze burned my skin as I removed my clothing completely, exposing myself to her. Her tongue swiped across her lip when her eyes dropped to my cock.

I didn't waste time before climbing on top of her, rolling her on her stomach, and tearing off her leggings. My love for her—and that mesmerizing gaze—made me feral. I shoved a pillow under her back before laying between her legs. Her sweet ass and glistening folds were on display, making my mouth water. My arms slid under her thighs to line her entrance up with my mouth and I dug in.

Fuck, she looks so good.

My tongue lapped her up, eliciting the melody of her pleasure. I was an orchestra conductor, each calculated touch responsible for its own note, and our song was visceral. I wanted to make music out of her for the rest of my life. I didn't let up until my face was drenched and she quivered in my hold.

"Can you handle more?" I said, lifting up.

"I'll hurt you if you don't give me more," she said breathily. "You won't get dinner either."

I laughed and kneeled on the bed. "That would be cruel, wouldn't it? Well, lucky for you, all I want is to be inside you." I slowly sheathed myself, her wetness coating me with each increasing inch. "You look so pretty wrapped around me."

"I know."

"That's my girl. Now, tell me how hard you want it."

Chapter 24

❧

JACE

On the third Thursday of November, Ruggiero and I brought Thanksgiving to Cleo. We collaborated in researching and preparing a Hungarian feast that would remind her of home. We made her *gulyás*, or goulash, a stew-like dish with beef and vegetables; *töltött kaposzta*, cabbage stuffed with meat and rice topped with a hearty helping of sour cream; *kifli*, a crescent-shaped yeast bread, glazed with butter; and *dobostorta,* a buttercream-layered chocolate sponge cake, which I left up to Ruggiero to make.

We stood outside of her room, waiting to walk in. The dork kept messing with his hair in attempts to fix it.

"Are you sure I look fine, *cara mia*? Or are you just telling me that?" he questioned, his eyebrows pulled together with worry.

I rolled my eyes. "Yes, Ruggiero, you're meeting Cleo, not the pope."

"You've been talking about her like she's the pope," he retorted. "I feel like I'm going to have to bow when I greet her."

"Shut up." With that, I turned the knob and pushed open the door, immediately swelling with joy when I saw her. She gave me a small smile before turning her attention to Ruggiero, squinting her eyes at him.

In a voice that was light and raspy, she demanded, "Good afternoon, you lovebirds. Come in." Obediently, we entered the room and joined her at her bedside. She reached out to me, grasping my hand. "Good morning, doll." She then let my hand go and grabbed Ruggiero's. "Good morning to you. I hear you've been making my Jace happy."

I could practically feel Ruggiero's worry diminishing beside me. "I've been trying," he replied, "I've been told you make her very happy, too."

"Well, not many people can handle her, so I'm glad she's found the two of us." She then patted an open space on the bed. "Sit, handsome. I want to know about you. Tell me a story from your childhood."

While we ate, Ruggiero shared stories about his youth in Italy, stories that even I hadn't heard. In turn, she told Ruggiero and me about her life in Hungary before she moved to the states to start a family. For the first time in a while, I was at true peace.

I always thought letting Ruggiero in would throw my world off its axis, ruining all the self-love I'd rebuilt, but it didn't. Spending time with him and Cleo felt surreal and I cherished the moment. If I could freeze time, I would do it now, with them.

At the end of the night, we hugged Cleo goodbye. She kissed both of us on the cheek and said, "*Család.* You two are family."

Some weeks later, I met my mom for breakfast at Blue Plate Café, a favorite of hers near Wolf River Harbor. With the goal of fostering a better relationship with my mom, I'd invited her the last time I saw her for our routine dinners.

I arrived before her but made a point to go to the bathroom first. There, I observed myself in the mirror. How noticeable was it that I was pregnant? My cheeks and my lips were colored rose pink and flushed from the chill outside, but I was happy the cinnamon-colored sweater that I borrowed from Ruggiero hid my figure. I applied some honey-flavored lip balm, took a deep breath, and walked out to meet my mom sitting at the table.

She looked beautiful today, her blonde hair pulled into a ponytail, showing off a pair of ruby earrings. Her blue eyes were emboldened by black mascara and she was dressed in an emerald-green sweater dress. For the first time in a while, I saw myself in her.

With a smile, I sat down across from her. She returned my smile and reached across the table to grasp my hand. "I feel like I haven't seen you much outside our dinners," she gushed. "I know I'm not your favorite, but you haven't forgotten about me, have you?"

"No, no, no," I assured her. It pained me that she thought that. "I've just been... I know I've been a little distant. A lot has been happening."

She rolled her eyes. "Must be that man you've been hiding from me. When do I get to meet him?"

"Perhaps Christmas." I paused, as the waiter, a gray-haired man named Hubert, came by. We ordered water to start and my mother ordered herself a black coffee. Once he was gone, I continued. "But he's only partially to blame."

She was staring at me a bit too hard as if she were searching for something. "Hiding something else from me?"

Before I could answer, the waiter came back around with our drinks. I ordered myself three pancakes with a side of country-fried steak. My mother ordered herself a three-cheese omelet with a side of hash browns and toast.

"I thought you would've ordered an omelet," she said, "that's what you usually get. The same thing as your old mama."

I gave her a small smile. "I'm not feeling it today."

My appetite was changing and not entirely in the best way. Just a few days ago, I had Ruggiero make me a bowl of vanilla ice cream with a dill pickle spear in the middle of the night. It was not anything I ever thought I'd eat, but it was delicious. When I finally came to terms with my own pregnancy and broke the news to my mom, I could ask her about her cravings. Until then, I'd keep them to myself.

"You do look a little red-faced." She leaned forward a bit, narrowing her eyes as she searched my face. Her hand left mine and she pressed it against my forehead. "Are you feeling okay?"

I gave her a nod.

"Jace, honey, your cheeks have gotten so fat!" That she stated with an amused smile. Her hand dropped from my face and she leaned back in her chair, setting her hands in her lap. "You getting fat on me? That boy has been stuffing you."

Slowly, I took a sip of my water. "What does that mean?"

"It means you're getting fat. And that sweater, dear. It's swallowing you," she said. Any other day, I would've taken offense, but I could hear the humor in her words. "I'm your mother. I'm going to love you no matter how fat you get. You were a fat baby, y'know?"

I couldn't help the smile growing on my face. "My man feeds me well," I disclosed. "He brings me lots of fatty and junk food, and he cooks for me."

"*Your* man?" she asked excitedly, "You're claiming him?"

"Yeah. He's my boyfriend." I looked down at the surface of the table, playfully avoiding eye contact. I was blushing, I knew. I also knew that she was probably staring at me with her mouth open. One glance confirmed it. "Close your mouth. You'll catch flies."

"You've been hiding so much, Jace!" she chastised. "What else *are* you hiding? How fat have you gotten?"

I rolled my eyes. "I look the same, Mom. I'm only wearing this sweater because it's my boyfriend's and it smells like him." That was only a half-truth, of course. It did, in fact, smell like him and his cologne. "You, on the other hand, look ravishing."

"Don't make me blush, Jace," she said, grinning. "I want to know all about your boyfriend."

Because he was quickly becoming my favorite topic to discuss, I obliged. Ruggiero was a blessing, and I wanted everyone to know it. So, when our food came, we enjoyed our meals and told each other of all the new updates in our lives. And surprisingly, it felt great to spend time with her.

Chapter 25

~~~~~~~

JACE

"Ready to go, *cara mia?*"

Ruggiero was dressed warmly in a dark brown sweater, a pressed pair of khakis, and a pair of sneakers. Though the temperature was dropping, I'd been running hot lately. This was evident by the navy blue long-sleeved mini dress and the opened-toed sandals I wore.

I grabbed my purse and nodded. "I'm ready."

"No jacket?" he asked, brows furrowed. "If you get too warm, you can always take it off."

"You're right," I said with a sigh. "Let me get one."

After I grabbed a denim jacket, we set off to the stores. Christmas was a week away, and I had a heap of shopping to do.

Buying gifts for my family was easy; their interests hadn't changed in years. All I had to do was throw in some variation. My parents were always happy with some sort of accessory while Jackson liked to be gifted a taste of his guilty pleasures. So, in addition to getting them each a giftcard to their favorite restaurants, I settled on CBD gummies for Jackson, a bracelet for my mom, and a leather wallet for my dad.

The person I was struggling to shop for was Ruggiero. Thankfully, he was off doing his own Christmas shopping for his parents, which allowed me the chance to think.

I shuffled around the men's section, waiting for something that just *felt like him* to jump out at me. And then I saw them—a pair of silk boxers that would wrap his package perfectly in his favorite color. He would look incredibly sexy wearing them.

Finding the boxers gave me newfound confidence in my task. His gifts would accentuate my favorite things about him.

A half hour later, I wound up with a sleek, black and gold watch with a beautiful museum dial and a leather band that would circled his wrist nicely, showcasing the veins running along his arms and his hands; a black leather belt because for some reason I couldn't understand, watching him remove his belt hardened my nipples; and a pair of Christmas-themed socks as a playful nod to his preference for wearing socks during sex. I hoped he'd love his gifts as much as I did. I couldn't wait to see what they'd look like on him. Or off him. I'd be happy either way.

I walked out of the store with bags in both hands and slumped into the bench near the entrance with a sigh. Aside from buying groceries, I didn't shop often. I saw it as more of a task than a leisurely pastime. The holidays were an exception and this year, I'd enjoyed Christmas shopping more than any year before.

I hadn't gotten to relax for long when Ruggiero came out of a different shop with a bright smile and a few bags of his own in tow. "What did you get me, *bella*?" he asked, stopping to stand in front of me.

"Oh, Rue," I said with a grin. "Would it still be a gift if I told you?"

"When the time comes, I can pretend I didn't know." He winked, offering his hand to me.

"Yeah, no." He heartily lifted me off the bench. A dull pain in my back, I rotated my shoulders for some relief as I stood. "We're not doing that. It looks like you're just going to have to wait."

He feigned a bothered huff. "What if I tell you what I got for you?"

I headed toward the parking lot as he followed close behind me. "Don't be ridiculous. Good things come to those who wait."

"You're lucky I'm a patient man."

On the way to his house, we listened to a shared playlist we'd started making the other day. It was an unbalanced blend of country, pop, and R&B, the lyrics a mix of languages. When the beginning notes of Danielle Bradbery's "Hello Summer" played, I jumped to turn the volume up and nodded to the beat.

"Ugh, this is such a good song! I remember the first time I heard it," I gushed.

He kept the brunt of his attention on the road but answered all the same. "Oh, yeah? Tell me about it."

"I was eating lunch at a Tex-Mex restaurant and shortly after my steak tacos came around, it started to play. I didn't pay attention to it at first, but the chorus hooked me."

I caught a slight frown from Ruggiero. "Have you really paid attention to the lyrics?"

"Of course, I have!" I giggled. "It might seem a little morbid, but this was a few months after my ex and I split. I thought he was going to be the one. Just as the singer says, it was goodbye to my broken heart."

He gruffed. "And how about now? What do you say to your heart?"

For a brief moment, I was reminded of my conversation with my therapist, Kaliyah, on our first session.

"It's understandable to be afraid of love," Kaliyah had said. "You said whenever your ex got upset at you, he would point out your biggest flaws."

I'd sighed and looked anywhere but the therapist's face. She was a kind lady, maybe a decade older than me, with deep brown skin and warm brown eyes. Her office had been cozy with cream walls and a few scenic paintings. The couch I sat in had a plush cushion that had soothed my aching back.

"Mhm. He'd say it was necessary for me to know those things so I could improve." I'd scoffed. "Don't know how telling me that I'm dramatic all the time is helpful."

"Do you worry that Ruggiero might do the same?"

I'd focused on the tabletop water fountain in the corner of the room. "Sometimes. I think I'm falling in love with him, and I've been trying to avoid doing that this whole time. I don't want to ruin what we have with my problems."

"You don't have 'problems.' You have trauma that you're trying to worth through and yeah, it's not always going to look great, but you don't have problems, Jace. He knows that. Trust him and trust yourself."

I bit my lip, focusing on the conversation at hand. "It's on the mend. I'll admit you're burrowing into my hateful, heavy heart."

"I like that, *cara mia*. You're burrowing into mine, too."

I drank in the sight of him. Hair combed back with his sunglasses, five o'clock shadow dusting his face, and hands on the steering wheel, he was a sight to behold. And he was all mine. For the first time in a while, I was spending the holidays with someone I might be in love with.

"Hey, I know I'm handsome, but I can feel you staring at me," he said, grinning. "If you take a picture—"

"It'll last longer. Very original, Rue. I expected a better line considering you studied literature and languages."

"Well, excuse me. I'm not in an academic setting, am I? I'm just some normal guy driving home with his girl, free of the constraints placed by literary prose."

"Dr. de Fiore, I expect better from you next time," I said, playfully stern.

"You're making me wish I became a doctor. Sounded very, very sexy leaving your mouth."

"How does your mind go to the gutter so quickly?"

"Your voice. Your eyes. Your lips. I mean, honestly, anything about you can send my mind to the gutter. Don't shame me. I don't shame you."

"No, no, you're right. I look at you and my insides go crazy. I can't even go Christmas shopping without thinking about you like that."

He shifted in his seat, the front of his pants tightening. "Now, I really want to know what you got me."

"Nice try, big guy." I laughed and patted his shoulder. "I'm still not telling you, but if you want, we can take care of him when we get to your house."

"I'll hold you to it. Maybe I'll be a gentleman and return the favor."

Neither of us had enough energy to make do on our promises. Instead, we shoved our gifts into a corner of his bedroom and lounged in bed with the lights off.

We'd cracked a window to feel the cool breeze and hear the gentle whisper of the wind.

He placed a hand on my hip, moving it slightly underneath my black cami. "I'm really enjoying you being my girlfriend."

"I'm enjoying it, too."

"Mmm, I love that." His body curved into mine, his head nuzzling in the crook of my neck. His forefinger drew circles around my navel.

I twisted my hand to caress his face and felt the prickly new growth along his jawline. "Of course, you do. You have the sexiest woman in Memphis."

He stopped drawing circles. "I have more than that."

"Sure you do. You have a baby on the way whose mom is a great cook and—"

I wasn't even finished when Ruggiero lifted his head and kissed me intently. He tugged on my bottom lip with his teeth, and I smiled against him, parting my lips to allow his tongue in. His hands grabbed ahold of my waist as he held me in place purposefully, fluidly moving his mouth against mine and then kissing at my cheeks and my chin.

"*Cara mia, sono felice*," he gushed. With him now on top of me, I was able to look into his honey brown eyes. He had beautiful eyes, and they were even more lovely when they were glossed over in moments of happiness.

With my hands on both sides of his face, I brought him down for another kiss, letting it linger. "I know. Me too."

He noised a satisfied hum before moving himself down further into my body, soon settling between my legs with his head resting on my thighs. I ran my fingers through his dark hair and he sighed contently.

"Do you like that it never snows here?" he mused. "I've only lived in Tennessee for six years, but I get tired of the dry winters."

I was glad he couldn't see my face well, for I knew the puzzled look I wore was ridiculous. "It does snow here... sometimes. It hasn't for a while time. Does it snow in Italy?"

He responded with a warm laugh. "Yes, it does. My family is from Friuli-Venezia Guilia, northeastern Italy. It snows quite a bit—much, much more than it snows here."

I closed my eyes, feeling comfortable underneath him, in his company. "That's... a lot of places to be from."

His laugh rumbled, vibrating against my stomach. "I guess?" Tendrils of his hair ticked my skin when he shook his head. "It's one of the country's many regions. If it gives you any context, I have family in Cividale del Friuli and Palmanova."

"Where were you born?" I asked. Honestly, I had no idea where any of these places were, aside from the fact that they were within that boot-shaped country. But it was always interesting to get to know more about Ruggiero and I loved his voice.

"I was actually born in Manzano, a city between the two. My *mamma* was very pregnant, and my parents were spending the day there when she went into labor," he said. "I don't know why she was pushing nine months pregnant while still trying to tour cities, but I can at least say I was born in a historic town."

"Mhmm... So, what are your Christmases like?"

"If I'm honest, they're pretty lonely. I have no family in the states and I spend most of my Christmases curled up with a good book."

That *did* sound lonely. I couldn't remember the last time I'd spent Christmas without my family.

He spoke again before I could reply. "Ironically, I participate in traditions even though I'm alone. I have a *presepe* that I've been setting up in the guest bedroom. It's a nativity scene I've had for a while. It's not as big as some, but it fills up the expanse of the dresser top."

"Tell me more," I said, stroking his hair. "What happens closer to Christmas?"

Usually, on the night of Christmas Eve, Ruggiero made himself a pot of tortellini, browsed his bookshelf for something that called out to him, and placed baby Jesus in the manger of his *presepe*. This year, he agreed to spend the holiday with me as long as we completed the nativity by the end of the night.

As we continued talking, I started nodding off and did my best to stay focused and awake. Some time later, I could no longer make out any of his words. Maybe he was mumbling or whispering, and the wind was too loud.

I snuggled my pillow with a sigh and the noise canceled out around me.

Chapter 26

JACE

I t was well-known that nursing homes could be less than enjoyable. Living there could stir feelings of depression and sense of lost independence. To their credit, Glendshire attempted to compensate for that by often hosting events for the residents, such as game nights, cooking sessions, or late-night activities.

For the holiday season, Glendshire went all out while also keeping decorations vague, given the wide range of holidays one could celebrate. It was the one time of the year that there was an event held every day. For Christmas Eve, though they just acknowledged it as the twenty-fourth of December, they were holding a dinner where residents were encouraged to dress up. I always enjoyed viewing the fun, vibrant photos that came from the holiday season, the ones that captured the residents in moments of joy.

Outside Cleo's door, I took a deep breath and knocked on the dark wood softly. Cleo's faint "Come in" could be heard as I opened the door, exposing Ruggiero and me to her slim frame.

She was beaming, arms spread wide. "Merry Christmas Eve, *babák*! You two are too good to me." Cleo's hair today was in a braided updo, secured with a green scrunchie with multi-colored ornament clips. She was wearing a red sweater that read *IT'S CHRISTMAS, B*TCHES*. In the center of the sweater was a knitted tree with small bells attached as ornaments.

"Cleo, *where* did you get that?" I bit back a laugh and greeted her fully with a hug.

She rolled her eyes. "Oh, Jace, you're always so sweet." *That* I knew was sarcasm. "I got it from Amazon! I thought it was funny, and I only spent fifteen dollars on it!" She pressed a kiss to my cheek before lightly nudging me to the side. "You get a hug, too, Ruggiero!"

After hugging us both, she crossed her arms, seemingly satisfied.

"Aren't your parents missing you today?" she inquired, cocking her head a bit. "Surely, here is not where you want to be spending your Christmas Eve."

I shook my head, attempting to reassure her. "They're not and here is where I'd like to spend my Christmas Eve. My family doesn't celebrate Christmas Eve together anymore, only Christmas Day."

By the look on her face, I could tell that she wasn't buying it completely. That was okay. I was telling her the truth. Christmas Eve had never quite been a Thompson tradition. At least, in my household. I couldn't speak for my extended family.

"You sure?" she asked.

I nodded. "Quite sure. It's not something we Thompsons do. Besides," I started, walking around towards the other side of the bed. "*You're* my best friend. Why wouldn't I spend it with you?"

Ruggiero simply smiled. He took a seat on small blue sofa that sat between the door and the sink, just as I was climbing in the bed next to Cleo.

I laid my head on her shoulder gently and she patted the top softly.

"Can you believe that Dorina and Kelemen haven't called?" she said.

While the news certainly made my spirits dim, I wasn't surprised; calling wasn't something they'd ever really done. Still, I knew that it hurt her.

"The Lukás-Moores certainly had a Christmas Eve tradition. I think it's really screwed up that they behave as if they don't know me, or as if I'm already dead." When I didn't reply immediately, she hurriedly said, "I'm sorry, Jace, Ruggiero, I don't mean to bring the spirits down. It was just something that was on my mind."

"You never have to feel bad for expressing yourself. Sadly, your children are missing out on a wonderful woman. From what I've gathered, your children take after their father more than they'd care to admit." Ruggiero's response warmed me, and I was lucky to be graced with someone with his compassion.

"Hand me that bag in the corner, please," she asked Ruggiero and sighed deeply as he complied without hesitation. "Oh, Jace, I see why you're having this man's baby." She opened the humongous bag and removed the silver tissue paper, neatly placing it in front of her on the bed. "Speaking of babies, these are kind of gifts for you, but not really." The first thing she pulled out was Margaret Wise Brown's *Good Night Moon*. I recognized the cover immediately—a lit fireplace against a green wall and a full moon peering through the red windowpane. My dad read it to me as a child. "This one," she said, gesturing toward the book, "is a classic. I *had* to." She handed it to Ruggiero, who looked at it as if he'd never seen it. I made a mental note to ask him about it.

I couldn't help the smile that my lips spread into. Intuitively, I had put a hand over my stomach, lightly rubbing circles. "It *is* a classic," I agreed. "My dad used to read this to me before bed. If my child is anything like me, they'll love it, too."

Ruggiero was still slowly turning the book over in his hands. "I don't know this one," he said. "I think the closest thing to something like this that I had was called *Filastrocche in cielo e in terra*, or *Nursery Rhymes in the Sky and on Earth* by Gianni Rodari, a famous writer in Italy. I think I will like learning this book with my *bebè*."

Cleo beamed with joy at Ruggiero. "Oh, well, don't get too sentimental yet! I have more, of course!" She reached into the bag with both hands and withdrew a stack of books. "Dr. Seuss is also a must. Baby Jace and Ruggiero will love to read, so I am trying to get you two started." She didn't hand the books to either of us, though. Instead, she set the Dr. Seuss books atop the tissue paper. "In that pile, there is *Green Eggs and Ham*; *Fox in Socks*; the counting fish book; *The Foot Book*; and *Oh, the Thinks You Can Think*. I tried to grab a few that won't be so common once schooling begins." Her hands went back into the bag to dig. "Because I love Hungary, though…" Cleo's voice trailed off as she became more focused on her search. "Aha!"

Cleo pulled out a book that was colorfully illustrated. She flipped it around proudly. On the cover of the book was a mouse, hanging from a rope in the sky. The title 'RUMINI' was printed in large text. It was my turn for unfamiliarity.

"This is a book that I read later in my adult years, once I'd already had children. Hungarian author Berg Judit's *Rumini* is a wonderful tale of a cabin boy on the fastest sailboat in Mouseland, and that's all I'm going to tell you!" She handed the book to Ruggiero and informed us, "I was nice and got you a version in English. Those are not easy to come by, but I figured my *unoka* might enjoy it."

My heart was so full and warm. I couldn't have been happier. My two favorite people were there with me at the same time, and I had my baby, too. I was overwhelmed by Cleo's generosity. I didn't know how to thank her.

"Oh, Cleo," I expressed, "this is all so sweet of you!"

Ruggiero sent me an earnest smile. "It really is, Cleo." He was careful as he gestured with the book in my direction. "Look at how happy you've mademy girl."

Cleo playfully rolled her eyes. "That girl? She's a sap." She hugged me tightly. "I'll do anything I can for my Jace, as she always does for me." The hug was but a ghost as she was quick to proceed.

Her hands sank back into the gift bag. That time, she withdrew a blanket. It was a beautifully woven blanket, red and pink flowers against a white background.

Ruggiero looked at her with a raised brow. "It's very beautiful."

Cleo, still smiling, answered, "It's a *Kalocsa*-style blanket for the baby. In the event we never meet, the baby will know that Aunt Cleo loved her still. It's also very soft and will keep them warm." The blanket was passed off to Ruggiero, who rubbed his hand across its surface. "Just one more thing." She withdrew a cloth of similar design but of thinner material. "This one is a tablecloth. Before you ask, yes, I want to be remembered*every*time*you eat on your table even though I'm a phone call away."

She handed the tablecloth to me. It was delicate and elegant. I appreciated the tablecloth; however as pretty and dainty as it was, I wasn't sure if it was something I wanted to have on the table 24/7. I'd be afraid of dirtying it. Nevertheless, I was grateful. "Cleo, I must admit, this is all a bit overwhelming. I didn't expect so many, let alone any, gifts."

Cleo hugged me again, her frail arms warm around me. "You have no idea,*angyalom*, how much of a gift your presence has been in my life." She held me tightly, almost as if she were afraid I'd disappear. "You have already thanked me. I love you, Jace."

At that, I couldn't help the tears that ran down my face. Cleo was right; I*was*a sap. I just didn't like people to know it. "I love you, too," I said. "Always."

Chapter 27

JACE

On Christmas, we arrived at my dad's modern style two-story home about twenty minutes until dinner began.

Ruggiero parked on the side of the street and jumped out of the car to open my door. With his help, I stepped into the grass. "Rue, can you get the gifts from behind the seat?"

While Ruggiero grabbed the gifts, I rang the doorbell and clutched my purse closer to me. He returned to my side just before the door was answered.

"Are you nervous?" he asked, his breath minty from the gum he'd been chewing on the ride over.

"No. I don't think so. You?"

"A little. It's been a long time since I've met someone's parents," he confessed.

"It'll be fine." I stood on my tippy toes to plant a kiss on his lips. As I did, the door opened.

My dad laughed with his usual throatiness. "Is that my daughter in love?"

I pulled back from Ruggiero, biting my lip. "Something like that. Dad, meet Ruggiero de Fiore."

My dad was a short, stout man, his belly full and stretched by quality whiskey. He extended his hand to Ruggiero. "Nice to meet you. I'm Jon." After realizing that Ruggiero couldn't shake his hand due to the gift bags, my dad pulled him in for a quick hug.

"It's a pleasure to meet you," Ruggiero said. "It is true. Jace has stolen my heart."

My dad ran a hand over his balding scalp. "Well, I'll be damned. Come on inside! Jackson's already here. We're just waiting on your mother to eat!"

As I walked into the house, Ruggiero trailed closely behind me. The smell of honey-roasted meat wafted into my nose. "Oh, Rue, doesn't that ham smells so good?"

He hummed in agreement.

I sauntered further to find Jackson already sitting on my dad's leather sectional, watching football. "Hey, baby brother."

"Sister," he said lovingly, standing to greet me. "How're you?" He hugged me and then looked at Ruggiero as he loosened his grip around me. "Hey, man. I'll help you with those."

"Thanks, Jackson. Great to see you." As they started chatting, I wandered to the kitchen.

My dad was in there opening the boxes of food, spreading them out on the island. "Hey, Jace," he said.

"Hey, dad. You got Steve and Wanda's?" I asked, putting the pie in the refrigerator. Their food was unmistakable.

He grinned proudly. "Sure did. Those two are too damn sweet not to support this time of year."

"And you got their ham," I gushed. "Steve and Wanda's ham is so good."

He couldn't help but laugh at me. "You've always liked their restaurant, haven't you? They would give us extra pecan pie because you enjoyed it so much."

"Makes sense why I had such a hard time losing my baby weight."

"Guess so. How long have you and Mr. Hotshot been together?"

"A while now. We met about a year and a half ago," I said. It wasn't a complete lie. Technically, we had known each other for a while, but I didn't want him judging us for moving so fast in such a short time.

"Good," he said. "He seems like a nice enough gentleman."

I nodded. "He is."

"How's Glendshire?"

"It's going well, thanks for asking." It wasn't an off-limits subject, but it wasn't something I really wanted to discuss. I enjoyed my job, but it was mentally and emotionally exhausting. "Where's Leah?"

Leah was my stepmother.

"Spending Christmas with the boys. Michael invited her and Noah's family to his place for the holiday." He unboxed the macaroni and cheese and looked in his utensil drawer. "I don't mind. It's just like when you were kids."

"That's true."

I helped myself to a glass of water and decided to return to the living room.

Ruggiero was sitting on the sectional next to Jackson. "Hey, Jace, turns out soccer in Italy is actually football," he said, seemingly enlightened. "I mean, I knew that, but it's different meeting someone who actually calls it that."

"Yeah? Anything else you want to share?"

"I like him," Jackson added. "He's a nice guy. He agrees your farts stink."

"Hey!" My cheeks warmed with embarrassment. "Ruggiero, you've never mentioned my farts before."

Ruggiero broke into a laugh. "It's never come up in conversation. I know that it's a natural function," he defended himself. "You are okay, I promise."

Jackson feigned hurt as he held a hand over his heart. "All this time, you've been seeing a mechanic, and you didn't tell me? You know, the Challenger eats my money."

I took the open seat next to Ruggiero. "I had to make sure he was the real deal."

" I met the man ten minutes ago and I know he's the real deal." Jackson turned to Ruggiero, his plaid button-down wrinkling slightly. "Would you trade a hundred-dollar gift certificate to Carlisle's for a one-year membership at my gym?"

"I'd love to," Ruggiero indulged, "but I'm not sure I'm allowed to do that. I think it goes against our ethics policies."

Jackson beamed his pearly whites at Ruggiero. "I'd tip every time?" Ruggiero didn't budge. "How about a two-hundred-dollar gift certificate to Carlisle's for a one-year membership for you and six months for all of your boys?"

Ruggiero licked his lips. "I'll see what I can do."

Shortly after, my mother rushed in the front door. "I'm on time, I'm on time," she shouted, a foiled pan in her hand. "Where's Jon?"

"In the kitchen!" he called.

Her black mule heels carried her to the kitchen quickly.

"Ah, the queen has arrived," Jackson announced. He flipped through the channels on the television before settling on *Modern Family*. "What do you think she made?"

"I don't know," I said honestly.

"What did you make for dessert?" he pried.

Ruggiero's hand grabbed mine, and his thumb caressed the back of my hand softly. "I found a recipe online. Something new."

"What is it?"

"Jackson," I dragged out. "Too many questions. You'll taste it after

185

dinner." I crossed my legs and focused my attention on the show.

"Someone must be on her period," he sang.

I didn't respond to his comment. Instead, I leaned my head against Ruggiero's shoulder. "Why did we come here again?" I asked him.

He nuzzled my head with his nose. "To spend the holiday with your family. Try to have a good time."

My father came into the living room, his olive-green polo stretching as he placed his arms on his hips. "Y'all ready to eat?"

Jackson nodded and jumped off the couch. "Come on, lovebirds. Let's get this grub on," he said. "This is my cheat day."

"Okay, Jack," I mumbled, smiling sarcastically. Ruggiero helped me from the couch.

"It smells good." He was close behind me, his warm breath fanning the top of my head.

"Yeah, it does."

My mother yelled as we walked into the kitchen. "Oh, my goodness!" She stood up from her stool at the island and approached Ruggiero and me. She extended her arms and closed them around us. "You must be Jace's boyfriend!"

Jackson scoffed with annoyance. "Wow, Mom, nice to see you, too."

She waved him off with one hand. "Hush. I see you all the time." She returned her attention to us and held her hand out. "Hi, I'm Eleanor, Jace's mother. What is your name, handsome?"

"Ruggiero de Fiore," he said, his voice silvery and velvety. "It is a pleasure to meet you.

She moaned dramatically and fanned herself with her hand. "Goodness!" she exclaimed. "That accent."

I rolled my eyes in irritation. "Behave yourself."

"Jace, honey, your boyfriend is an attractive man, that's all," my mom explained. She smiled and returned to her seat. "Sit down, children, so we can pray and eat."

Ruggiero and I took the seats across from my mother on the island, Jackson taking the chair next to her.

"Who wants to pray?" Jackson asked.

"I'll do it," my dad spoke up. "Close your eyes and find a hand."

I did as I was told and grabbed ahold both Jackson and Ruggiero's hands. I closed my eyes as my dad prayed for us. Once he was done, we murmured "Amen" in unison.

The food smelled wonderful and, geez, I was hungry. I grabbed two spoonfuls of mac and cheese, three slices of ham, a helping of collard greens, and two rolls. I almost felt bad for eating more than one portion, but I was eating for two.

I ignored my mom's curious eyes as I closed my lips around a forkful of greens. Before I knew it, I was halfway done with my plate. Ruggiero's hand landed on my thigh and lightly squeezed. I stopped chewing and looked toward him, raising my eyebrows.

"Slow down," he whispered.

"How's the food?" Dad asked, wiping his mouth with a paper towel.

Jackson nodded as he finished his bite. "Delicious as always. They outdo themselves every year."

"So good," my mom said, catching my eye and winking.

"Delicious," Ruggiero agreed.

"Jace doesn't need to say anything. You can tell it's good by how she hasn't swallowed at all," Jackson teased. "Have you put your fork down to breathe?"

There Ruggiero's hand was again, lightly squeezing my thigh.

"Leave your sister alone. I'm sure she's just hungry," my dad cut in.

"Yes, hungry," my mom agreed, yet she scrutinized me with a knowing look.

"Just finish your food, Jack," my dad told him. "So, Ruggiero, tell me about yourself."

Ruggiero finished his bite and then smiled softly. "I'm from Italy, but I moved here a while back. I work as a mechanic at Carlisle's." He sipped his water. "I'm twenty-nine, thirty in April."

"Ooh," she cooed. "That's a good profession."

My dad nodded in agreement. "It is. I'm an accountant, but I enjoy cars." He then smiled. "I've got a black '73 Chevy Corvette parked in the garage. It's a coupe. Bought it for a hundred fifty grand a couple of years back."

"Gorgeous car," Ruggiero agreed. "How many miles?"

"Fifteen thousand," he said. He shook his head with a laugh. "It doesn't get better than that."

Ruggiero shared his humor. "It really doesn't. He got robbed."

"More like he robbed himself," Jackson chimed in. "Dad let me drive it to my senior prom. Little does he know, that's where I got my first road head."

"Jackson," my mom cut in sternly. "That's really not appropriate for the table."

"Road head?" Ruggiero asked.

"My date gave me a blowjob while I was driving," my younger brother elaborated. "Almost crashed, sorry, Dad."

I furrowed my brow, tilting my head towards Ruggiero and pointing my fork at Jackson. "He's gross, isn't he?"

"Jackson! Hush up and eat, mom shouted.

With a shit-eating grin, he returned his focus to his plate. "Yes, ma'am, sorry."

Following dinner, we moved to the living room to exchange gifts. "Should we do oldest to youngest?" my dad asked.

My mom smiled and nodded. "I think that's a good idea, Jon."

"Amazing," my dad said, clearing his throat.

We made quick work of distributing our gifts. "Okay, guys, let's open up!" my mom said excitedly.

"Wait," Ruggiero pleaded, holding a hand up. "I had one as well." He took the small bag from his lap and passed it to me. "For Jace."

"We ready now?" she asked.

We nodded.

"Open up!"

Ruggiero's eyes watched me with loving amusement as I opened the gifts from my family.

My mother bought me a warm, baby blue cotton pajama set. I wasn't upset with it at all. My father got me a pair of stud earrings. Without asking, I knew they were diamonds. I found myself pleasantly surprised with Jackson's gift; it was a velvety blue weighted blanket. Between my pregnancy pains and the few nights I'd spend without Ruggiero, I could see myself making use of it.

"Those are all good gifts," he observed.

I nodded in agreement. "Yeah, they are."

"Open mine," he urged. "Please."

"Ruggiero," I whined, meeting his gaze. We had agreed to exchange gifts for each other back at his house.

"Jace, please."

I rolled my eyes and dug my hand into the bag. *What the fuck? Is this a box?* I pulled it out to find that I was correct.

I stared at it. It wasn't large at all, only about the size of a Rubik's cube.

I held the box to my ear and shook it gently, hearing the soft clinging of metal. Okay. It was jewelry, perhaps.

With a deep sigh, I held the box and popped it open.

It was a necklace with a round floral pendant. In the petals, there seemed to be gemstones. I eyed it more closely. Without a doubt, it sparkled in the light. Were those diamond accents?

"Let me see," my mom said. She stood up from her seat on the couch and found the empty one to my left. "Absolutely beautiful. Thank you, by the way. I love the bracelet you got me."

I didn't respond, only smiled.

Ruggiero studied me intently. "Do you not like it?"

"I do," I assured him. "I just wasn't expecting it, as all."

"She's not good with receiving gifts," my mom explained. "She gets all weird about them. Always been like that." She rubbed my back before standing up. "Anyone down for a game of Spades?"

Jackson and my dad were in immediately. Ruggiero, on the other hand, had a face full of hesitation. "I don't know what that is," he whispered.

His confession brought a laugh out of me. "No?" He shook his head. "It's a card game."

"I know several card games, but that isn't one."

"Just watch us play a bit. It's not hard to learn."

"Great." Jackson stood up from the couch and rubbed his hands together. "Jace, I want you on my team. Let's kick some old Thompson ass."

A half hour later, Jackson and I had gotten the thirteen books we promised. A second game was played before I excused myself and Ruggiero took my place, teaming up with my dad while my mother and Jackson tried their hand at collaborating.

I watched from the end of the couch, my head resting on the arm.

"You've really never played Spades?" Jackson asked Ruggiero. "I'm having a hard time believing that."

"I promise. There are card games I play back home," he explained. "I believe it's your turn."

"Yeah, Jack," my dad taunted. "Get your head in the game."

I sighed. Ruggiero was everything I didn't realize I wanted in my life.

I thought about life before him. I had a routine, for the most part. Still did. I slept around ten. I woke around seven, had breakfast, and went to work. After my shift, I'd come home, shower, have a snack, and watch some television. I didn't have many friends, but I had Cleo. I had biweekly Sunday dinners with my family.

After Garret, I couldn't really see myself with anyone else. While I wasn't distraught when we split, I was sad. In many ways, I had loved him. However, we had already been growing apart.

Unfortunately for me, commitment was hard. It was something I had been diligently working on, trusting people, opening up to people. I had chosen to trust my gut with Ruggiero.

So far, I wasn't wrong.

He got along well with my family, laughing with them and putting up with Jackson.

A decade ago, when I was alone in that hotel bathroom, numb after I had been taken against my will, wishing it were all over, I'd never imagined that this moment was ahead of me. A moment filled with love—love that was unbridled and unbound. I couldn't have imagined this was the life I had waiting for me, nor that Ruggiero was the person that had been it for me all along.

It all seemed too good to be true.

Chapter 28

JACE

We made it back to Ruggiero's house around a quarter 'til eleven. Between the drive from my dad's house in Rocky Villa to my apartment and my apartment to Ruggiero's neighborhood, I was almost ready to doze off. Almost.

Knowing that Ruggiero and I still needed to exchange gifts was a motivator to stay awake and alert for a little while longer.

Unfortunately, we had a few slight inconveniences to take care of before we could share our small Christmas gifts. For one, there were plenty of things in the car, such as foiled to-go plates and gift bags. Two, most of it needed to be taken in the house.

Ruggiero got something out of the trunk and then he went around and opened my door, offering a hand to me. "Here, baby, just take the plates in. I'll get everything else."

"Thanks." With a smile, I grabbed his hand and allowed him to help me to my feet. He then grabbed the plates out of the seat and passed them to me along with his house key.

He pressed a kiss to my forehead. "I'll be in soon."

"Okay," I told him. I started up the concrete driveway and to the porch.

Shifting the plates to my left hand, I stuck the key into the door and let myself in. I shut it with my backside, kicking out of my shoes.

All I wanted to do was slump on the couch and close my eyes, but I pushed myself to the kitchen. I put our slices of eggnog pie and my mother's peppermint bark cheesecake in the fridge. I drank a glass of water.

"Jace!" he called. I could hear the bags rustling as he brought them inside.

"In the kitchen," I responded, making sure my voice was loud enough for him to hear me.

A while later, he walked in. He flicked the light switch on before coming to stand in front of me. "Hi," he said softly, lowering his forehead against mine.

I eyed him as I drank a sip of my water. "Hi."

"How're you feeling?" he asked, lazily placing his hands on my hips.

How *was* I feeling? Tired, certainly, but there was another emotion I couldn't name. It rubbed on the side of being an anxious excitement. "I don't know," I answered honestly. With a sigh, I loosened myself from his arms, setting the glass on the counter.

He didn't follow me, allowing me the space I sought. Ruggiero stood there, tall, dangerously handsome in the dimly lit kitchen. "How does a bath sound? I made sure to grab some salt for you."

I'd almost forgotten about Ruggiero's offer to run me a bath. Thus far, he'd been a man of his word, so I didn't know why I hadn't seen that coming. A bath did sound good, though. My feet were killing me.

I said nothing in reply, but Ruggiero moved anyway. "I'll go start the water. Have a seat," he told me. "You look terribly tired."

Grabbing my hand, Ruggiero led me back to the living room, gently backing me onto the couch.

"Relax, *per favore*," he said, kissing me on my forehead. "I'll come back and get you when it's ready."

I did as I was told, laying on the couch. Though it didn't bring much relief to my back, it did feel good to be off my feet for a bit. "Thank you," I murmured, "really."

He smiled at me and gathered the bags in his hand. "It's my pleasure. *Per te, niente è troppo.*" Before I could complain about not understanding, he said, "For you, nothing is too much."

All I could do was grin as he disappeared up the stairs.

Just as I begun to relax, I heard Ruggiero's footsteps. "Ready to get washed up?" he asked me.

I sat up on the couch, using my arms to push myself to my feet. He awaited me at the end of the staircase, a patient hand extended out to me. Plastering a smile on my face, I met him where he stood, placing my hand in his.

"Are you okay, Jace?"

He, of course, never missed a beat. Still, I could be okay for him. So, I nodded. "I'm okay."

I followed Ruggiero up the carpeted stairs. Fatigued and worn-out, I held on to the wooden railing for support. As we neared the second floor, I could hear the muffled sound of the running bathwater. Stepping up to the platform, I trailed Ruggiero to the right.

He pushed open the bathroom door and I was shocked at what I saw.

The lights were off, but the bathroom was lit by a small, white ceramic wax warmer plugged in near the sink, situated on the counter. Rose petals were scattered about the surface of the water.

Ruggiero slid to the side, allowing me to peer further into the bathroom. That's when I noticed two wine glasses on the edge of the tub.

"What's in that?" I demanded. "I'm not drinking—"

He placed a hand on my waist, lowering his mouth to my ear. "It's cranberry juice."

"Oh," I said, dumbfounded. "Duh."

I imagined him rolling his eyes as he hugged me from behind, his growing arousal firm against my backside. Warm, wet lips pressed a kiss behind my ear. "Yeah," he whispered. "I know that baby means no alcohol."

I turned around to see him begin to unbutton his shirt, regarding me with dark eyes aglow. I knew the look like the back of my hand— lustful, passionate, licentious. Judging by his hardness, he wanted me badly.

"Fuck," I groaned. "Stop staring at me like that." As always, I found myself tempted, but I was already spent. I wasn't sure if I had the energy.

Ruggiero chose to play, furrowing his eyebrows. "Like what, *cara?*" He slid the shirt from his long arms and focused his attention on the zipper of his pants. "I'm sorry," he murmured, sounding apologetic, "Just, *voglio quelle labbra su di me.*"

I knew by now not to trust Ruggiero's innocent acts. And although I had no clue what he'd said, the way he lifted his eyes and smirked told me it wasn't innocent at all. "Come again?" I asked, trying to hold back my own smirk.

"I said, I want your lips around me," he remarked, loosening his pants around his hips, a simper on his face.

"You want my lips around you?" I repeated. I rolled my eyes, running a hand through my hair. "That the only reason you ran me a bath?"

"No," assured Ruggiero. Seeming to be taking his time undressing, he leaned towards me and pressed a kiss to my forehead. "The bath was definite. Your mouth on me? Well, that's fifty-fifty."

His fingers played at the hem of my dress before he bunched it around my waist. "Aren't you romantic?" I complied with his efforts, raising my arms toward the ceiling. In just thirty seconds, the dress was hung next to his shirt.

"I know, Jace." His hands were at the waistband of my panties. Keeping his eyes on my face, like the gentleman he was, Ruggiero slid my panties down. I placed my hands on his shoulders to keep myself steady as I lifted a leg for him. "But trust me, you deserve everything I have to give you."

"Okay, quit it," I huffed. "Let's just get in the bath."

He stood there, staring at me.

"Are you going to move?"

Then, for whatever reason, he laughed. "Yeah. I think you should take your bra off, though."

I looked down at my chest. Of course, he was right. I glanced back up at him, trying to ignore the tinge of heat I felt on my cheeks. "I guess I should then."

Once I was submerged in the bathtub, it amazed me how quickly the day's tensions wore off. The entirety of the bathroom smelled like lemongrass, warm and citrusy. I laced my legs with Ruggiero's, catching red petals in the palms of my hands.

"You didn't have to do this for me," I mumbled. "It feels good, but—"

He groaned, leaning back in the tub. "If it feels good, then what is the problem?"

Good question. What *was* the problem? How about the fact that all of it felt so real?

He immediately followed with, "Have I done something wrong today?"

I quickly shook my head. "No, Ruggiero, it's just—" I stopped myself and breathed deeply. "I just have a lot of nerves recently."

"That's okay," he said. He took my hands in his, entangling his fingers in mine. "There's a lot going on. If you feel overwhelmed, that's normal."

I sighed. His words made things sound as if they could be so simple. Why couldn't things be that simple?

"Do me a favor, Jace," he started. "Close your eyes." Because I trusted him, I did as he instructed. "Now, inhale deeply, through your nose." I inhaled. "Hold it. Now exhale through your mouth." I exhaled, obeying his instruction. "Lean back in the tub, until your shoulders are under the water, and relax."

The latter of his instructions were harder to perform, but after some shuffling from both of us, I managed to do so.

"Isn't it exhausting always being on the go?" he asked. "Don't you deserve some of that time for yourself?"

"Ruggiero," I breathed, my eyes still shut.

"Yes?"

"Take your own advice, please. Close your eyes. Relax."

"Okay."

I was sitting on the edge of his bed, a plush bath towel wrapped around my body. Ruggiero was searched through his closet. "Come on," I complained, "tell me you do *not* still want to open gifts."

"I do," he said, keeping his back to me. "You opened everyone else's, *cara mia.*"

"You already gave me one," I tried to reason. "Ruggiero, I'm beat."

For a quick second, he spun to face me. "Let's pretend you're not." Three more minutes of rummaging and he was closing the closet door, emerging with two bags in his hand. He dropped them beside me on the bed. "Okay, open them."

Wearing nothing but a black pair of boxer briefs, Ruggiero stood in front of me, his arms crossed. I snorted at him, but he held his posture.

"Open them, Jace," he urged.

"Fine," I said. I grabbed the first bag, silver and shiny. After pulling out the white tissue paper, I dug my hand inside. I could tell that it was some sort of fabric.

Maybe an article of clothing? With a deep breath, I withdrew whatever it might be. The fabric unfolded in my hands. Heat rushed to my cheeks. It was a black lace babydoll, and it was very sheer.

"Go on," he said, "there's more in there."

More? I sighed, and with a grin I couldn't fight back, I fished another piece of fabric out of the bag. It was a matching pair of panties. "Ruggiero," I murmured. "What is all of this?"

He rolled his eyes playfully. "It's something nice and romantic for you to wear for me," he explained. "Your panties have a playful backside."

"You naughty man," I teased. "Thank you. They're... sexy." I could imagine myself wearing them, my round derriere making an appearance through the cutout in the back. "I know there's a shit ton in those bags, so just give them here."

Ruggiero licked his lips and handed me the remainder of the gifts. Who knew he'd be so generous when it came to gift-giving?

I tried to make the rest of the process go by quickly. As grateful as I was that he felt moved to buy me so many beautiful things, I was tired. In addition to the lingerie, he bought me a matching baby blue pajama set and a few more things just for me. As he stood there with a shit-eating grin, swaying side to side, he eyed me with a playful curiosity.

"What?" I prodded.

"I have one more," he said.

I furrowed my brow at him. "One more?"

He nodded. He sauntered toward his dresser, pulled open the top drawer, and grabbed something.

"Close your eyes," he told me. I did as I was instructed. "Hold your hands out." A few seconds after I did, something was placed into my palms, cold and hard.

"Can I open my eyes?"

"Yes."

I looked to see what he'd placed in my hands. It was a house key, small and bronze at the teeth and the head painted an electric blue. "Is this mine?"

"Who else would it belong to, Jace?" He leaned his face down to press a kiss to my forehead. "Of course, it's yours. I want you to be able to come home, whenever you want to."

And just like that, a wave of emotion hit me. He'd given me my own personalized key.

"Fuck," I said, biting back the urge to cry. "Ruggiero, this is so sweet."

"My home is yours."

I closed the key in my hand and pressed my mouth to his. "Mine."

He returned my kiss in fervor before kissing my forehead. "Yours. Now, get some sleep. I'll open your gifts in the morning."

Chapter 29

⚜

RUGGIERO

As I read over the invoice, making sure everything was in order, heavy boots approached. A hand slapped the door frame. "Hey, boss, I'm here to take over for you," a deep voice, one that I knew as Wayne's, said.

Wayne was an alluring guy. He hadn't been the first to catch my eye in the shop, but I knew he was safe to make a pass at. I almost did before Jace tumbled back into the picture.

I glanced quickly at my watch before I met his eyes with a smile. "Thank you, Wayne, I really appreciate it." I stood up, smacking my hand on the paper. It was half-past, so I needed to get going. "This invoice goes with the 1998 silver Supra. They dropped it off around noon, only wanting an oil change, so I'm guessing it'll be done in another hour or so. Though, Kyle and Lucky suggested they could use more work."

"I'm guessing you left a summary under the invoice," he commented, walking further into the office.

"I'd be no good if I didn't. Am I okay to leave?"

200

"Yes, go on, boss. I can handle this," he assured me, giving me a hearty pat on my shoulder.

As I made my way out of Carlisle's, I thought about the surprise that I was planning, one that would bring me face to face with my mother. Though it had been over a decade since she'd said them, her words had never left my mind: "*Sei la vergogna della famiglia.*" Translation? "You are a disgrace to the family."

I didn't expect my mother to understand me. She was reserved and well-guarded as if an army of thorns were protecting her. While she was the same woman that raised me, something changed when I turned eighteen. I couldn't pinpoint what it was, nor did I ever ask my dad about it, but I could tell her disgust for me ran deep.

She was ashamed of me and those feelings heightened the longer Martina and I were very visibly together. I didn't believe in hiding my love, whether I was with a man or a woman, and I was adamant to show off Martina proudly. Despite her being more than two decades older than me, I loved Martina. She accepted me—all of me—and she never once made me feel bad for anything. When we separated, it wasn't because we no longer loved each other, but the opposite.

The news of her illness was blindsiding. A few weeks before her forty-seventh birthday, she became noticeably symptomatic. Her appetite became nonexistent. Still, she continued to eat as best she could with a smile on her face. The second indication came during sex. For us, it confirmed something was wrong. Over the three years we were together, we had a more than healthy sex life. We were open about our desires and explored them comfortably until sex started to bring Martina excruciating pain.

Soon after, she was diagnosed with ovarian cancer. Still, it was considered a late diagnosis, her tests and scans showing that cancer had been around for more than a few weeks; it had been around for at least three years. To make matters worse, it was spreading to her cervix. Martina didn't want me to stick around while she went through chemotherapy. She didn't want me to witness the hair loss, weight loss, and sickness that she'd endure. I begged her to let me stay by her side, to support her, to love her, and she demanded I go. "You're too young to give your life up for me," she'd told me. "It would be selfish for me to allow you to stay. This will fuck you up."

A few months later, I migrated to the United States of America. Despite loving my home country, I was ready for a new terrain. Saying it hurt to leave Pa would be an understatement, but he assured me he understood. He knew that there was no way I could stay in the same place as Ma and Martina, at least not then.

After leaving Carlisle's, I ran some errands. Sometime in the beginning of December, I'd purchased plane tickets for Jace and myself to Italy. Thanks to her brother, I knew she had a passport. I hesitated to give the tickets to her on Christmas. The gifts she gave me were modest and practical, and I worried about overwhelming her with too much.

I planned to reveal them to her today. I'd waited long enough. Christmas was a week ago and our anticipated plans happened in a few weeks. Fuck, I hoped she said yes.

By the time I'd gathered everything for tonight's surprise, I had only a half hour until I needed to head home and I had to make a stop at Lucky's. His apartment building wasn't too far from my house, but I needed to make it quick.

I got out of the car and straightened out my shirt.

I headed up the stairs and knocking on his door. A couple of seconds later, he opened the door clad in a tank top and some pajama pants. His blond hair was dark and straight as if he'd just gotten out of the shower. "Howdy, friend," he greeted me, motioning for me to come in.

"Hey, Lucky." I stepped inside but stayed by near the door. I didn't want to let myself get carried away. I didn't come to Lucky's apartment often, but whenever I did, he knew how to sit me down on that corduroy couch and liquor me up so I'd be here for hours, talking and laughing with him.

"I'm not even gonna ask if you want a beer 'cause you look antsy already," Lucky said.

I rolled my eyes. "Whatever you want to call it, but you're right. No beer today. I'm certain that Jace made dinner and I don't want to keep her waiting."

"Alright, alright, I'll be right back. Let me go get your package."

I nodded as he disappeared down the dark hallway. I didn't know how Jace liked her flowers, but after looking at his sister Sadie's catalog, I tried to pick some that reminded me of her. I could only hope were as nice as they were on the website, though Lucky swore that his sister sold nothing but the best.

I let my eyes scan the front room and waited for him, tapping my foot against the wooden floor. His expansive flat-screen TV played an episode of The Blacklist at a loud volume.

She was just about to head toward the motel when Lucky's footsteps sounded. I snapped my head up to look at him. I was distracted by the stunning bouquet in his hands.

Que bello!

I'd picked an arrangement of white roses, the beautiful white Madonna lilies, dark blue iris flowers, and dark purple Calla lilies. I then noticed Lucky's wide grin as he held the flowers proudly.

"They're perfect, aren't they?" he said to me.

I couldn't help but smile. "Of course, they are." Just thinking about giving them to her made my heartbeat quicker. "I love you, Lucky, thank you."

"No need to thank me, pretty boy, the smile on your face is worth it." He stepped closer, pushing the bouquet into my hands. "Go see your girl and have fun on vacation, will ya?"

"Wish me luck. I really hope she likes it."

"Dude, come on, I know she'll like it because she likes you. And who wouldn't want to go on a romantic rendezvous with you, a big, strong man?" he teased. "But seriously, Ruggiero, you're worried for nothing."

"I'm not worried, Lucky—I'm a big, strong man. You should try it out some time," I poked.

"Alright, that's enough. Get out of my house. Go eat your dinner." Lucky pushed me towards the door and reached behind me to open it. "The next time I hear from you, you better be in Cancún!"

"We're not going to Cancún," I protested.

"Wherever you're going," he responded, narrowing his eyes at me. "I love you, get out of here, Ruggiero."

"Bye, Lucky," I managed to say before he closed the door on me.

I drove home with a permanent smile on my face, knowing that in t-minus sixteen minutes, I'd be seeing my gorgeous Jace.

Chapter 30

◦◦◦◦◦

JACE

Excited for the surprise I was planning, I made my way to the grocery store. I sat in the parking lot for a little while, searching the web. I wanted to cook Ruggiero a meal that tasted like home.

It wasn't easy to decide what to cook. From the readings, I learned the food of Friuli-Venezia Giulia wasn't what I thought of as traditional Italian. While there were certainly Italian influences, most of their food seemed to resemble that of its surrounding countries. Situated in northeastern Italy, the region was neighbored by Slovenia and Austria. I read some more, eventually narrowing down my choices to dishes from its capital, Trieste. That still didn't prove easy, as I discovered Trieste used to be the main port of the former Austro-Hungarian empire.

I could now see why it was so easy for Cleo and Ruggiero to get along. They'd come from similar cultural backgrounds.

I was relieved to know that the meal didn't have to be a perfect recreation. His home's cuisine was a result of cultures bleeding into one another and creating something unique. So, I settled on a dish called *jota*, a hearty soup of sauerkraut, beans, potatoes, and pancetta, as our appetizer; *agnello al cren*, lamb prepared with horseradish, and a side of polenta as our entree; and *gubana*, a cake made with nuts and dried fruits, as our dessert. Since I had no idea what any of this would taste like, I hoped for the best when I finally ventured into the store. This meal would take some time to prepare well, so I needed to make this trip quick.

I searched the meat section for lamb chops, wanting to find the best deal. I picked up a pack and flinched at a sudden warmth beside me.

"Jace?" My name came from someone I'd never forget—Garret.

I scrutinized him as I dragged my gaze from his cargo shorts to his white t-shirt. "Hello, Garret," I said kindly. Little did he know, I'd set him on fire with my eyes if I could.

It had been almost two years since I'd seen him and I wouldn't have minded going longer. He was still handsome, his blond hair grown out past his ears. Those deceiving, brown puppy-dog eyes were the same as they always had been.

"Hey," he said, "how're you doing? You look... different but really good."

"I'm doing okay. How's Katherine? Are you excited about your wedding? That's coming up, isn't it?"

He pretended to be shocked. "You remembered? Will you be there?"

I sighed deeply, selecting a pack of meat and setting it in my cart. "I don't think so, bud. Anyway, I gotta go." I took that as my opportunity to walk away and leave him where he stood.

A few seconds later, I looked over my shoulder and saw that Katherine had come to him, a confused expression on her face. I felt bad for her, but I was glad to find that I was completely unaffected by him now. My only priority was having a good night with Ruggiero.

I made it to Ruggiero's a quarter till five and immediately went to work on preparing the food. Since I'd chosen to make three separate courses, I'd need all the time I could get. I only had a little more than three hours before he'd be home from work.

I listened to music as I cooked, alternating between Thomas Rhett and Jason Aldean. I could only hope that I was making everything correctly and that Ruggiero would be pleased with the meal.

So far, our baby was being cooperative, not yet sending me to the bathroom. It seemed like they liked it when we had a productive day. When I spent hours lying in bed, they complained, seemingly telling me, "Mom, get up." Over the past month, I'd learned that our baby liked to take short walks; cook with me; car rides with Ruggiero; eat bananas, cottage cheese, and peanut butter, either all together or separate; and watch TV. I also learned that they liked when I rubbed my belly, when I listened to music I enjoyed, and when I took warm bubble baths. It was in these moments that they were the calmest.

I swayed to the music as I diced the vegetables for both the appetizer and the entree. Ruggiero always came home a little after eight, and I assumed tonight would be no different. We didn't need to have a three-course meal, but I wanted to treat him to a special night, one that showcased my appreciation for him.

Once I prepped the vegetables, I started on the dough for the *gubana*. Compared to the many cake recipes I'd encountered, this one ranked low on the basis of difficulty. The dough was a simple flour, milk, and yeast mixture with sugar to add sweetness. I was glad I brought my mixer over from my apartment; while I liked kneading dough, doing so manually was time-consuming. I watched the dough carefully as it spun in the stainless-steel bowl, adding the egg yolk and butter. Shortly after, I let it sit to the side and began the filling.

The time seemed to fly by as I cooked. It was seven o'clock before I knew it. The good thing was that everything was going as planned; all the food would be done by eight and Ruggiero should be returning from work a little after.

Brushing my hair behind my ear, I grabbed a pair of oven mitts and took the freshly-baked *gubana* out. It smelled wonderfully sweet, the aromas of cinnamon, nuts, and cocoa swarming the kitchen. I carefully placed the pan on top of the cast-iron trivet on the counter. Sliding the oven mitts off, I returned my attention to our appetizer and our entree.

On the front eyes, I had the jota on the left and the beginnings of the *agnello al cren* on the right. The former was nearly done, only needing about another half-hour on the stove. After giving the *jota* a quick stir and checking for bay leaves that were ready to be taken out, I dropped two tablespoons of butter into the Dutch oven—which I was extremely excited to find in his house since I hadn't yet bought myself one—before adding in the myriad of spices. After ladling the broth in, I gave everything a good stir. Per the recipe, this step would take ten minutes. So, I busied myself by setting the table. I set down the sets of regular silverware and searched for accompanying dinnerware. I was pleased to find that in his China cabinet, he had a set of beautiful, Italian-style porcelain dishes. The blue motif of fruit around the rim appeared to be hand-painted. However, since I didn't know their significance, I left them alone and opted for a plainer set, one with a vibrant image of a chicken in the center. Since these, too, could mean something special, I hoped I wasn't overstepping.

Once the timer went off, I added the cuts of lamb and transferred the pot into the oven. Per the recipe, the lamb should be cooked for forty-five minutes over low heat. I took that as my chance to freshen up and prepare myself for the night.

Chapter 31

RUGGIERO

The unmistakably savory aroma of *jota* wafted to my nose when I pushed open the front door. The familiar scent both threw me off and intrigued me. It smelled like my childhood home in Udine during the holidays. Keeping the bouquet of flowers securely in my hand, and the tote bag on my shoulder, I shut the door behind me softly.

I kicked off my work boots and followed the smell and the sound of country music further into the house.

The closer I got to the kitchen, the more the house smelled like a diner in Friuli. Over the past few months, I'd learned she could replicate any meal with enough effort. She was a phenomenal cook and had proven so time and time again. I didn't doubt her ability to replicate Friulian cuisine without error. If the aromas swarming the house were to be believed, she had.

The music grew louder as I padded through and I reached the dining room. The table was set for two and my woman sat at the head of it, presenting a spread of covered dishes. Surprised, I glanced along the

209

spread of food before meeting Jace's gaze.

Her shoulders were covered by a silky black robe tied around her waist in a bow. Honestly, it wasn't covering much. I struggled not to drop the items I held and swoop her into my arms as I stood at the edge of the table.

"Jace," I murmured, "*Sei meravigliosa.*"

"Ruggiero," she returned, a small smile spreading across her lips and a glimmer in her blue eyes. "Are those flowers a centerpiece for the table?"

I shook my head, trying to ignore the sweat collecting in the palm of my hands, and cleared my throat. I didn't want her to see that I was nervous. "No, Jace, they're for you."

"Oh, they are?" Her lovely smile grew wider. She pushed her chair out and stood up. "What's in the bag?" My eyes scanned the length of her torso as she sauntered toward me. The garment wrapped her body faultlessly, doing a wonderful job at accentuating the swell of her breasts and her curves. She looked like a present ready to be unwrapped.

"I'm more concerned with what's underneath those lids," I told her, gesturing toward the table with my free hand. "I know these smells very well and I'd like a confirmation."

Jace ignored me and moved closer. She was so close I could smell notes of warm vanilla bean and hazelnut. She rubbed her hands down my shoulders and caressed my arms. Goosebumps rose along my skin. "How come there's hardly any grime on your uniform?" she asked. "Were you not at work today?"

"I was at work, but only until one-thirty," I admitted. "I had to prepare something." I dragged my gaze from her body and met her ravenous eyes.

"Prepare what, if I may ask?" Jace stepped closer until there was only enough space between our chests to keep from crushing the flowers.

210

I wanted to hide my surprise a little longer. "I'll tell you once we've eaten your delicious dinner.".

"I guess that's fair." Her hands slid from my wrists to my hands clutching the stem of the bouquet. Closing her eyes briefly, she inhaled. "Wow, Rue, these are very nice."

"*Bella*, they don't hold a candle to you," I promised.

With a soft tug, she pulled the flowers toward herself. With a small smile stretching her lips, she said, "Have a seat, Ruggiero, I'm going to put these in a glass and come right back."

My eyes were glued on her ass swaying as she walked out of the dining room. She was a magnet, and I was helpless against her pull. Not even five minutes in the same room as her, and my blood was rushing south. The music she was playing wasn't helping. The singer's warm bass voice pleaded with his lover to wait up for him, that he'd be coming home soon to be with her.

Taking a deep breath, I hung the bag on the ear of the chair and sat down. I shifted in my seat as I observed her handiwork and attention to detail. The plates she set the table with were the *pollito* collection my parents bought me when I first moved out of the house. My mother wanted to ensure I had dinnerware of my own. The set had been with me for nearly twelve years, and this was the first time they were being used.

Jace had a habit of going above and beyond. This night was no exception. I was giddy just knowing that she'd spent the past few hours making this for me. Jace expressed her love through her cooking, and nothing made me feel more loved than her making e a meal fundamental to my culture. I smiled widely, all teeth, not bothering to hide my nervous excitement as she walked back into the dining room with serving utensils in hand.

I quickly stood up from my seat and pulled her chair back for her. "Miss me?" she asked, sitting down.

"Of course, I did. What's not to miss?"

"Good. Now, take a seat. I'd like to show you what I made." Biting her bottom lip as she focused, she lifted the lids from the three dishes. As I'd suspected, *jota* was one of them. Just by the look of the soup, I knew she'd made it perfectly. She peeled back a corner of foil stretched across the top of the Dutch oven next. Steam traveled from the opening and the smell of roasted lamb filled the air.

My mouth dropped open as she uncovered the last dish.

Her brows pulled together in concern. "You okay, Rue?"

I nodded quickly. I didn't want her to get the wrong idea. "You baked *gubana*," I explained, "I haven't had this in nearly two decades." In my family, preparing and eating *gubana* was a tradition reserved for weddings and other special occasions.

"Is there a reason why?" Jace frowned. Her eyes darted back and forth between me and the dish.

"We had a family gathering when I was thirteen. My nonna baked enough *gubana* to last a week. My *nonni* were happy to have all their children and their grandchildren together." It was the last time they'd seen us all together like that. I loved the dessert, but after my grandfather passed, she stopped making it. She couldn't stomach it. "The tradition died with my *nonno*."

Chapter 32

JACE

I didn't know what to say. Ruggiero's eyes were wet with emotion as he observed the dessert. "I feel like I should apologize for baking this then. Baby, I had no idea—"

"Jace," he quickly cut me off, shaking his head. "Please, I am incredibly moved by this. This means more to me than you know. It just…" He trailed off and I understood he must be searching for the right words to say. "It surprised me, that's all."

He was probably asking himself, *how do I tell her I hate this?*

I sank into my chair. I'd wanted to surprise him, and it seemed I'd only managed to upset him. "Rue, baby, I really feel bad for making this. Out of all Friulian dishes, I could've chosen one less—"

"Less, what? Meaningful?" Despite his glossy eyes, his tone was light and jovial. "Jace, I love *gubana*."

"You do?"

He nodded. "I do. I also love *jota* and *agnello* and *cren*. I love sauerkraut and pancetta. I love my home," he gushed. "This is so sweet of you."

I tried to let myself smile. I still wondered if he was telling the truth. "Well, it seems you deserved it considering you got me flowers."

"Do you like them?"

It had been over two years since anyone had bought me flowers. Though I could tell that this was a bouquet from a flower shop, it was obvious they were flowers of his choosing.

"I love the flowers, Ruggiero. It was a nice surprise," I said honestly.

A tear escaped his left eye as he gave me a closed smile. "This is an incredible surprise. I knew you'd make dinner, because that's just you, but Jace, *cara mia*, you put your love into this."

I should've told him he was right; I did put my love into the meal. Instead, I retorted, "You haven't even tasted it yet."

He rolled his eyes and wiped the tear with the back of his hand. "I'd love to eat, then, if you're ready. I've been itching to taste it since I walked in." It seemed his body betrayed him as more tears streamed.

"Ruggiero," I said, dropping my voice to a whisper. "Are you sure you're okay with... all this?"

"Oh, yes. I'm more than okay." He paused to grab a napkin from the table and blotted his eyes. "I don't mean to cry. This just feels like a dream. You, *Jace*, feel like a dream."

I reached across the table and grabbed his free hand. As he'd told me before, I said, "I'm real, y'know, I'm completely tangible."

He squeezed my hand in his. "I think I'm finally starting to believe that. This has all just happened so—"

"Fast. I know," I finished for him. It hadn't even been five months since we'd found each other again.

He nodded. "Yes, it's been fast. I always fear that this will be taken away from me at any moment. Not even half a year has passed and yet we're creating a family."

I opened my mouth to speak but soon closed it. I wasn't sure what to say. I'd been mulling over the same thought for weeks now.

His thumb rubbed the back of my hand soothingly. "I'm grateful for you, *cara mia*. Your affection feels so wholesome, and I believe that's why it can be scary that we've moved so fast."

I managed to smile at him a little. "I would've waited to get pregnant if I could have, but I don't regret doing this with you." Dropping my gaze down to our joined hands, I admitted, "It's extremely scary for me."

"I hope we can work through this fear of ours together."

"Me, too." Though I wanted to sit and hold his hand longer, I didn't want to get lost in my thoughts. I let go, standing up. I doubted he was scared of the same thing I was. He seemed like he'd be a naturally good parent. "Are you ready to eat?" I asked, forcing myself to look into his glossy eyes.

I didn't entirely believe him when he said he was okay.

"I'd like to eat, yes," he assured me. He narrowed his eyes at me and chewed on his bottom lip.

I stared back at him, searching his eyes. I couldn't believe I made him cry.

"Unless you'd like to starve me now for crying," he said, laughing lightly.

I huffed, hastily looking away and grabbing the serving spoon. "That's not funny."

"You were the one trying to stare into my soul."

"Can you pass me your bowl?" I asked. "Please?"

"Of course, Jace." He then handed me his bowl, waiting patiently as I spooned jota into it.

I blushed and gestured for his plate.

We didn't talk again until we both were served.

"Have you tried the food yet?" he asked. Though his eyes were still puffy, they were void of tears and sadness.

I shook my head. "You want me to try it first?"

215

"I'll try it first," he said, and spooned a portion of soup into his mouth. He closed his eyes, humming joyfully. "That's really good." He ate another spoonful. "Really. Try it."

Under his instruction, I spooned some into my mouth. It was warm and savory. I was surprised by how well the sauerkraut went with the pancetta and the beans. "It is really good," I agreed.

Ruggiero was taking his time with his soup, but I dug into the lamb next, eager to know if that, too, tasted so good.

I closed my mouth around the spoon with an appreciative moan.

It tasted amazing. I hadn't eaten or prepared lamb before, but I did a pretty good job. I was blessed to not be a picky eater and to be skilled at cooking, because that meant I could try whatever I wanted whenever I wanted to.

"I'm guessing you like the food?" he asked, a grin on his face.

"It's delicious, Rue," I answered, putting my hand over my mouth so he couldn't see all my half-chewed food. "I feel like I'm eating multiple cuisines in one."

"You practically are. Our food is representative of Italy, Austria, and the surrounding Slavic cultures." He took a second to clean his face and then continuing. "It's what I love most about Friuli, aside from the art. I love traditional Italian food, but I really, really love food from other cultures, too."

"So, it's like you have the best of many worlds?"

"Exactly. But I have you, too, so I think I have the best of all worlds," he said, a gleam in his eyes. "Speaking of which, what made you cook such a special dinner?"

I shrugged. "I wanted to do something nice for you. What made you buy me such nice flowers?"

He mirrored my actions. "I wanted to do something nice for you, but I think your something nice blew mine out of the water."

"Really? What's in that bag you brought home?"

"Hush your mouth, Jace, and eat your food so I can eat mine," he retorted, a playful grin on his face.

Initially, I wasn't super interested in the bag, but his secrecy made me curious. Maybe if I exaggerated a little, it would move him. "I can barely eat because I am wondering what's in the bag."

"Jace," he said, more sternly than usual. I straightened my back in the chair. "I will show you after dinner."

I rolled my eyes. "Do I have to wait until after dessert, too?"

"I might make you," he said. "Eat the delicious meal you've prepared, and we can explore the bag afterwards."

I huffed, feigning annoyance. "I guess."

Thirty minutes later, once we'd finished our meals and each had slices of the cake (Ruggiero had two; I had four), we still hadn't explored this bag of his. Honestly, I didn't think we were going to.

The two of us were in the kitchen, putting away the food together. The bag still hung on the ear of the chair.

I understood I was nosy, but ever since he came in the house with it, I couldn't help but wonder what was in it. It wasn't often that he brought stuff home besides food, if ever.

We were quiet as we straightened up the kitchen. I didn't know about him, but I was a mess of nervousness and excitement. Between his presence and the mystery of the bag, I was overwhelmed. As I put the soup into a large container, I thought about the first time I heard his voice over a year ago and a half.

It had echoed mine as he asked for a screwdriver. Shortly after, he'd introduced himself to me, his name rolling off of his tongue like butter: "I'm Ruggiero."

Sure, I was probably crazy, but I knew then that he was someone special.

Something remarkable was happening between us. How crazy was it that we found each other again? And how crazy was it that we both thought to surprise each other today?

"Jace," Ruggiero called softly, his voice breaking into my thoughts.

I gave him a small smile. I realized that while I finished putting away the food, he must've left and come back. The tote bag was on his shoulder. "Yes?"

"Are you ready to go upstairs? We can explore the bag there."

Chapter 33

❧

RUGGIERO

I hated making Jace wait, but her giddiness made it worth it. She had no clue what I had in store, and while I didn't have much, I knew the ambiguity of it excited her. She sat quaintly on the edge of the bed, feet flat against the ground, legs pressed together, hands clasped. I wanted to drop down to my knees and part her legs, but that would be selfish; I had put off her questions long enough. Her curiosity was bound to make her explode.

I stood in front of her, maintaining a few feet in between us. I, too, tried to appear proper, keen on making sure I stood up straight. "Are you ready?"

"Can't you tell?"

"Yes, I can tell." Smiling, I removed the bag from my shoulder and handed it to her. "Explore it. Everything in this bag has been handpicked for you."

There were five things, each of them significant to our trip. The trip that she unknowingly prepared a perfect meal for.

I kept quiet as she reached into it.

Jace was magnificent. Radiant. Gorgeous. I loved the way her eyes and nose crinkled with excitement when she retrieved the first item from the bag. Her brow furrowed as she unfolded the piece of paper: a plane ticket.

"I'm going to Venice?" she asked slowly. "We're going to Venice?"

"Yes, baby, but keep going. There's more."

She rummaged through the bag. I smiled as she pulled out the next item: a brochure. She crossed her legs as she unfolded the pamphlet. "Okay, I'm confused," Jace said after a while. "According to this, we're going to Udine, but the plane ticket says Venice."

I laughed lightly. "I know what it says. What do you think it means?"

"Maybe I'll find more clues in the bag?"

I said nothing more, only shrugged.

Jace rolled her eyes and continued to look. She opened the bag fully pulled out a medium-sized rectangular box. She set the bag aside and focused on unwrapping it. "Y'know, every time you give me a box, I'm scared it's a ring. Although, this one is too large to be a ring."

I frowned. "I doubt you want to marry me so soon. It's not a ring, *cara mia*. It's something a lot less serious."

"I do want to, I think, but I'm happy to know it's not a ring. I'm not ready for that yet." She stuck her finger into a flap and tore the paper away.

I tried not to show how much the conversation was affecting me. "I do, too," I admitted, "but I'm not ready either."

Jace smiled. "That's okay. There's no rush."

She was peeling back the tape now and opening the flaps of the box. I was nervous for her to see my gift. But if she loved it, that was amazing, and, well, if she hated it, that was okay, too.

Jace turned the cardboard box upside down and put a hand below to catch whatever fell out. Her eyes widened as another slightly smaller box slid out first, all black and rectangular, and then a pocket-sized book.

Jace tossed the former box and focused her attention on the black one. I crossed my arms as she turned the box around, observing it.

Slowly, she gazed up at me. I enjoyed her curious eyes and the glimpse of fire behind them. "Is this a dildo?"

I smiled at her. My heart was beating quicker. I had no clue what she'd say next.

"And it vibrates?" Her voice softened as she finished her thought. "Rue, this is naughty."

"Well, you are a naughty girl," I said. "Do you hate it?"

Jace bit her lip, tucking a strand of hair behind her ear. "No, I've just never—" she paused, laughing a little. "I know I'm, like, almost thirty, but I've never really used toys. I mean, I have, but a long time ago."

I was silent for a moment. "How long ago?"

She shrugged. "I don't know. Probably like five or six years."

"I wish I could say the same," I divulged, "I have a small collection of toys."

"How come I haven't seen any of them?" She sat up, eyes full of curiosity.

My ears and cheeks warmed. Licking my lips, I stepped closer to her. "We can explore that later on. Besides," I said, politely taking the box from her, "they're personal toys."

"Yeah, personal," she mumbled.

I sat beside her and grabbed the book from her lap, bringing it to her attention. "You probably didn't notice because of the dildo, but there's a dictionary, too. I figured you'd want to walk around and know a little bit of what's being said."

"That's really great, but I think I saw one more thing in there," she said, scooting closer to me so that our shoulders touched. I breathed in that sweet, dessert-like scent of hers.

"I'm certain you did."

She opened up the tote bag one last time and pulled out an envelope. The sap I was, it had a red wax seal imprinted with a rose. Her eyes widened as she investigated the envelope as much as she could without opening it. "What's in here? A golden ticket?"

"No, I just wanted to make it extra special."

"Fine. I'll open it."

I didn't take my eyes off of her as she tore through the seal. I smiled as she withdrew the card.

With a deep breath, Jace opened the card and ran a hand through her hair. "To my beautiful woman," she began reading aloud, "I know it hasn't been very long, but that doesn't mean that you don't deserve the best. So, I spent hours designing and curating the perfect vacation for us. Thanks to your family, I know you have a passport." She stopped reading to look at me, a nervous grin taking over her face.

I gestured for her to continue.

She cleared her throat. "In a few weeks, we'll be boarding a flight to Venice, where we'll spend four days in Dorsoduro exploring the area. Then, we'll take a train to Udine, Friuli where we'll stay for five days. The brochure will come in handy. If you study it a little closer, you'll find that it doubles as an itinerary." She laughed. "Of course, you made an itinerary."

"Our time in Italy will be a perfect time for you to use everything I've given you, including this. Attached to the back of this is a visa gift card. I know it's not a whole lot, but I wanted you to be able to get yourself some things. For one, it's pretty cold there. Nothing like Memphis."

"I'm looking forward to taking this vacation with you. Being with you in my hometown will be a dream come true." By the time she finished reading, she had a huge smile on her face. "So, you're really taking me to Italy?"

"That is correct, I am taking you to Italy." I put my arm around her waist, pulling her closer. "It almost felt like you knew for a second, especially given dinner."

Jace shook her head. "Surprisingly, that was a coincidence, but I'm excited. Extremely." She set the card in her lap, her brows furrowed. "Do I have to meet your parents?"

"Only if you want to, Jace. I won't force you," I said.

"Well, you've met my parents. I feel like it's only right that I do. That is, if you want me to."

"Of course, I want you to."

Truthfully, I didn't mind her meeting my dad. My mother, on the other hand... I wasn't confident she'd like Jace. Hell, she barely liked me. At the end of the day, though, it didn't matter what she thought.

I loved Jace and she was good for me. I wouldn't let anyone tell me otherwise.

However, at my words, her smile faltered.

"Everything okay?" I asked, placing a finger under her chin.

She attempted a smile again. "I'm fine, Ruggiero, just are you sure? Like, you really want to go with me?"

I spoke without another thought. "I'd love to go together."

"Mean, emotional, scared-to-be-a-mom me?" She no longer tried to smile. I understood she couldn't. Her feeling like she wasn't good enough was a fear I realized wouldn't go away for awhile. I'd do my best to change that.

Choosing my words carefully, I said, "You forgot amazing. Mean, emotional, scared-to-be-a-mom, amazing *you*. I promise I planned this trip for us. I'm not leaving without you."

Jace focused her gaze on her lap, her fingers played with the edges of the envelope. "Okay," she said. "I am really excited."

I sighed, relieved. "I can't believe I thought you'd be disappointed, or worse, not want me." I kissed her forehead, a moan slipping out when her hand reached inside of the underwear and gripped me hard.

223

She brought her other hand to the nape of my neck as she rubbed me harder. "Ruggiero, you've never once disappointed me."

I lifted my head slightly as she put her mouth to my collarbone and kissed up my neck.

"You've always made me so comfortable and so fucking happy."

"You've made me so happy, too," I said, taking hold of her hips, pulling her closer to me.

"Good. Show me how happy I make you." Her hand dropped lower to fondle my balls, and I groaned.

The anxiety I felt moments ago was fading into an eagerness to please her.

"That's it, Rue. You know I've always loved how big you are, how much you stretch me."

I loved the fire that coursed through my veins when she encouraged me. Overwhelmed with emotion, I grabbed her face and kissed her.

I moaned into her mouth as she gripped my cock. Eager to know what was under her robe, I backed her onto the bed, keeping my lips on hers as I dropped my hands to the bow she'd tied.

"Rue, you're making me so wet," she remarked as I loosened the knot. "Can I feel you in my mouth?"

Fuck, I loved when she called me that.

I shook my head, doing my best to maintain my composure. She wouldn't dominate me right now. Not yet. I brushed aside her robe. "Can you show me what's under here instead?"

"You're always so eager," she cooed, looking at me bashfully as I took in the sight before me. She was wearing the light blue babydoll and the matching panties I'd chosen specifically for their open back.

"Someone was planning to get fucked tonight, weren't they?" I teased, lowering my voice. I reached my hands under the dress to where her ass was exposed, pressing my lips to hers again.

Jace smiled against my lips and opened her mouth to let my tongue

224

in. She squeezed me hard before dragging her hand along my length. She swallowed my moans as she thrust me in her grip.

I rubbed her thighs and took her ass in my hands, kneading the skin. I wanted to sink my fingers into her and curl them against her walls until her legs shook, but I wanted to do it slowly, to savor the moment. "Fuck, Jace, I want to fuck you so badly."

"I'll let you fuck me if you let me suck your dick." She took her hands off me and climbed further onto the bed. My desire swelled as he let the robe fall from her shoulders and laid on her side.

"Jace," I groaned. I needed to be inside her.

"I like sucking your dick. I like how you feel in my mouth, how smooth you are against my tongue, choking me." She reached for my hips and dragged me in front of her, inching my boxers down. Her eyes, heavy and dark with desire, stayed focused on my painfully hard cock as she freed it from the fabric.

"Go ahead," I gave in. I just wanted her to touch me, to bask in her attention, to be hers to do as she pleased. She kept her eyes on mine as she wrapped her hands around me and brought my tip into her mouth.

Jace spread her legs wide for me to see all of her. "Fuck, Jace." If my dick didn't hurt before, it definitely did now.

She nodded, popping my cock out to smile. "Do you like it?"

I gazed at her lazily as she covered me with her mouth again, loving how soft and alluring she looked with her lips around me, those big blue eyes full of lust. The babydoll was a perfect fit for her. The fabric showcased her body, giving me a lovely view of her breasts and her hardened nipples. I groaned loudly as she took me further into her mouth. "Mhm, baby, this feels so fucking nice."

She moaned and pulled my hips closer. Wanting to feel what I was doing to her, I sucked two fingers into my mouth and slid them down her slit. She whined around my cock and spread her legs even wider for me. I circled a finger around her entrance, loving how she writhed against the bed.

Jace closed a hand around my balls once again and I sucked in a sharp breath. I didn't want to cum in her mouth, but I was dangerously close to doing so. While I pushed two fingers into her dripping core, I wrapped my hand in her hair and forced her away from me.

"Ruggiero," she complained, pouting, "give it back to me."

"Hush," I ordered. I let go of her hair and put my hand on her chest, pressing her down. I didn't want her to be able to move as I pleasured her, thrusting my fingers in and out of her. To say she was wet was an understatement and nothing was better than knowing it was because of me. She didn't have to listen to me, but she did, relaxing against the bed. I focused on her lips, loving how they parted when she moaned loudly. "Baby, you're so good," I praised, adding a third finger.

Her chest rose up and down, her gaze fixed on me. My thumb applied pressure to her clit as I fucked her with my fingers.

"That's it, baby, you're doing so well. You can handle a fourth, can't you?"

She smiled, her teeth biting down harshly on her lips as she nodded. I stuck my pinky deeply alongside the others. Jace was clenching around them, whimpers spilling from her lips, bringing her hands to her breasts. She squeezed her nipples as I massaged her clit.

"God, you are so fucking gorgeous. I want to bury my cock into you. Would you like that, *cara mia?*"

Chapter 34

✥

JACE

"Please, fuck me," I begged.

I wanted him to stop teasing me.

"Oh, but baby, you're so close. You can wait, can't you?" He shoved his fingers in deeper and thrust faster, curling them upward. "Or are you wanting to cum with me inside you?"

"For fuck's sake, Rue, please, put your dick in me." I reached for him hastily and used my thumb to rub his precum around the tip. "Please. Can't you feel how crazy you're making me?" Upset I'd been reduced to begging, I squeezed my hand hard around him.

I could tell by the look in his eyes that he was giving in. "Mhm, Jace, you've been so kind lately. I think you deserve it." He pulled his fingers out of me before grabbing my hips and dragging my body to the edge of the bed. His hands moved to my thighs and pushed my legs apart, but he only put the tip in. He was enjoying watching me moan beneath him, his eyes laden with passion. After sucking a thumb into his mouth, he pressed it to my clit.

"You are so fucking evil," I groaned. "Why do you want me to beg?"

He sent me a smirk. "I don't, but I do want to savor this, baby." He rolled his hips into mine, greatly surprising me as he sheathed his length inside of me. "Why would I want to make you beg to feel this?"

My mouth dropped open in an inaudible moan as his thumb rubbed circles against my hardened bud. I dug my fingernails into the skin of his waist, stunned at the sudden fullness.

He kept talking as he drove himself in and out at an antagonizing slow pace with tortuously deep thrusts. "Why would I make myself wait to feel your warm pussy around my cock?" He lowered his lips to my neck and licked the skin behind my ear. "Why wouldn't I give you exactly what you want when you're carrying my child, my brave woman?"

I almost came just from his words and was only able to respond by clenching around him. The sounds of our centers meeting, hot and wet, were a constant rhythm in my ears.

"*Mi fai impazzire,*" he murmured against my skin, pressing kisses on the base of my neck. "Fuck, Jace." His lips left wet kisses along my collarbone before they found the mound of one of my breasts.

"Fuck, Rue," I echoed. My body was hot, my blood pulsing through my veins and drumming in my ears. All I could think of was him, how good he was to me, how good he made me feel.

I squeezed my eyes shut and arched into him as he took a nipple into his mouth and swirled the bud with his tongue. He pushed himself deeper into me, moving his hips with more urgency. Ruggiero fervently shifted his attention to the other nipple, sucking it and biting it softly.

The sensations transported me to cloud nine, the sensations of his sweet assault growing tenfold. His warm mouth sucking my nipples, his hands smoothing up my body, his warm, pulsing dick thrusting in and out.

I was in Heaven. I didn't want him to stop. I wanted him to ride my body until I couldn't take it anymore.

"Harder," I pleaded, "fuck me harder."

"Like this?" he asked, his fingers pinching my nipple as his lips rested against my neck.

Each perfect thrusts his hips pushed me closer to the edge. "Deeper," I breathed, moving my hands to his ass and coaxing him forward.

"Ahh, Jace, you're trying to make me cum."

I buried my nails into his side. *"I'm* trying to cum."

He muttered a "fine" and slid his hands down my body, leaving shocks of electricity in their path, and grabbed my ass, pulling me down toward him until he couldn't anymore. He sucked on my neck, nipping and biting as I wriggled underneath him, grinding against him. "Like that?" he mumbled.

"Fuck, Rue," I whimpered, "just like that."

I could feel every ridge and vein of his beautiful dick, especially its twitching when I called him Rue. He'd never voiced out loud that he liked the nickname, but I knew that he did.

"Mhm, Jace, you feel so good, so fucking perfect," he groaned, hands squeezing and massaging my ass cheeks.

A rush of emotion flooded me as he pulled out and then thrust hard. I cried out as he did it again before burying my teeth in his shoulder. I was trying so goddamn hard to hold back, my walls clenching and my legs shaking around him.

"Fuck, baby, you going to cum for me?" With his lips still ravishing my neck, he slid his rough hands from my ass to the backs of my thighs, spreading my legs wider. Ruggiero moaned loudly as he pushed himself deeper, his balls firmly against my ass.

I whimpered, nodding. I was losing my mind, barely processing anything other than him riding me and the blissfully painful strokes of his dick.

His fingers on my clit made me throw my head against the pillow, my nails breaking skin as I grounded myself. Ruggiero continued to stroke my clit and thrust into me as I squeezed my eyes shut in surrender to the orgasm ripping through me.

He stilled, holding his body above mine. "Yes, baby, milk me," he urged. His warm fluid filling me prolonged my orgasm, waves of pleasure washing over me steadily. Ruggiero lifted his head, peppering kisses along my chest as I came undone. "Fuck, you're so good, so, so good."

I let go of him as he pulled out of me and rolled off of me, resting next to my side. I took a deep breath and turned to face him. His cheeks were red, a film of sweat coating his forehead. "Thanks for a thorough fuck," I whispered hoarsely, my throat dry.

He smiled with those pearly white teeth, pushing damp hair from his face. "Anytime, *cara mia.*"

Chapter 35

❧❧❧

JACE

A few days later, my mom and I went on an impromptu shopping trip.

"So, where're we going again?" my mom asked, putting her shades on after buckling in. She sat comfortably in the passenger seat of my car. Comfortably, meaning she adjusted the temperature of the heat and didn't hesitate to mess with more things.

I gave her a small smile as I pulled away from her house and merged onto the highway. "The mall."

"Why're we going there?" She was fiddling with the radio, more than likely looking for the old country station. She wasn't into country pop like I was.

"I needed a shopping buddy," I admitted.

I didn't spend much time one-on-one with my mom, but with the baby coming, I wanted to build a stronger relationship with her. I'd need the support.

"Well, isn't that something?" She continued to surf through the stations until the Statler Brothers' "Hello Mary Lou" came through the speakers. "What're we shopping for?"

I couldn't help the smile that took over my face. "I'm going on vacation, Mom. My honey is taking me to Italy."

My mom squealed. "Italy? Oh, Jace, that is awesome! I've always wanted to go to Italy. You'll have to take lots of pictures for me. When are you leaving?"

"Next Tuesday. We're flying to Venice and I need some more clothes. It's colder there." I took a moment to glance at the GPS. We had another nine miles to go before we'd reach the mall. "Rue gave me a gift card to get whatever I need."

My dramatic mom gasped and pressed the power button of the stereo. "Shut up! That's so cute."

"Relax, Mom, turn the music back on," I mumbled, feeling bashful.

She shook her head and obliged. "Well, anyway, thanks for bringing this old lady. Maybe I can look around for myself. I've got a date on Friday."

Now, it was my turn to be dramatic. "Oh, do you? And who's that with, young lady?"

"Oh, some guy I bumped into at church a few weeks back. It'll be our third time meeting outside of church."

I almost asked her if he was single, and if so, if she was sure of it, but I left it alone. I didn't want to jeopardize a good morning. "You've been hiding this from me."

"Well, I didn't want to get excited about nothing. I had to make sure he wasn't another cheating scumbag."

Bingo. Question answered. "Didn't want to be the other woman, huh?"

"I've never wanted to be the other woman. I just wanted to find a good man. There's not a whole lot of good men in God's land."

"Okay, so what about this guy?" I asked.

My mom laughed a little. "I'm thinking he might be one of remaining few."

I slid a quick glance her way. "You gonna tell me his name or what, Eleanor?"

"Shut up, don't use my name like that." Despite her scolding, she still laughed like a schoolgirl. "His name is Wilmer, but to you, Mr. Strand."

"Mr. Strand? I'm an adult, Mom, I'm not calling him mister anything."

She smacked my knee. "It's not about you being an adult. It's about respect. When you meet him, please call him Mr. Strand. Don't call him Will or Wilmer. He wouldn't like that."

"So, we'll be meeting him?"

"I sure hope so. Y'all meeting him will mean the world to me because it'll let me know if this is a good idea or not."

"And why's that?"

"My girlfriends always tell me that kids just have an instinct, y'know. They know if something's off right away."

I snorted, shaking my head. "Don't know if I agree with you there. Also, I'm not a kid."

"You're my kid and that means that when it comes to me, and other grown folks that are more grown than you, you still have that instinct. Remember Markus?"

"I fucking hated that guy."

"I really wish you wouldn't talk like that," she griped. "It's not becoming of a lady."

"And yet I'm still a fucking lady. I love you, Mom, but cursing doesn't mean I don't respect you." I flipped through the stations, wanting to hear something more upbeat. "Besides, this is my car. I can speak freely."

"I'll let you have your free speech if it means you'll buy me lunch."

Stealing another glance at the GPS, I said, "I was already planning on it. What kind of daughter would I be if I invited you out and didn't feed you?"

"Hmm, what about ice cream then?"

"Does buying you ice cream mean you won't make me censor myself for the day?"

Though I wasn't looking at her, I knew she had her hands clasped together in her lap. "You can say whatever you want as long as you don't say the Lord's name in vain."

"Well, my goodness, Eleanor, we've got ourselves a fucking deal," I laughed, finally pulling my hand away from the radio when it landed on the chorus of "Kiss Somebody."

"Now who's this, Jace? Can't tell me this is better than the Statler Brothers."

"It's Morgan Evans, but there's also a Morgan Wade… and a few other Morgans."

"I'll be honest, I don't know what the hell you're talking about." She laughed. "You can list off as many Morgans you want to, and I won't know a difference."

"Whatever, whatever. Let's just sit back, enjoy the ride, and bop our heads to some country."

"I'll sit back, but I don't know if I'll enjoy the ride. This isn't the country I bop my head to."

"Well, you're going to learn how to today," I told her, turning the music up.

I couldn't believe I was saying this, but shopping with my mom was fun. It had been over a decade since we'd last shopped together. When I was a teen, either my dad took me shopping or I took myself.

In the past three hours, we'd managed to acquire five bags apiece. I doubted that I needed everything I bought for vacation, but I wasn't complaining.

Ruggiero did a bad, bad thing by giving me all this money. Rarely did I splurge on myself because once I started, it was really hard to quit.

That explained why I'd ransacked a store's sweater collection, spent an hour in the dressing room trying on must-have pants, and then went to another store to pick out some more cute, wintry outfits. But I still had some money remaining on the card. I itched to find ways to spend it.

"Ooooh! Turn around!" my mother shouted, throwing her arms in the air.

I laughed as I complied with her request and spun in a circle. "Are you sure this isn't too... like, I don't know, much?"

"Oh, hush! There's no such thing as too much when it's your man. There's no sin in getting spicy with one special person."

My cheeks warmed as she looked me up and down. Her eyes lingered on my stomach for a few seconds, and I pretended not to notice, but she said nothing. I held my arms behind my back, struggling to not cross them.

"I know you aren't acting shy," she said with a laugh. "I couldn't ever get you to cover up when you were a teenager."

"Yeah, but back then, I was showing skin to get attention. I'm sure you know that by now." I retreated back into the dressing room, pulling the door closed. I gave myself another look in the mirror. The blue number hugged my curves and even gave my small breasts a boost. "Besides, when it comes to being in the bedroom, I prefer to be naked. That's how I got pregnant now."

"Sneaky way to tell me, but I was growing suspicious." I smiled when I realized how kind her voice was. "Congratulations, baby. You're going to be amazing."

"Thanks. We're happy. You sure this looks good on me?"

I wasn't too excited about lingerie, but I knew Ruggiero would be.

He was a fun of undressing me. I wasn't too hot about it because I still had my jeans on underneath the one-piece, making the crotch look ridiculous, and I was starting to show. At the moment, I could pass for being bloated, but that wouldn't be true for long.

At least my mom knew, and it didn't need to be a long-winded conversation.

I titled my head, trying to imagine what it would look like without my pants. It was a simple teddy with a low plunging neckline covered in a floral pattern that gave sneak peeks at bare skin. The back was nearly non-existent as it descended toward the thong that sat against my jeans.

"Your father always loved when I bought special pieces, though he always pulled them off within minutes," she said through the door.

I gagged loudly so she could hear me. "I didn't need to know that!"

Little did she know, I wasn't even thinking about her, nor the two of them together. I was thinking of Ruggiero and me, the flight we'd be boarding in a couple of weeks, and our worlds finally colliding at full force.

As my reflection stared back at me once more, my mind drifted to the Italy gifts I had opened, right before he opened the gift I prepared for him. I'd never been one to put much thought into lingerie, but nothing had excited me more than the anticipation of letting him unwrap my robe. Especially after seeing the toy he'd picked out for me.

I squeezed my legs together and fanned myself with my hand. It was suddenly very, very hot in the dressing room as I remembered the events afterward. The bold confessions. The intense groping of each other's bodies. His dick in my mouth. His fingers inside me. His dick inside me. His voice in my ear.

I sat on the bench and leaned my head against the wall. I needed to get a grip on myself. I could *not* be getting hot and bothered in the dressing room of a lingerie store.

But I am so hot and bothered.

I shook my head. Not here. Not now.

"Mhm, Jace, you feel so good, so fucking perfect," he'd said. "Fuck, baby, you gonna cum for me? Yes, baby, milk me. *Dolcezza*, you're so good, so, so good."

A loud knock sounded on the door and I jumped. "Jace? You doing okay in there?" my mom asked, her voice sweet. "I hope I didn't make you uncomfortable. The outfit looks good, but don't feel pressured to get it."

I took a deep breath, pressing my hands to my rapidly beating heart. "I'm okay, mom, thanks. Just give me a second."

It had been nearly two weeks since that night and I was still daydreaming about it.

I stood up, beginning to shimmy out of the teddy. "Oh, and Mom, it's coming home with me. I think I'll get two more in different colors." "Oh?"

I pulled it off of my feet and set it on the bench. I quickly put my shirt back on before sliding on my jacket. "Yeah, you should get one, too. I think Mr. Strand will like it. Maybe a nice red or yellow. It'll bring out your eyes." After grabbing my purse and the teddy from the bench, I opened the door.

"You think so?"

I gave her a smile full of teeth. "I know so." From my experience, wearing something sexy worked for me. My man liked it very, very much and it benefited me. That, and I didn't want to be the only person embarrassed from daydreaming in the dressing room.

"Sure," she said, smiling, "let's grab some. And then ice cream for the three of us, of course?"

"Yes, and then ice cream."

Chapter 36

JACE

With our focus homed in on packing for our trip, the rest of January seemed to pass in a blur. Our trip approached faster than I expected and soon our only priority was enjoying the last night we'd have in our bed for a while. We were in bed earlier than usual, but that didn't stop a sense of delirium from capturing us.

I told myself I was tired, but deep down, I knew that it was him that made me delirious. His smell, his touch, his taste, his love.

Ruggiero pushed me down into the mattress and kissed my neck. "Are you sure you don't want dessert? I'm really craving some strawberries and ice cream."

I snorted even though dessert did sound good. "You sure you're not the one pregnant, Rue?"

"I think so," he said, his hands sliding up the sides of my abdomen and lingering beneath my breasts.

"I'm too excited to eat. I'm sure you can hear my heart knocking against my chest."

Ruggiero lowered his head and listened for my heart. "I can. Why so excited?" His thumbs brushed the base of my neck and my heartbeat picked up.

"Cause we're going to Italy," I gushed. I moved my hands up his back, resting them at the nape of his neck. I bucked my hips forward to press myself against his growing erection. "I'm still shocked."

He thrust, rubbing himself against me. "It's just another country." Even with his sweats on, I could still feel all of him. Every inch of him.

I pulled him down for a kiss and savored the moment his soft lips met mine with the same sense of purpose. Ruggiero's rough hands roamed my chest, my stomach, and my back, holding me to him.

I smiled against his lips. "It's not just another country. It's my first time in another country and it's with you."

I didn't know if it was the trip or the pregnancy hormones, but all I wanted to do was be close to Ruggiero, to thank him, to savor him.

"I guess," he said with chuckled. "But I'm telling you now, it's only kind of cool." He licked his lips, grinding into me again.

"Fuck," I whined. The friction sent a wave of warmth throughout my body. A heartbeat manifested at my core.

I dragged my hands up his neck and pulled on his hair; he dragged his hands down my body and pulled down my underwear. "I'm glad you're excited, I love that I can feel how excited you are," he said, the tips of his fingers meeting my clit.

I leaned into his hand as his soft touches kindled ripples of fire under my skin.

"*Dio mio*, you're so reactive," he said with a smile. I buried a loud moan in his chest when he thrust his fingers inside me.

He worked with a perfected skill and my eyes closed as I gave in to the pleasure. He gripped my waist with the other hand, holding me in place as he always did.

Ruggiero nuzzled his face into my neck and peppered kisses along it. "Are you this wet because we're going to Italy or because I'm on top of you?" he asked, his lips brushing my ear.

I managed a breathy laugh. "I don't know. Maybe it's because I'm going to Italy with you." I urged his fingers deeper as I circled my legs around his waist.

"Mmm, I think you need more than just my fingers."

"Me too, Rue. I don't want to beg."

"Alright, alright, *bella*," he said, taking his fingers out to push down his pants.

My eyes followed his movements with devotion, eager for the reveal I'd seen so many times. He slid his boxer briefs down and I swallowed, nearly salivating at the offering before me.

"You're so beautiful, Rue," I told him, admiring his naked body.

Ruggiero lips curled upward into a smile. "And you're so beautiful." He kissed his way to his destination, taking time to suck and bite at the skin.

I rested my hands on his shoulders, laying my head against the pillow as soft moans left my mouth. "Don't tease me," I whined, tightening my grip.

"Not teasing," he mumbled. He settled between my legs, putting his arms underneath my thighs and grabbing my hips. "Fingering you isn't enough. We both know that."

I had no chance to fuss as his warm mouth met my pussy. Ruggiero's eyes met mine as he slid his tongue upward and circled it around my clit. His eyes didn't leave mine, not even as he licked my clit and buried his tongue inside me.

"Oh, you feel so good," I panted, moving my hands to his hair.

He moaned into me and I whined in response, his deep hums sending vibrations through me. He returned his mouth to my clit, flicking it with his tongue. I jumped against him, causing him to tighten his hold on me.

240

"I swear to God, stop teasing me."

Ruggiero groaned and lifted his head a bit while he licked his lips. "Baby, you'll have to learn patience. I'm so fucking hard it's going to be difficult not to cum."

"Rue, what—"

"I'm not trying to embarrass myself, okay? I know you love getting fucked, so I'll fuck you, but right now, I'm trying to eat your pussy. You're going to cum before I fuck you, okay?"

I smirked. "What's wrong? You already leaking?"

He rolled his eyes at me. "You are an incredibly sexy person. It's not my fault."

"Alright, then," I said, pushing his head down as a shudder ran down my spine, "Get back to work, Rue."

He licked his lips, his eyes darkening. "As you wish."

We stayed up late into the night, giggling like we'd drunk a whole bottle of wine, touching each other with so much zeal you'd think we'd never shared a bed before. We paid the price the next morning when our alarms rang at seven o'clock, our heads smarting as if we had hangovers. Ruggiero and I weren't morning people, but if we slept in a minute too long, there was bound to be some unforeseen accident that would prevent us from catching our flight. We shuffled out of bed and got ourselves ready in under an hour and then loaded into the car with beverages in hand. Ruggiero's choice was coffee, mine hot chocolate.

I sipped at the hot liquid, keeping my hands around the cup to warm them. I could understand how Ruggiero missed the snow. It was February. Christmas and New Year had passed, and I was going to Italy. My giddiness grew as we drove closer to the airport, my foot tapping on the mat.

"I see your enthusiasm has broken through your tiredness."

"I can't help it. I'm so excited my stomach hurts." It was true. I thought maybe the baby was excited, too, and our mutual excitement was too much to handle.

"I'm glad," Ruggiero said, reaching for my hand across the middle console. "I thought it was a good idea for us to get some air. Memphis is a little stuffy right now."

I kept my arm looped around Ruggiero's as we bustled through the airport. I'd fantasized about the airport being the calm, picturesque place presented in movies. It was anything but. It was so goddamn busy. I should've known that it would be. It was a Tuesday morning and the holiday season was still alive.

"Remind me why we're here again?" I mumbled. "All of these fucking people."

His smooth laughter filled my ears. "To go to Italy."

For someone who claimed he wasn't all that excited, he had a lovely smile spread across his face. If we'd had time to stop, I'd take a picture to capture the moment. "I know, just—it would be great to just teleport there."

"If you can figure out how to do it, I'd happily teleport with you, *bella*." He stopped abruptly at a turn before pulling me along. "I think our gate is over here."

"You're good at navigating this place. All I'm thinking about is how to get out of it."

"Feeling claustrophobic?"

I nodded, pushing myself closer to him. "Painfully so."

"Well, come on, we'll find a spot for us to eat. I can't promise that it'll be quiet, but we can try for a spot with fewer people."

True to his word, he bought us a meal after he led us gate 10. We sat at a table in a corner close to our terminal, but far enough from others that I could breathe.

He'd promised not to laugh at my cravings, but he failed horribly at keeping his word. I'd ordered a basket of chili cheese fries and sides of pickles and mac and cheese to dump on top of it.

It was magnificent. I couldn't believe I hadn't done this sooner.

He shook his head, his nose scrunched up in a mixture of intrigue and disgust. "I can't tell if that looks good or not."

I covered my mouth with my hand as I chewed. "It's good, needs more pickles, but it's good." I finished my bite and then I spoke again. "Want to try it?"

He pretended to think for a moment. With a nervous smile, he picked up his fork. "Sure, I'll try a bite."

"Brave, brave man. You won't regret this." I lifted the basket and held it towards him. I enjoyed the look of unease on his face as he pushed his fork through the fries.

Once he had some of everything on his fork, he carefully held it up to his mouth. "Sure this won't kill me?"

I rolled my eyes. "Stop that. You like everything separately. You might like it together."

He took a deep breath and mumbled something in Italian before putting it in his mouth. I watched closely as he tasted the food, waiting to see if his nose scrunched up again or if his mouth pursed. Neither happened. Instead, a small smile crept onto his face. "I did like it."

"You must be pregnant, too." I giggled. "There's no way you liked that."

He laughed with me. "I did, I really did. Almost better than this Philly cheese steak."

"You're funny. How much longer until we board?"

He glanced down at his watch. "About two hours."

"That's exciting. I wonder how much more I can eat in that time."

Ruggiero furrowed his eyebrows. "You're not still hungry, are you?"

I bit back a smile. "We're hungry often, Rue."

"Understood, *bella*. We'll explore to pass the time. Eat that first, though."

"Gladly," I said, digging back into my fries.

Chapter 37

❧

RUGGIERO

Jace slept soundly against my shoulder. She looked so snug in her cable knitted sweater. If I'd eaten as much as she did, I'd be tired, too. She was lucky to have no one behind her—a real miracle—so she leaned her seat back and cushioned her neck with a pillow.

The plane cradled in the soft cotton of the cumulus clouds. For a moment, I lost myself in the peace of being suspended in the air.

I watched the clouds until they were no longer white puffs and instead stretched threads blotted with gray. And then the sky grew dark, the water below us seeming small yet infinitely menacing. I dared not to look down, to take in the immenseness of the ocean. It could swallow me easily.

Despite how hard I tried to resist peering down at the water, at the waves crashing, my eyes were drawn to the way the moon illuminated the blue ocean and reflected off its surface, the same way they were drawn to Jace's eyes.

So blue, so lovely, so dangerous.

It felt like we were swimming, both toward and away from each other. Our relationship was fluid—we operated as we had before. Somehow, we seemed to fit one another. Things just clicked with her. Even then, I dreaded telling her how I really felt about returning to Italy. It had been almost seven years.

Wherever we chose to meet, my father would greet me with open arms, but my mother wouldn't share his reaction. I expected her to scowl, mutter or say an insult—it just depended on how bold she might be feeling—and demand my father leave with her. If she did none of those things, she wouldn't take kindly to seeing me again after seven years of being away.

I hoped Jace wouldn't want to meet my parents at all. Maybe I could talk her out of it.

Fuck. Why hadn't I picked somewhere else? Somewhere neutral like… I don't know, Canada? But I knew Jace might want to go see where I grew up. I knew that I could give her an experience she'd surely remember if only I was feeling my most authentic. I loved Jace and I was at home with her, but nothing was like being at home in Italy.

Now, if only I could pretend like my mother didn't live there, too.

I hoped meeting my parents wouldn't break us. Despite the tender night we shared a few weeks ago and the fluid movement of emotions between us, our relationship sometimes seemed as fragile as tissue paper, its edges thin and brittle and flammable.

We'd experienced so much and so little together—Thanksgiving with Cleo, the budding life we created, Christmas Eve with Cleo, Christmas with her family, a quiet New Year's at my house. Throughout all of this, somehow the two of us stayed afloat, hands and legs and hearts entwined. Then there was how we began, how first she ran, and then, when fate led me to her again, she pushed me out.

And then… she opened up.

Would she run again when we were in Udine, sitting across the dinner table with my parents? Would she think I was too complicated and want out? Want better for her and our baby?

Jace shifted in her seat and snaked her arm around mine. I drew my eyes away from the window and set them on her. I was prepared to see her face, soft and peaceful, as she snoozed the time away. But instead her eyes were open, blue as the ocean waves, and they seemed to be searching for something I couldn't place.

"Hi, Ruggiero," she said, her voice soft and husky with sleep.

I licked my lips. "Good evening, *cara mia*." She was beautiful in the dim lighting of the cabin, her skin looking rosy and refreshed.

"Have you slept at all?"

I considered lying to her. "I haven't."

She walked her fingers up my arm and leaned closer to me. "What've you been doing instead?"

"I've been thinking."

"All this time? Rue, baby, you need sleep. We've been on this plane, for what—"

"Eleven and a half hours."

Jace shook her head and let out a light laugh. "I can't imagine sitting and thinking for that long. You've got to be tired."

"I'm a little tired, but maybe not as much as I should be."

"Grab yourself a drink next time they come 'round with them. Maybe that'll help." Jace smiled and kissed my cheek.

I turned my head and caught her lips, pressing mine to hers with a sense of desperation. "I don't know that a drink would quiet my thoughts of you."

She withdrew some, her lips wet and pink. "You've been thinking of me?"

"Jace, I'm often thinking of you."

The sly smile returned to her face and she gripped my other hand in hers. "Have you joined the mile high club yet?"

247

"What is that?" I'd never heard of the mile high club, and I'd flown a lot.

She giggled and pulled her bottom lip under her teeth. "It's a classy band of people that travel on planes and take luxury in their high altitude."

"Yeah, like we're doing right now. We're enjoying our seats and the free snacks."

"I'm talking about the additional luxury of orgasming a little more than six thousand miles above land." She dropped her voice, probably so that the others sitting near us wouldn't hear her. "Some people do it right here in the seats, others sneak off to the bathroom."

I grimaced. "Plane bathrooms are obnoxiously small." Still, I entwined my hand in hers, wanting to be as close to her as I could despite the armrest between us.

"Yeah, but that doesn't matter when you're horny. You don't seem like you've had sex in any bathroom, though."

"That's a lie. I had sex with you in your bathroom after you gave me perfect head." I smirked.

She groaned as if she were tired of me. "Any *public* bathroom."

I shook my head, not bothering to hide my disgust. "I haven't found a need to yet." My disgust turned into curiosity as I thought of the implications of her question. "Have you already joined the mile high club?"

Her hand left mine momentarily to adjust the blue pillow that curved around the back of her neck. "Surprisingly, I haven't, and I've had sex in a lot of places."

Though I didn't really want to have sex in a public bathroom, I always wanted to have sex with Jace. I couldn't help that I reacted a little below the belt.

"See? That is how sex in public bathrooms happens," she said, referring to the growing erection I was trying so hard to ignore.

"Keep your voice down. Our neighbors don't need an announcement of my little inconvenience."

Her eyes held a glint of mischief. "I don't know if I'd call it little." She moved closer to me, putting her mouth to my ear as she whispered, "It's pretty damn big, I'd say."

She was trying to rile me up and it was working. I was growing painfully hard, pushing against my zipper. If she were any other person, I'd be embarrassed at how turned on I got just from the thought of being inside her.

"I could help you out with that," she cooed. She slid her hand into my lap and rubbed the inside of my thigh.

"Do you have to do this here?" I mumbled, irritated and aroused.

Jace ran her tongue across her bottom lip and smiled. "This is innocent. I know what public decency means. If anything, you're the one being indecent." She stroked higher and higher. Her hand approached but never touched where I strained against the fabric. "Would you like me to stop?"

"I don't know," I muttered. "It happened without you touching me. I'm not sure if it would matter either way."

"I'll stop torturing you," she said. She removed her hand and set it in her lap. "I'll have plenty of time to do it once we're in Venice."

I inhaled sharply and shifted in my seat. We'd talked briefly about our preferences. Letting Jace bind me and being at her mercy did sound pretty nice, though I wasn't sure if that's what she meant. "Sounds pretty dominant of you. Are you going to order my food for me, too?"

"Nooo, Rue, no. I don't even know any Italian."

"But didn't you use the word *salsiccia* in reference to my cock the first night we met?" I dug, licking my lips. "You only know the dirty words?"

Her cheeks reddened and she squirmed in her seat. "Why do you remember so much from that night?"

"Because I'd never forget the day I met you, Jace." I held her gaze, hoping she could see how much love I had for her.

The first night I saw Jace, I thought I was in a dream. I'd been in Memphis for years and I'd never seen someone as beautiful as her. She didn't even have to try. It was just in the way she carried herself, in those fearless blue eyes and that slick mouth of hers.

How could I forget? Just like you couldn't forget meeting an angel, I couldn't forget meeting her. Even after I went a year without seeing her, her face and her voice kept popping into my mind.

Jace's eyes were welling up with tears. "You're so goddamn cheesy," she finally said. As a tear rolled from her eye, she grinned widely at me. "I couldn't forget you, either. I could never forget you. You're the nicest person I've ever been with."

I closed the distance between us and kissed her. For a moment, I forgot about my worries. I forgot about going home. All I thought of was her, our lips moving in sync, her fingernails pressing into my skin, her hand on my thigh again. This is where I wanted to be, where I wanted to stay. Six thousand miles in the air with her, with the clouds keeping us afloat.

When we pulled back from each other, I was lightheaded, as if I'd poured all of myself into her. Jace stared back at me, face and lips flushed. She reached up and took the neck pillow off, looking around her quickly.

"Get up," she said, "we're joining the mile high club."

What kind of man would I be if I denied her? Sure, the bathroom was small, but we'd make it work.

Jace was right. Joining the mile-high club was satisfying, but admittedly a little cramped. I managed to nap for the remaining three hours of the flight and awoke to her shaking my shoulders when it was time to get off.

I didn't know that I'd do have sex in a plane bathroom again, but several different versions of it appeared in my dreams. The dream started with us huddled in the small bathroom together. She sat on the toilet lid, sucking my cock as I stood in front of her. Her tongue swirled around the head of my cock before running over the slit. Then the scene morphed to replicate our real-life moment.

Her hands on the wall as she rode me. My hands on her waist holding her in place. My cock deep, deep in her wet pussy.

"What were you dreaming about, mister?" Jace asked me as we walked through the tunnel leading inside the airport.

My cheeks warmed. "You, Jace Always you," I confessed.

"Of course, you were." She gave me an appreciative smile. "Enough dreaming, lover boy. I want to get out of here."

We didn't waste a minute collecting our luggage from baggage claim and heading outside. The sooner we left the airport, the sooner I could get some real food in Jace's stomach. My babies needed it. The flight had some refreshments and decent food, but it wasn't first class. Nuts, fruit gummies, canned drinks, and what tasted like microwaved meals only did so much for a person.

Jace wrapped her arm around mine as we were greeted by the cool breeze. "Fuck, it's cold out here."

I breathed in the air, a smooth blend of the saltwater of the city's canals and fresh dark roasted coffee beans that warmed me down to my toes. I loved afternoons in Venice. "It's cozy." I leaned down a little and pressed a kiss to her forehead. "Are you hungry?"

She looked up at me with those big blue eyes. "Of course, we're hungry."

I smiled back at her. "I think I know the perfect spot."

We took a taxi to a family-owned restaurant near our hotel. It wasn't fancy, but it was delicious. My family and I used to come here whenever we traveled to Venice. Jace ordered a beef filet with roasted rosemary potatoes, and I had a grilled eel with polenta.

She took a sip of her water before stuffing a potato in her mouth. Watching her eat was more enjoyable than the plate of food in front of me. I dug into my polenta, my eyes never leaving her face.

Jace winked at me and covered her mouth with her free hand. "Y'know," she said between bites, "if you take a picture, it'll last longer."

"Is that your way of telling me to stop staring, *cara mia?*"

"Yes, Rue. Stop staring and eat your food. I can't look *that* good."

"I'd disagree. You look good enough to eat," I promised. This woman didn't seem to understand that she occupied every cavity of my mind. My heart had been beating for her the past few months.

I'd make sure she knew. Soon. I just had to wait for the perfect moment to say those three words.

Chapter 38

꧁꧂

JACE

"**W**ow," I mumbled as I stepped out of the taxi.

"Wow, indeed," Ruggiero said, grabbing our luggage from the driver with thanks.

There was only one way to describe the hotel in Dorsoduro and that was fucking luxurious. It was a rustic three-story building, its rear bordered by the Grand Canal. On our way into the hotel, Ruggiero had beamed as he told me it also functioned as a stop for the water bus.

After spending almost a full day on planes, I craved the comfort of soft bed sheets. To my delight, we grabbed the room key and then collapsed on the bed shortly after.

"I still can't believe you grew up in Italy," I said.

Ruggiero rolled over to face me. "I can" he said, throwing an arm across my back. His hand relaxed on the curve of my waist. "It's beautiful, isn't it?"

I couldn't help but smile at him. "It's incredible. What's the plan for tomorrow?"

"Come on," he scoffed. "I gave you an itinerary."

"I don't feel like grabbing it. You can just tell me."

He scooted closer and kissed my cheek. "I think we're going to be tired in the morning, so it's just me and you eating breakfast in this comfy bed."

"And after that?" I asked.

"We're going to pull out your new toy," he said.

I rolled my eyes, laughing. "You're joking, right?" I was very curious about the toy, but I'd never used a dildo before. My experience was limited to one small blue bullet vibrator—five years ago when I was an undergrad.

"I'm not joking." Ruggiero squeezed my waist with one hand and used the other to brush my hair out of my face. Mischief glinted in his eyes. "Is that alright with you?"

His words coupled with my curiosity sent an unexpected pulse between my legs. I managed a nod.

He cradled my face in his hand. "You love penetration, so I know you'll love it."

Heat raced along my skin. "What're we doing after that?"

"Depends on how long we'll be in bed. If we're out by lunchtime, we'll go to a restaurant nearby and Saint Mark's Basilica."

He was being completely innocent, yet the pulsing didn't stop.

"And if we're not out by lunchtime?"

Ruggiero grinned. "Then we eat lunch in bed, finish our one-on-one time, then go to the basilica."

"I want to hear more about this one-on-time."

"It'll be a moment to get to know each other a little better. I'll find more ways to make you squirm." He brushed his thumb across my bottom lip.

"I don't think that part was in the itinerary that I didn't read," I said.

Ruggiero chuckled. "If you didn't read it, how would you know, *cara mia?*" He pressed a kiss to my lips. "How would you know I didn't write how much I want to taste your lips," another kiss, "and then the curve of your neck?" His hand trailed from my jaw and smoothed down my neck.

I relaxed into him. He looked so good. Smelled so good, like cedar wood and saffron. Still, I couldn't bite back the urge to jest with him. "That must be one incredibly detailed itinerary."

"I had to use a really small font to get all the dirty details in it. I hope you brought your reading glasses with you."

I rolled my eyes. "Shut up. You're just trying to fuck me."

"I am often wanting to fuck, but no, I'm not trying to right now. I'm increasing your anticipation for tomorrow. I think it's working," he said, smiling. "I can feel your pulse under my hand."

"So, what are you waiting for, Casanova? Pull down my pants and tend to me," I said, only half-joking. If he actually did it, I wouldn't resist.

Ruggiero smiled wickedly at me, his hand sliding down to my waist. "The only tending I will be doing is tucking you into bed. I'd advise saving your energy for tomorrow. You'll need it."

"I am really tired," I admitted. And it would be so easy to fall asleep cuddled up to him.

His dark hair was ruffled, his white shirt wrinkled after what felt like the longest day in the world. His love for me dominated his brown-eyed gaze.

How is he so handsome?

He nuzzled his face into my neck, the scruff of his beard tickling my skin.

How is he so perfect?

He wrapped both arms around my waist and pulled me into him until my breasts were pressed against his chest.

How did I get so lucky?

"I am also very tired. I barely slept on the way over."

"Were the seats really that uncomfortable for you?" I said, frowning. I remembered waking to find him gazing out the window during our second flight. He hadn't slept during the layover in Chicago, and our layover in Frankfurt hadn't been long enough to sleep through.

He hummed into my neck. "Yes, they were, but laying here with you is incredibly comfortable, Jace." He pressed a kiss to my skin. "So, so comfortable."

His breathing was beginning to slow. I ran my hand through his thick hair, scratching his scalp lightly.

"Fuck, that feels good."

"Good. Then I won't stop," I assured him. "Try and sleep."

"It's so early in the day here," he complained. "I'd hate falling asleep before the sun goes down."

"It's almost four o'clock. Considering we just spent twenty-ish hours on and off planes, I think it's perfectly fine to sleep right now."

"Let's set an alarm. There're still some things I want to show you before we call it a night." He lifted his head. "It's also nowhere close to being nighttime."

I huffed in annoyance. "You're the one that brought up sleeping in the first place. Our baby and I have no qualms against being tucked in and going to bed."

"That's it," he said, loosening his arms from around me. "I'm setting an alarm for half past six." Ruggiero rolled over and sat up, throwing his feet over the side of the bed. It hadn't even been thirty seconds, and I missed his warmth already.

"And what are we going to do after six thirty?"

He threw a smile over his shoulder. "You'll just have to see."

As promised, Ruggiero woke me up at six-thirty sharp to explore Venice's nightlife. He dragged me to a jazz club with live music near our hotel.

Ruggiero nursed a couple of beers, and because I wanted this to feel like a normal night out, I downed a few mocktails. We danced for hours until our feet hurt before we returned to the hotel and crashed into bed for good that night.

Chapter 39

JACE

I woke up with a squirm. Something wet and large was between my thighs, tickling my skin. Not ready to open my eyes, I plunged a hand between my legs in search of the culprit. My hand dug into a mass of hair, strands tangling themselves around my fingers. A masculine groan sounded under the covers.

"Good morning, *bella*." Ruggiero's voice vibrated against me, his breath fanning my bare pussy, and then his tongue swiped upward.

I inhaled sharply and tightened my grip on his hair. "Morning, Rue," I moaned.

He hummed in satisfaction. "I hope you didn't think I'd forget the itinerary."

I peeked an eye open and sat up slightly. "How aren't you jet-lagged? How can you think the word 'itinerary' this early?"

The covers slipped away as Ruggiero lifted his head. "It's almost noon, baby." He didn't take his eyes from mine when he sucked a finger into his mouth and then sheathed that finger deep inside of me. "Are you still game?"

Realization dawned on me as his slow, rhythmic thrusting awakened all my senses. "You said I'll like it, so I'm game."

"You sure?" he cooed. Mischief sparkled in his brown eyes. "It'll feel like me, but a little cold, a little slimmer, and battery controlled."

I nodded and laid back against the sheets, relaxing in his hold. Just as he warned, the cool head of the phallus pressed into me. It wasn't the girth of my Ruggiero, but it felt oh so good as he inched it inside of me. "Oh, that's nice," I breathed.

"It looks really nice, too. Your pussy is swallowing every bit of it." Once the hand gripping the base of the toy met my lips, his mouth descended on my clit. His tongue swirled the bud, and my breath hitched as I lifted my hips in a lame attempt at friction. "Patience, baby. I'll give you what you want soon enough."

"I want it now," I whined. "I don't want to wait."

"Good things come to good girls who wait." He slid the toy out and started a slow back and forth thrust. It wasn't enough. I reached down to grab his hand and force him to work faster.

He stopped his torture on my clit to glare at me as he let go of the dildo and caught my wrist. "Jace, *cara mia*, I will stop altogether if you plan to take over. I have no problem watching you fuck yourself, but I want this orgasm if you'll give it to me."

"Fine," I agreed. "As long as you don't stop."

"Thank you. Hands in my hair are allowed, but you don't touch yourself, understand?" His eyes didn't leave mine as he awaited my response.

"Yes, fuck, Rue. I understand."

Ruggiero smiled, pleased with my surrender, and rewarded me by moving the toy inside of me with a mind-shattering pace. I threw my head back on the pillow as he gripped my thigh, spreading me wider. "You look so fucking sexy, baby."

I didn't care how I looked. All I cared about was the magic happening between my legs. Eager for his mouth to be on me again, I planted my hands in his hair and pushed his head down. He was equally eager to comply.

It wasn't long until I needed to cum. Just as I was reaching my peak, he turned the vibration on, stimulating a part of me I didn't even know existed, and white-hot bliss erupted.

"Fuck, fuck, fuck," I blurted, doing my best to scoot away from him yet helpless against his grip on my thigh. It was perfect and almost too much at the same time. I was wrecked by another orgasm before I could take a breath.

"Shit, Jace, you're pulsating," he said, flicking the vibration off and slowly withdrawing the toy. "Fuck, that was so sexy."

I felt hollowed out, but I didn't care. I was boneless, all of the tension released from my body. "I don't know if I can move."

"You don't need to move." The blue surface of the dildo glistened with my arousal as he held it up. "I'm going to bring breakfast to you. I just had mine." He rose on his knees, the blanket falling away to reveal the hard planes of his bare chest, and brought the tip of the toy to his mouth.

I propped myself up with my elbows. "You're not going to lick that, are you?"

The fire in his eyes answered my question. "Why risk wasting this precious juice? Hell yeah, I'm licking it." His gaze was hard on mine as his tongue licked from the base to the tip before he drew it in his mouth to suck off the excess. "Delicious."

Watching him made me consider another round.

I think he just unlocked a new kink.

He climbed off the bed as if he didn't just do one of the most erotic things I'd ever seen. "I'm going to wash this and then I'm going to bring you breakfast. Don't go anywhere."

I nodded and sighed in bliss. With the state of my limbs, I couldn't go anywhere even if I wanted to.

After a hearty breakfast of waffles and sausage in bed and some time spent cuddling, we mustered up the energy to go to the basilica as planned. The beauty of a Saint Mark's Basilica trumped my first impression of our hotel in Dorsoduro. It was grander than I imagined, an amalgamation of European architectural trends. Its interior wasn't any less impressive.

"I wonder how long it took to paint this place," I mused, slowing my pace to gaze at the art. We'd been in the basilica for over an hour, and I was becoming well-familiar with the Byzantine-style mosaics narrating the life of Christ that decorated the walls and ceilings.

"Centuries and centuries," Ruggiero said. He looped his arm around mine, holding me close. "Here's a fun fact; only a third of the mosaics in the basilica can be considered original because they've been redone so many times."

I was quiet as I took in the scene above me that signaled that we were in the Dome of Ascension. Christ was at the apex of the along with a quartet of angels. Ruggiero had been leading me around the Western facade, softly narrating the events to me. I didn't consider myself to be very religious, but it was hard not to be enthralled with the basilica. It was beautiful, the craftsmanship impeccable.

He kissed my cheek before staring up at the scene with me. "I was speechless the first time I came in here, too."

I shifted my gaze to Ruggiero. He was even more beautiful than the art that illuminated the basilica. His handsome features relaxed as he admired the dome. I wanted to run my hands through that dark hair of his. "How old were you?"

"Sixteen," he said, lowering his head to look at me. "I visited with my father."

"It seems like you have a really good relationship with your dad."

"I do. I'm lucky to have him." His eyes softened. "I don't know where I'd be without him."

I smiled up at Ruggiero as we continued to stroll through the building. "I'm happy you have him. I'm closer to Jackson than either of my parents, but my dad has always been supportive of me. It's nice to have that."

"It really is. I'm excited to see him in a few days." He squeezed my bicep lovingly.

"Good. We're having dinner with them on our first night in Udine, aren't we?"

"Yeah. It should be fine. My mother can be a bit… much," he said with a grimace. "But I already told my father about your pregnancy, so there'll be no surprise there."

I shrugged. "I think I'll be able to deal with it," I assured him. "I'm not easily intimidated."

"I know you aren't, *cara mia*. For now, let's enjoy our time here," he said. "There's so much to see and four days is hardly long enough to do so."

From the basilica, we ventured for gelato—mine strawberry, his pistachio—before we paid for a gondola ride on the Grand Canal. To accommodate for the evening chill, Ruggiero wrapped me in his coat, braving the weather in a thick jacket. Venice was bustling along the canal, but in the boat with him, time seemed to slow down. It was only us, even the gondolier fading into the background.

My back rested against his chest. He held me in his arms, his hands on my belly—our baby. The bump was becoming more noticeable.

I love you.

The words were on the tip of my tongue, but I didn't dare say them.

I love you.

I wanted to tell him, but I had to know what I really meant to him. For some reason I couldn't explain, I wanted his parents to like me.

I wanted to be the girl he could write home about. It was ridiculous and stupid, but I couldn't say it without knowing if they liked me.

I relaxed in his hold, covering his hands with mine.

I love you.

Chapter 40

~~~

RUGGIERO

Our days in Venice flew by and before I knew it, we were only a few kilometers from Udine. As the train pulled into the station, my heart began to pound. The thought of facing my mother again after six years was terrifying.

Beside me, Jace seemed to sense my unease and squeezed my hand. The weight of anticipation hung heavy in the air, casting a shadow over what should've been a joyous day.

We disembarked and made our way through the bustling streets of Udine. As we walked, I couldn't help but think about the confrontation I had long dreaded. While a part of me yearned for closure and reconciliation, the other part feared facing my past.

My past wasn't kind. It burned like alcohol on a fresh wound.

After a few blocks, we reached the rental flat that would be our home for the next five days. I withdrew the key from my pocket, my hand hovering near the doorknob.

Jace placed a hand on my shoulder. "Everything all right, Rue?" she asked, shooting me a concerned glance.

I offered her a weak smile and unlocked the door. The rental flat greeted us with a sense of warmth and familiarity, yet even in the cozy room, I couldn't help the fear that gnawed at my insides. My heartbeat pounded in my ears. I took a deep breath, doing my best to push down the anxiety.

"I'll be right back," she said once we were inside. "I'm going to find the bathroom."

"Okay, Jace. I'll start unpacking our bags."

She nodded and disappeared down the hall.

I leaned against the wall, placing my hands on the surface to ground myself. I practiced deep breaths. The wall cooled my hands. I remained for a few moments, letting my heart rate slow down. I exhaled one more long breath before I pushed off the wall.

I grabbed our suitcases and rolled them to our bedroom. *Get it together*, I scolded myself. *Don't ruin this night for her.*

Midway through unpacking, I was warmed by Jace's breasts and growing belly on my back and her arms circled my waist. I relaxed in her arms. The fear of seeing my mother again was very real, but so was Jace's presence.

"Thanks for bringing me here," she said.

I dropped the clothes in my hands and turned in her arms. I couldn't resist pressing a kiss to her forehead as she looked up at me. "No, thank you, *cara mia*. I can't believe you came with me."

"I wouldn't want to be anywhere else." She tightened her arms around me and laid her head against my chest.

A few hours later, Jace and I walked hand in hand to the restaurant. As we stepped inside, I noticed my dad sitting at a table near the window, a warm smile lighting up his face as he saw us.

"Ruggiero! Jace!" he called out, rising from his seat to greet us with open arms.

I rushed forward to embrace him. The scent of his cologne was comforting and familiar. "Pa," I greeted him warmly, my voice thick with emotion.

Beside me, Jace smiled at my dad, her eyes sparkling with affection. "It's so nice to meet you, Mr. de Fiore," she said, extending her hand.

My father ignored her hand and enveloped her in a warm hug. "Please, call me Pa," he insisted.

"Nice to meet you, Pa," she said, hugging him back.

As we settled into our seats, my nerves began to resurface. I glanced across the table at my mother, her expression cool and detached as she eyed us. I could tell when my mother was disappointed, and this time was no different.

"Mamma," I greeted her tentatively.

She offered me a curt nod in return, her lips pressed into a thin line of disapproval. "Adamo," she acknowledged.

I clenched my jaw, struggling to maintain my composure in the face of her disapproval. No matter how hard I tried, it seemed I could never live up to her expectations, could never earn her approval.

My mother turned to Jace. "And who are you?"

"Mamma, this is—"

"With all due respect, ma'am, your husband just said my name," Jace spoke. Her hand found mine under the table and squeezed. "I'm Jace Thompson."

"Jace Thompson," my mother repeated, her tone laden with distaste. She turned to look at me. "Really, Adamo? An American?"

I nodded. "She *is* an American, but I don't care about that." I squeezed Jace's hand again, appreciating her presence.

"Did you think I'd be proud?" my mother asked.

My dad cleared his throat, running a hand through his long hair. "Enough, Rossana. These two traveled a long way to get here and will enjoy their dinner." He began to unwrap his utensils from the napkin. "Besides, Ruggiero, you don't need our permission to decide who to love."

My mother turned up her nose, but remained silent.

Fortunately, the waiter approached soon after. I wasn't stupid enough not to notice that Jace's hand was squeezing mine tightly and I was grateful for the reprieve. *"Benvenuti,* friends," he said, "can I start you off with beverages?"

"I'll just have water, please," Jace ordered, managing a smile for the waiter.

I brushed my thumb against the back of her hand. "A glass of white wine, sir," I said.

"Sì certo." As the waiter turned his attention toward my parents, I stole a longer glance at Jace.

"How're you?" I asked, keeping my voice low.

I don't know, she mouthed, breaking her gaze.

My stomach churned. I was so excited to have Jace in my life that I hadn't thought this through entirely. I wouldn't be surprised if Jace wanted nothing to do with me once we were back in Memphis. Our trip to Italy would surely be ruined by my mother's machinations.

I felt my mother's gaze on me once the waiter walked away, assuring he'd be back soon with our drinks. I did my best to avoid her eyes and looked at my dad instead. "How have you been?' I asked him. "I've missed Udine."

"We've been good, son." My father smiled tenderly. "I've been keeping myself busy with the shop. You'd be surprised by how much business this old man still gets."

"I'm not too surprised. Customers at Carlisle's love me and I learned from the best."

Jace squeezed my hand again. "It's so good to meet the man that taught him so much."

"Did you meet at his job?" my mother asked.

My eyes snapped to my mother's, unsure of how to approach her question.

"No, ma'am, we met a while back at a bar. Ruggiero was just so easy to talk to." I looked at Jace, who was wearing a forced bright smile.

"I am sure that he was. He has always been very tender for a male." My mother's eyes boring into the side of my face caused a burning sensation. "It's a wonder he was able to create a child, assuming the child is his."

My stomach dropped. Though all I wanted to do was scoot my chair back and flee from the dinner table, I forced myself to respond. "The child is mine, Mamma. I know that for a fact."

My mother narrowed her gaze. "It is laughable to me to think that you, a man who's never been much of one at all, would have the power to father a child. You are *un finocchio*, are you not?" Her red-painted lips spread in an impish smile. "This woman does know that, doesn't she?"

"Rossana," my father snapped, grabbing my mother's arm. "We are in public. Please behave yourself."

Jace's hand remained in mine as we watched my mother yank her arm from my father's.

"We could be in a cathedral, and I would still not hide my thoughts for my son," she snarled. "Especially not in front of someone as pathetic as this girl. She's as unfit as all your past partners."

I shouldn't have come here. We hadn't even ordered our meals, and the dinner was already going horribly, horribly wrong.

Chapter 41

❦

JACE

This woman was—

No. I wouldn't think anything foul about his mother. I'd only met her once. Surely, I'd just gotten the wrong first impression.

You don't need a second impression to know someone's a bitch.

She'd already been walking a fine line when she pretended not to know my name, but her insulting Ruggiero's manhood crossed the line. Insulting me crossed another line. To refrain from giving her a piece of my mind, I'd excused myself to the bathroom to take a breather.

Now that I was back at the table, I tried to keep a smile on my face as the waiter set down our food. I'd ordered goulash Triestino and gnocchi. While the food smelled amazing, I could barely focus on meal.

Who did she think she was to look me up and down like that? Did she know who I was? Did she know that if she wasn't Ruggiero's mother, her mouth would meet my fist?

Cleo would know the right thing to say right now. She'd know how to make me feel better. I closed my eyes, tried to think of what she'd say as she'd take me into her arms and hug me.

Don't listen to her, I imagined her saying, *she's just a jealous old bitch*. It was possible she'd be nicer than that, or harsher, but it made me feel better nonetheless.

But was his mother really a jealous old bitch? She had nothing to be jealous of! His mother was beautiful, not a single gray hair on her head nor any wrinkles on her face. Laugh lines and crow's feet had already latched themselves onto my face. I was probably half her age yet she looked better than I had since my early twenties.

A shoulder bumping into mine drew me from my thoughts. I looked up from my plate, meeting Ruggiero's eyes.

"Are you going to eat, *cara mia*?" he asked quietly.

How did I tell him that despite how good this food looked, eating was the last thing on my mind? I wanted to punch his mother's teeth out and cry at the same time. I arrived in Udine happily this afternoon and she was turning this day into a nightmare.

I was pregnant, for crying out loud. I was supposed to be glowing, not being shit on by my boyfriend's mother!

Ruggiero laid a hand on my thigh and squeezed gently. "Jace," he whispered, "Let's talk."

I allowed him to be my guide as he grabbed my hand and excused us from the table. I followed him quietly, biting my tongue until we reached the hall that led to the bathrooms.

In the dimly lit hallway, I leaned against his tall frame and took deep breaths.

"I'm so sorry. She is not the friendliest of people."

"But your dad is so fucking nice, Rue, I can't believe this," I rushed out, pushing my face into his chest. Tears were pricking my eyes and I didn't want him to see, to know that she'd made me cry.

He pulled me close to him and nuzzled his face in the crook of my neck. "As they say, opposites attract. Growing up with her as a mother was a good example of how not to treat people."

I continued to cry into his chest. "That woman—she is—"

"She's awful, I know." He lifted his head and put some distance between us to look at me. "Fuck, I'm so sorry."

I frowned, taking in his sad, brown eyes. "No, it's my fault. I said I didn't mind meeting her." I dragged my hands across my face as I tried to dry my wet cheeks. "I said I could handle it."

"No," he said firmly. "This isn't your fault. I knew how terrible she could be and I still let you meet her."

"But she's right," I whispered, "I'm not good enough for you."

"Jace, don't ever say that. She's rarely right about anything and she's definitely wrong about you."

Ruggiero paused and pushed open the door to the family-sized bathroom. He drew me inside, shut the door firmly, and locked it.

Ruggiero dropped to his knees and circled his arms around my waist as he leaned his head against my legs. "You are everything to me," he said, peering into my eyes. "Everything."

My frown deepened. "Everything?"

"Must I say it again?"

I noticed then that he was crying, too, his eyes glossy with tears ready to fall. It was too much for me. I couldn't do this.

I fervently shook my head as he stared up at me. "There's no way I can be everything."

"But for me, you are."

I felt like I was going to throw up. "No, Ruggiero, get off of me. I don't want to be your everything." I wanted his hands off of me.

It was funny to think that Ruggiero could be endgame for me. It was going so well, but I still should've known better. It was common knowledge that I wasn't good enough for him.

As he always did, he complied right away, backing up from me and leaning against his hands. "Jace?"

"I'm sorry," I sniffled, backing towards the sink. I turned around and stared at myself in the mirror. It hurt that I got all dressed up just to be deemed not good enough—again. "I just can't do this right now. We should've never come here in the first place."

He nodded from where he sat on the floor. "I agree."

"So, you didn't want me here?" I asked, glaring at him.

"*Dio*, Jace, stop jumping to conclusions." He laughed dryly. "I did, but as you can see, I left for a reason. I don't know why I thought things would be different if I returned, especially with you."

"And what about me?"

"Well, you're an insanely beautiful woman, for one, and you're smart, sexy, and blunt," he answered quickly, giving me a small smile. "So, I thought maybe she would be happy."

I blinked at him a few times. "That was a terrible plan, Ruggiero."

"It was, I know, but we behaved like adults. My mother didn't," he said. "Can you accept that?"

Taking a deep breath, I crossed my arms. The tears slowed but now they streamed leisurely down our faces. "Your mom really is a bitch."

He crossed one leg over the other and sighed. "She can be worse. I won't let you see worse."

"Do we have to spend time with them again?"

"You tell me. I came to Italy to spend time with you, not them. Pa, I'd consider, but not her." His unwavering gaze told me he meant it. "She said some pretty awful things to me, too, after you excused yourself to the bathroom earlier before our food came."

I pulled my bottom lip between my teeth. "What did she say?"

Ruggiero straightened his back and pulled his knees up, hugging his arms around them. His eyes left mine and he looked off to the side, then to the ground. "She asked me why it was so hard for me to do something right, and why I even bothered to come back."

She said *what* to him?

Cleo, I mentally prayed, *please know that I want to scratch this bitch's eyes out. And God? Please, give me the strength not to.*

I closed my eyes and took a deep breath. I needed to pick my next words carefully. I knew he loved my bluntness, but hearing my violent thoughts about his mom probably wouldn't help the situation.

My therapist would be proud of me. I wouldn't let my emotions get the best of me.

When I opened my eyes, my anger only grew. I hated how easily she could make him go from the strong, carefree man I knew to one crying from the heartbreak of constant rejection. "Rue, I don't want to see them—her—again."

His head snapped towards me and his eyes instantly met mine. "Do you really mean that?"

The hurt in his voice was unbearable. I never wanted to see him so hurt and so broken again. And I would make sure I never had to.

"Of course," I quipped. "We're not dealing with that bullshit."

I closed the space between us and cupped his face, relishing in the feeling of his stubble caressing my palms. "We're going to leave here and enjoy the rest of our time in Udine. After we have them box our food up. Sound like a plan?" He stared up at me and nodded. "Lovely, now, please get off the floor."

He scrunched his nose up. "This is a public bathroom, isn't it?"

"I bet you're thinking about how dirty the floor is, aren't you?"

He stood with a lame smile on his face. "*Sì*, but we can shower it away once we get back to our rental."

He brought our lips together in a kiss and I held him tightly in my arms. We would be okay. We had to. And I wasn't letting that woman mess it up for us.

Chapter 42

⁂

RUGGIERO

I sat in bed, my head resting on the headboard, reading John Medina's *Brain Rules for Baby*. I'd managed to snag a copy of the book at a local bookstore in Memphis a few days before we left for Venice. Right now, it was the perfect distraction.

The energy hadn't felt the same since we returned to the rental. We'd been… quiet. We ate our leftovers with minimal conversation over an episode of *Keeping Up With the Kardashians*, took turns showering, and occupied ourselves.

While I was reading, she'd been watching a comedy show on her phone.

"Tonight was something, wasn't it?" she finally said, breaking through the silence.

I dragged my attention away from the book and towards Jace. Her hair was pulled back in a low ponytail, rogue flyaways framing her face. She eyed me expectantly, awaiting my reply.

"Yes, *bella*, it was." I folded the top corner of the page I was on and closed the book. I set it aside on the nightstand to give her my full

274

attention.

The night's events were fresh in my mind. Three hours had passed, and I was still upset by how I'd handled it.

It was our first day in Udine and I was already on the verge of fucking it up. How dare I let my mother talk about Jace the way she did? What the fuck was I doing on the bathroom floor? Why did we even—

"Did you hear me?" Her jaw clenched.

Idiota, you're looking right at her.

My ears warmed in embarrassment. Shaking my head, I said, "No, I'm sorry. What did you say?"

"I said, thank you for giving me the choice to leave. I've sat through an uncomfortable conversation in the past," Jace said.

"Don't tell me it was—"

"It wasn't Garret," she said quickly, shaking her head. "No, it was some time ago, but still. I know how it feels to have to do that."

"Oh, Jace, come here," I said. As she scooted towards me, I gathered her in my arms. "I would never force you to sit through something like that. I'm so sorry we even went."

She reached a hand up and ran it through my hair. "No more apologizing, Rue. We've already talked about it. I just wanted to thank you."

"I understand, but I could've done more for you. I could've—"

Jace cut me off again. "No more apologizing," she said firmly. She put her hands on either side of my face, forcing me to make eye contact. The softness that was usually in her blue eyes was absent. "Promise me you won't apologize anymore for this night."

"Jace, you can't expect me not to utter a single apology about how tonight went. It was disastrous," I countered. I moved my gaze to her collarbone. I didn't want to see her disappointment anymore. "I didn't defend you the way I should have."

"Ruggiero, look me in the eyes and promise me," she demanded. "Promise. Me."

I met her gaze once again.

Reluctantly, I said, "I promise."

I swallowed the lump in my throat. I wanted to break down, but I wouldn't do it. Not tonight. Not again. At least, not in front of her.

I tried to look away, but she kept her hands on my face, a silent refusal to let go. I blinked, a tear rolling down my face. She was so beautiful, so perfect, and I let her down. Her empty gaze didn't leave me for a second.

Without saying another word, her soft lips met mine in a kiss. I closed my eyes and melted into her. I anchored myself with the smooth curves of her hips. She dropped her hands from my face and rested them on my shoulders. I pulled her even closer until she was in my lap and her legs were around my waist. Her hands rubbed wide circles into my skin.

I groaned appreciatively. My hands snaked under the hem of her silky cami so that I could touch her skin.

She pressed into me, her ample breasts against my chest. Her face hadn't softened.

Breathlessly, she said "I want you" against my lips. She ground herself against me, the friction of her hurried movements and the underwear between us kick-starting my arousal.

"I don't want your pity," I huffed, unable to stop my cock stiffening in my pants.

She broke our kiss to slide her top off.

"No need for you to worry about pity." Jace steadied herself with a hand behind her. The other palmed one of her breasts drew my attention to her hardened pink nipples. "Like what you see?"

"No," I said quickly. I shoved her on her back, shamelessly watching her breasts bounce as her head met the sheets. "I fucking love it." I dropped my hands to her thighs and spread her legs apart. I grinned at the wetness between her legs. "I guess you were being honest about the pity."

Hands relaxed at either side of her, she stared up at me with a smirk. "Not something I'd lie about, Rue. I don't pity fuck. You should know that."

"Yeah, yeah."

I hovered over her body, a hand at her waist, the other pulling her panties to the side. I reveled in the soft cry that left her mouth as I pushed a finger in her. I silenced her cries with my mouth, kissing her, tasting her plump lips, pumping my finger in and out of her. Her back arched, the peaks of her breasts grazing my chest.

I slid another finger in and kissed down her neck. "You look so beautiful, you're taking my fingers so well." She was so wet my fingers glided in and out without any resistance. I traced her collarbone with my tongue before I bit down gently, just hard enough to give her a tinge of pain with her pleasure.

I licked from her neck to the valley between her breasts. I loved the taste of her skin, sweet and heady. Her moans were unapologetic as I thrust into her harder, faster until she was writhing on my fingers. "Fuck, you feel so good," she said, her breath ragged.

I withdrew my fingers and lowered my head between her thighs, haphazardly pulling her panties down. I replaced my fingers with my mouth, flattened my tongue, and swept it up her slit. With the sounds of her pleasure like music to my ears, urging me on, I rubbed her clit with my thumb.

I savored her like a bite of ripe blood orange on a sweltering summer day. I rested my hands on the insides of her thighs and relaxed in between her legs, laying my stomach down on the sheets. Eyes closed, I lapped at her, my guttural moans vibrating against her skin, until she fell apart underneath me, her legs trembling around me and her cries filling the air like a sensual melody.

I pulled away from her and rolled over on my back to catch my breath, endorphins flooding me as I regained oxygen.

I looked down to see my cock tenting my boxers.

Jace didn't hesitate to climb on top of me, spit in her palm, and put the hand under my waistband. My breath hitched when she grabbed my shaft, using her other hand to push my boxers down.

Lubed with her spit, her hand felt amazing moving up and down my cock, squeezing the base every so often. I bucked my hips, desperate for more. She swiveled around until her back faced me as she straddled me, giving me a perfect view of her ass as she lined her center up with my cock.

I groaned helplessly when I felt the heat of her pussy around me, tingling down to my toes. I cupped her ass in my hands, massaging, kneading as she rode me, paying close attention to my cock thrusting in and out of her.

Dio mio, I love her.

I laid my head back on the pillow and closed my eyes. She felt so fucking good. And yet... I couldn't help but think of the unspoken words between us.

We made up in the restaurant's bathroom with a kiss and a hug, her gestures full of sadness and an emotion I could not name. Now, she was closed off, showing no glimpse of her feelings.

She'd had a similar demeanor when we first met.

Smug. Sure of herself. Sexy. Unavailable.

Her pussy clenching around my cock pulled me from my head and back into the present. I sunk my nails into her skin, bringing my knees up so that her thighs pushed further apart. Her pants were rhythmic as she continued to ride me skillfully.

I opened my eyes to watch.

She lowered herself to the hilt before lifting slowly and then slamming herself back down. I groaned, willing myself not to cum too early. With her hands on my thighs as support, Jace continued with her hard rhythm, clenching around me every so often.

I grabbed her hips in an attempt to slow her pace. "Fuck, baby, you're going to make me cum." The waistband of my boxers was smothering my balls, and the pressure was wavering my resolve.

"That's the point, Ruggiero," she huffed, likely with a roll of her eyes.

"*Mi scusi.*" I tightened my hold on her and thrust with deep strokes. I forced my ruminating thoughts away, only focusing on her.

Jace's skin glowed with a sheen of sweat. With each stroke, I could smell her conditioner's vanilla and lavender fragrance in her slightly damp hair. The smell, the touch, the taste, the sound of Jace was intoxicating.

Unable to hold back any longer, I came, tightening my grip on her waist to anchor myself. Ecstasy spread through my veins, my entire body buzzing and tingling. Suspended in bliss, my mind went blank as she continued to ride me.

My body and grip relaxed, I opened my eyes just as Jace peeled herself off of me. "I'll come to bed in a bit," she told me, keeping her head low. She grabbed her panties off the bed and sauntered to the bathroom.

"Alright, Jace," I said, feeling the chill of her absence. As much as I wanted to dig into her change of mood, it'd been a long day, and I'd already burdened her enough. I couldn't bring myself to do it again.

Chapter 43

❧

JACE

I was an asshole. Since meeting his parents two nights ago, I'd been less eager to talk and quicker to become irritated. I was the one who said we'd still have a good time in Udine despite the way dinner had gone, but I'd been making the rest of our trip unenjoyable.

It was noon and I'd spent the majority of the day in bed, the same as yesterday and the day before, only getting up to eat and use the bathroom. After I kept shutting down his efforts to converse, Ruggiero gave me space. But he was right.

I *had* wanted to come to Italy. After seeing his reaction to the dinner I'd made, it felt wrong not to come.

My mind was jumbled. I wanted Ruggiero, this baby, *our* family. I didn't want to let his mother's words ruin what we'd become. Whatever I believed about my mom, I could see that his mother was worse.

Being told that I wasn't good enough—again—hurt. Seeing how she hurt Ruggiero stung even more. Which brought me back to my realization.

I was an asshole. Despite what happened the other night, his kindness toward me never faltered. His mother broke his heart, but he was worried about my heart more. It wasn't my heart that needed mending, it was his. The one person someone thought would love their child most seemed to hate him.

I slammed my head against the pillow and screamed.

"*Cara mia?*"

I jolted, looking up to see Ruggiero with a takeout container, my ears burning hot. "Hi," I managed.

"You okay?" He set the container down on the table and shimmied out of his jacket.

"Yes," I mumbled. "No. I don't know."

I was frustrated about me, about him, about this fucked up situation we were in. The most frustrating part about this was that I knew loved this man. There was no longer a question about it. I loved Ruggiero with all my heart.

So, why did I feel farther from him than ever? Why did I want to run away?

The bed dipped as he sat beside me. "I was thinking, we should get out of this room for a bit. It's suffocating, if I'm being honest."

"Where would you like to go?"

"Well, since you enjoyed the gondola ride in Venice, I think you might enjoy a boat ride in the Fusine Lakes. It's quiet, scenic—a good place to breathe."

A good place to breathe. Maybe that was what we needed.

"That sounds nice," I said. "When do you want to leave?"

He smirked. "Sometime within the next five hours, but preferably before the sun sets."

"Hmph. That doesn't sound like *anytime*."

"I'll admit it's a short window. You'll understand when we get there. It's a beautiful place," he assured me. "Would you like to eat or do you plan to become one with the sheets?"

I stuck my tongue out at him, happy that he could still be his good-natured self alongside my coldness. "Are you saying I stink, Rue?"

Ruggiero shook his head and smiled in earnest. "I love how you smell. It's you," he said. "Now, if it were like thirty days or so…" He leaned over to kiss my cheek.

For the first time since that awful night, I didn't object to his affection. His nose nuzzling my neck, he breathed in. "Are you smelling me?" I asked softly.

"I am." As if to prove his point, he sniffed me again and traced the path with his tongue afterward. "You smell and taste delicious." His warm breath against my damp skin gave me goosebumps and I let out a small sigh of pleasure.

"You're gross."

He chuckled, his hair tickling my ear. "You're grosser. I took a shower this morning."

"Sorry," I mumbled. I knew he wasn't judging me, but he wasn't wrong. I hadn't showered since that night, either.

"No need to say sorry, I'm only teasing. Like I said, I love it." He shamelessly inhaled again.

I was suddenly aware of how yucky I felt. I'd been sitting in bed, hopelessly wallowing away. I didn't remember brushing my teeth yesterday or this morning. "Okay, well, I don't," I countered. I wriggled away from him, scooting to the other end of the bed.

Ruggiero leaned against the headboard, his arm lazily draped over a pillow. "Shower's free, *cara mia*. The water's hot, too."

I rolled my eyes as I climbed off the bed. "No need to be a smart ass."

"Alright, Jace, go take your shower," he said with a nod.

I narrowed my eyes at him and stripped out of my clothes. "What does it look like I'm doing, Captain Obvious?"

"Giving me a show, maybe." He rolled onto his stomach and rested his head on folded arms. "All you'd have to do is spin around and bend over a little." He was poking fun at me and I couldn't help but entertain it.

I winked at him before turning around and giving a halfhearted shake. "Is that enough of a show for you?"

"Not sure. I might need another tonight. Go wash up before I make you," he said, lowering his voice until it sent a shiver down my spine. "Our food's getting lonely."

"Alright, alright. I'll stop playing," I said, the chill of the air starting to get to me. With a final wink, I crossed my arms in an attempt for warmth and headed towards the bathroom.

While Ruggiero was out grabbing food, he also rented a Volkswagen specifically to go to the Fusine Lakes. I guessed he'd known I'd say yes. Smart guy, he was.

He didn't push me to converse on the ninety-minute ride. Instead, he was more focused on enjoying the change of terrain just like I was. There were icy blankets of snow on the trees and grass.

It was still early enough in the afternoon that I wasn't bothered by the weather once we got there. Though the sun was guarded by a few clouds, it shone through, reflecting beautifully on the water's surface. My cashmere sweater, as well as Ruggiero's body heat radiating underneath his merino wool sweater and the blanket he was adamant about bringing along, would be enough to keep me warm.

When I stepped out of the car, I closed my eyes and inhaled deeply. The air was fresh, earthy, the smell of pine filling my nose. As Ruggiero had said, it was a good place to breathe. The built-up tension from the last few days slowly ebbed away.

I opened my eyes at the sound of Ruggiero's voice and the heat of his body telling me he was near. "This is the smaller of the two lakes—

Lago di Fusine Interiore." He spoke smoothly, sliding a supportive arm around my waist. With the other, his hand pointed to a group of boats along the shore. "We'll pick up our boat at that end."

We walked towards the shore hand in hand and I took in the scene before me. Visiting the Julian Alps or even Italy was something I never planned to do, but I was glad I was doing it. Ruggiero was showing me his world, inside and out, and it moved me in a way I never thought possible.

All this time, he'd been strong for me. I never thought to be strong for him, even when we were just messing around. I'd always thought of him as a mountain—solid, confident, calming. The last few months have shown me that a mountain could be moved and it could collapse. My mountain had collapsed and it was up to me to do the damage control.

As he helped me into the boat, my resolve settled. He needed to know how I felt.

Chapter 44

RUGGIERO

I couldn't take my eyes off her as I rowed us into the water. Wisps of hair blew softly around her face, her cheeks tinged with pink from the chill's kisses. Her eyes were wide with awe as we traveled further from the shore. For the first time in days, she looked like she was truly at peace.

The fresh air was doing her good.

I wished I could say the same. My stomach had been in knots since the minute we'd stepped off the train in Udine. Maybe she was at peace because she planned to run far, far away from me once we returned to Tennessee. I wouldn't blame her if she did. She'd never have to see me or my family ever again.

The last thing I wanted to do was trap her by telling her I loved her. She'd finally seen the boy that ran away from home all those years ago. I didn't want her to stay with me out of pity.

I forced my feelings down and checked to make sure we wouldn't hit anything on our way through the lake. "It's nice out here, isn't it?"

"It really is," she said. "This is a good idea. I feel like I can breathe, y'know?"

"I know," I lied. "It's nice."

"I have to tell you something."

The words cast a wave of nausea over me. I swallowed the urge as I met her gaze. I couldn't read her expression. "Tell me."

"I love you," she whispered. She shook her head and repeated herself, louder this time. "I love you, Rue."

My heart skipped a beat. "You what?"

She shuffled towards me carefully, cautious of the boat's balance. "I said I love you, you fool. I couldn't wait to tell you anymore. I've been an asshole. I wanted validation from your parents, from *a* parent, but I have it in you. I want you to know you have me, too. I want you and I'm tired of fighting it."

Why couldn't I say the words? I'd been dying to tell her and I had the chance, but the words were stuck in my throat.

She doesn't want you.

I wanted to believe her. I had to believe her. She hadn't given me a reason not to. And though I knew she was also overwhelmed with what had transpired, all I could think about was my mother's words and how Jace shut me out afterward.

She can't love you.

"Stop overthinking it, Ruggiero," she said. Her hand cupped my face and forced me to look at her. Tears shimmered in her eyes. "I can see you overthinking it. I love you. I'll say it a million times if you need me to."

The promise in her words freed mine. "I love you, too, *cara mia*, today and every day. I don't want you to leave. I'm scared you'll run away after the other night."

"I'm not running. I don't want to run. I love what we have, and I don't give a fuck what anyone else thinks."

"You heard what my mother said. I'm not sure I can be the man you need."

Her brow furrowed. "Dammit, Ruggiero, I don't care about her. You and our family is all that matters. We don't need her. *You* don't need her."

I couldn't hold back the tears that fell. "I need you, Jace. If you tell me you don't want this—"

Jace silenced me with a kiss, her hands on either side of my face, showing me what my mind refused to comprehend. My body—my heart—couldn't deny her. It all belonged to her. She washed away my doubt with her tongue stroking mine. She kissed me until I was putty in her arms.

She loves me.

As we parted for breath, she ran a hand through my hair and locked eyes with me again. "I want you—all of you. You're mine, Ruggiero de Fiore. I'm not letting you run from this either."

"You'll be stuck with me until we die," I warned, attempting a half-smile. "Are you sure, *cara mia?*"

"I've never been surer."

Chapter 45

❧

JACE

Ruggiero and I made the most of the rest of our time in Udine. After our afternoon at the Fusine Lakes, we had dinner at a restaurant not too far away. Even if things hadn't gone awry with his mother, I'd be giving birth by the end of summer. We had bigger fish to fry than worrying about the disagreeable woman.

Besides, things weren't all bad. Ruggiero's father invited us to breakfast the morning of our flight, wanting to say his final goodbyes.

"I'm so sorry for my wife," the older man said, squeezing my hand in earnest when Ruggiero excused himself to the bathroom. Just like his son, his demeanor was calming. "There's no excuse for her behavior. You will always have a place in my heart."

I shook my head with a smile. "It's not your fault, Pa. You're not responsible for your wife's behavior. Believe it or not, we still had a good time."

"That's what matters then, right?" He winked. "I always tell Ruggiero *se sono rose, fioriranno*. If they're roses, they'll bloom. You two, *mia figlia*, are blooming before my eyes. Your love is radiating."

288

My cheeks warmed. "Are we really that obvious?" I asked with a laugh.

"Yes, but there's nothing wrong with that. I'm happy he's found you. You're good for him."

"He's good for me, too," I said, returning my hand to my lap.

"Who's good for you?" Ruggiero pulled out his chair, sat down, and leaned over to give me a quick kiss on the cheek.

"You," his father said. "We were talking about you."

Ruggiero scooted the chair in a few more times until he was satisfied with his seating position. "Ah, *sì certo.*" Under the table, his hand found my thigh. "I love you, too, *cara mia.*"

After our meal, his father saw us off to the airport with promises to call. I knew one thing for sure as we left Udine. Despite what happened, we had the love and support of his father. It was made apparent after we texted a copy of the ultrasound print to our friends and family this morning as a subtle announcement of my pregnancy. Our phones had quickly flooded with congratulatory messages.

We were able to leave the country with our hearts full and our minds open, ready—albeit scared—to start our new life together. Unlike our journey to Italy, Ruggiero slept peacefully on our way back when he wasn't deep in one of his books. I slept as the baby allowed.

Things only got better for us as time passed. Along with working and spending time with my family, I added psychiatry, therapy, and OB appointments to my routine. Ruggiero remained his hardworking, flirty self, but moved with a lightness that hadn't existed. During one of our OB visits, we learned we were having a baby girl.

Now that Ruggiero and I were loud and proud about our love, I saw Lucky a lot more than I ever thought I would. Turns out, they really were best friends. Even worse, Jackson was starting to hang out with them.

Before I knew it, I was six months pregnant and preparing to move into Ruggiero's house once my lease ended at the end of the month. The majority of my belongings were crammed in boxes, and a great deal of my furniture sat in the bed of Ruggiero's trunk, waiting to be dropped off for donation. All we had left to deal with was the kitchenware and my bedroom.

"*Dio mio*, what can I do to keep you off of the floor?"

I looked up at Ruggiero from where I kneeled beside the bed. "My things aren't going to pack themselves, Rue."

"Tsk, tsk," he said, shaking his head. "The OB *and* your therapist prescribed rest."

"Blah, blah, blah," I said. "I don't remember them telling me activity was bad."

He smirked and crossed his arms. "Both can be true, *cara mia*. It doesn't matter. You have to get up anyway because we promised to have dinner at your mother's."

I groaned and threw one more pair of shoes in the box I was working on. "Is it almost seven already?"

"Sure is. Might be a good idea to get dressed and freshen up," he advised. He walked into the room and extended a hand.

With the way my back was feeling, I didn't hesitate to let him help me up. "We don't really have to go. There's always next time."

"Nice try." He chuckled, steering me towards the bathroom. "Do you need me to undress you, too? You know I love an excuse to get my hands on you."

"Considering we'll never leave if I let you have your way, I'd better dress myself." He hadn't become any less attracted to me as my body adjusted to make room for the baby. If anything, he'd become more attracted to me, matching my increased libido with his own.

"I think you're right, *cara mia*." He slid his hand down to my ass and squeezed. "I don't think I'd want to stop."

Electricity danced along my skin as he hardened behind me. "I don't think I'd be able to either. I love you too much."

"I know. Me too." He winked and shut himself out of the bathroom.

We were late to dinner, but it wasn't my fault. Though Ruggiero initially played as the responsible party, he was also the scoundrel that insisted on eating me out to ease my mind. His reasoning was bullshit, but I enjoyed it all the same. The downside was that it was half past seven and we'd promised to be on time.

"She's going to be pissed," I muttered, leaning my head against the window as we pulled into my mom's neighborhood. "She never wants to eat before everyone arrives."

His left hand remained on the steering wheel while the other squeezed my thigh. "Lighten up. I've already eased your mind, remember? You should reward me later for thinking ahead."

"You're ridiculous." I grinned.

"What're all these cars?"

I glanced ahead to see my mom's driveway littered with an assortment of cars. I only recognized hers, Jackson's, and my dad's. "I'm not sure."

"Seems like your mom forgot she was throwing a party when she invited us to dinner." He parked in an open spot along the street and then helped me out of the car. "Might as well see what's going on, huh?"

I sighed, ready to get this over with. The only things on my agenda were eating and going to bed at the end of the night. "I guess so."

Ruggiero guided me up the driveway, a stupid smirk on his face. Meanwhile, I searched—to no avail—for a reason why it looked like my mom invited half of the neighborhood to her house.

"This isn't weird to you at all?" I asked, my steps slowing as we neared the front door. It wasn't often that my mom's house was packed with people.

"I mean, we're not walking into a haunted house nor a crime scene. It's not too weird." He pressed a kiss to my forehead and rang the doorbell.

When the door opened, it wasn't my mom behind it. Instead, it was none other than Jackson and Lucky. I groaned, eyeing the two of them. "What the fuck is going on?"

Chapter 46

RUGGIERO

"What the fuck is going on?" Jace's bewilderment was almost reason enough for me to spoil the surprise. I didn't tell her that the cars she didn't recognize belonged to my friends, nor that there was a house full of people waiting on us. I bit back a knowing grin as she stared at the pair with wide eyes.

"What are you two doing together?" she asked, looking to and from Jackson and Lucky. "And where the hell is everyone else?"

"Wow, Jacey, hello to you, too." Jackson elbowed Lucky in the ribs with a laugh. "Pregnancy hormones, am I right?"

"Jackson," I warned. "Please, don't poke the bear."

She narrowed her eyes at her brother. "Still a douche, I see."

I gave Lucky a hug as Jace pushed herself into the house. "Can't believe I'm going to be an uncle soon," Lucky sniffled dramatically. "You'll name them after me, right?"

"In your dreams, Lucky."

I entered the house just in time to see Jace approach the living room and freeze at the threshold. Our friends and family stood together in front of the couch with smiles on their faces. I joined Jace and hugged her from behind, my hands cradling her stomach as I peered over her shoulder at our loved ones. "Surprise, *cara mia*," I whispered. "Happy baby shower."

She turned to face me, the iciness in her blue eyes melting away. "This is great, Rue. I should go say hello to people then, shouldn't I?"

"We'll do it together," I promised, kissing her forehead. "First, I need to introduce you to my pain-in-the-asses. They're my only form of family here in the states."

Jace nodded and followed me across the room. She eyed Jamie and Chris cautiously.

"Gentlemen, please meet Jace, my lover and baby mama."

Jace playfully rolled her eyes at me and smiled at the men. "Hi, I'm Ruggiero's baby mama, Jace. I've heard a lot about you guys."

"Trust, we've heard about you, too," Jamie said. "I'm glad. You seem like a great person to miss poker night for."

"It was one time, J. I didn't even miss it, I was just late."

Chris crossed his arms and shook his head with a grin. "Just know that we'll never forget it." He turned his attention to Jace. "It's so nice to meet you. In all my years of knowing him, I've never seen this guy smile so much."

"Leave the lovebirds alone." Lucky joined the group, patting my shoulder. "Or at least shit on them while opening your wallets. Diapers are expensive."

"He's right," Jace agreed. She was fully relaxed now, her confusion replaced with excitement. "Prepare yourself, boys. We'll need a lot of them."

Next, we headed toward Jace's relatives who were huddled together in the other room. Her parents greeted us with hugs and well-wishes. Even her stepmother, Leah, hugged me just as tight as she hugged Jace and told me she loved me. Once hugs were out of the way, her mom forced everyone to gather into the dining room and served us lasagna. Jackson took the open seat next to us with his usual goofy smile on his face.

"When little Jace grows up and asks how you guys got together, just know I'm taking the credit," Jackson said. "We'll pretend that the Halloween party was my best matchmaking idea yet."

As the night progressed, our family reaffirmed the promise that we belonged with them, that we had a home with them. From this moment on, I knew that I'd never have to worry about being loved. I had a second set of parents, a brother, and a group of friends that only wanted the best for me in addition to my father. I had a partner willing to weather storms with me. And in just three months, Jace and I would meet our daughter.

I felt Jace's joy in my bones as we opened gifts and she held up the various sets of baby clothing, diapers, and pacifiers. With the way her black dress hugged her curves and rounded belly, my cock felt it, too. The only thing that kept my lust at bay was the fact that the spotlight was on us and I didn't want to flash everyone with a hard-on. This was a PG event, after all, and pictures were constantly being taken.

By the end of the night, Jace and I had so many gifts that we chose to leave most of them at her mom's house until I emptied out my truck. With the move, we didn't have a lot of space to put much of anything, and likely wouldn't until after the baby was born. Merging households within months of Jace's due date was a little reckless, but when hadn't we been reckless during the past eight months?

If it weren't for our recklessness, we might've never fallen in love. I wouldn't change anything about how we came to be. She accepted me as I was, and all she asked for was love in return.

"You okay, Rue?" Jace asked, snuggling closer to me on the couch as everyone winded down to watch a movie. Her hands absentmindedly rested on her stomach.

"I'm okay, *cara mia*," I promised. I kissed her forehead and placed a hand on top of hers. "I'm just thinking about you and the future. Oh, and how much I love you."

"I love you, too," she said, kissing my cheek. "We're going to be fine."

"I know."

Like my father always said, *se sono rose, fioriranno.*

What we had were roses. Through any storm, they'd bloom as long as we watered them.

Epilogue

❦

JACE

FOUR YEARS LATER

"Jace, honey, stop doting on her and get ready for your date," my mom exclaimed. She rushed toward me, arms wide, ready to take Giulia.

I swept to the side quickly, evading her. Giulia clapped her little hands and giggled. "Nana is funny, isn't she?" I said, rubbing my nose against Giulia's.

For the longest time, I was scared to have a daughter due to fear that she'd be like me. And yet… Giulia was born with my eyes, nose, and wavy blonde hair. And she was perfect.

"Mommy has to go, pumpkin." I held her close to me and she nuzzled her face in my neck. "Dada and I'll be back in a few hours."

She cheesed, flashing all of her teeth. "Okay, mommy," she said. She hugged me one last time before I put her down. "Nana, it's time to watch the movie."

"Let's go, sugar." My mom enthusiastically grabbed Giulia's hand and started toward the living room, where *Rio* and bowls of popcorn were waiting for them. She looked at me. "And you, ma'am, are about to make the two of you late."

On cue, Ruggiero came down the stairs, fully dressed and ready to go. At thirty-four, he was sinfully handsome. The sight of him still took my breath away. He leaned against the staircase post, crossing his arms together, his dress shirt tastefully fitting his biceps.

Licking his lips, Ruggiero teased, "Are you going to stare at me or are you going to get ready?"

I rolled my eyes playfully. "Since you and my mom are so adamant, I guess I'm getting ready." I brushed past him on the stairs, making sure to caress his arm.

Ruggiero caught my wrist and pulled me back down to meet him. Body close to mine, he pressed a kiss to my lips. As I stumbled to get closer to him, my cheeks warmed. "Go get ready, *amore mio*," he said, breaking the kiss. "Or else we might not make it."

Once in his truck and on the way to the restaurant, Ruggiero gave me a mischievous grin, turning down Ginuwine's "Differences."

"What's up, Rue?" I asked, side-eyeing him.

He looked back to the road. "We're not late. Reservation is at eight, not seven-thirty."

I shook my head, laughing. "You sly dog. It's almost like you knew I'd run late."

"I also know how much joy you get from spending time with our daughter." Ruggiero placed a hand on my thigh, squeezing lightly. "She has both of us wrapped around her finger."

It was an understatement to say that we spoiled Giulia. While we'd worked hard to strengthen our relationship despite our internal battles, Giulia's birth had strengthened us in ways we never imagined. She was here because of us, because of our love, and we wanted her to grow up with nothing but love for herself and the world around her.

We were lucky enough to have Cleo around for the first two years of Giulia's life. At her passing, we were blessed to inherit Cleo's home, priceless keepsakes, and timeless photos of her holding Guilia.

"She deserves it," I told him, giving him a cheerful smile.

He kept his eyes on the road and inched his hand higher. "You deserve her," he said. "Excited to eat?"

"I'm sure it doesn't seem like it, but yeah. Always." I'd been primarily consumed with Giulia, but I'd never turn down good food and alone time with Ruggiero. I placed my hand on top of his, intertwining and splaying our fingers. "Surprised you can't hear my stomach grumbling," I teased. "The girl steals all the food off my plate."

"Well, don't you worry. I'll make sure you're fed tonight," he said, his tone promising.

I didn't miss the double entendre. Food wasn't the only thing I'd be eating tonight. Little did he know, I'd be doing a lot more than that.

Following dinner, I walked closely behind Ruggiero as he slid the key in the door to our hotel room for the night, smiling to myself as I thought of the secret I held. Before we left the house, I'd made sure to slide a few silk ties in my purse.

Over the past few years, Ruggiero and I had been exploring each other in every way possible. I had learned about more than a few of his kinks and I was finally ready to initiate some kink play on my own.

"So, what's the plan, Rue?" I asked, not yet ready to reveal my intentions. "Did you rent this room just so we'd have some time to ourselves or because you intend to have a marathon in bed?"

"I think both sounds good," he said, starting to unbutton his shirt. "I dropped some toys off earlier."

Even after four years together, we still fucked with the libido of horny teenagers.

I hummed appreciatively. "I hope you brought some of your own, too." My plans partially hinged on whether or not he'd included the toys meant specifically for his pleasure. Even if he hadn't, I had fingers and lube of my own.

The playful sparkle in his eyes confirmed that, yes, he had thought of himself, too. "What do you plan to do with them?"

"Personally, I plan to pleasure you," I said, pulling the ties from my purse. "At your expense, of course."

"Is it truly at my expense if I like it?" he teased. He dropped his shirt to the floor, exposing himself to me.

How the hell did he still look this good?

"I'll be the judge of that, Rue. Now, if you don't have any other ideas, I'd advise you to finish undressing and lay on the bed." I kicked my heels off and stripped off my dress.

"Fuck," he said with a groan. "I love when you take control."

"I know you do," I murmured.

His eyes were wide with lust as he removed the rest of his clothes. We hadn't even been in this room for ten minutes and his dick was already straining against his underwear. Unfortunately for him, I wouldn't be removing mine until I had him right where I wanted him.

It all depended on how long it took him to reach his first orgasm with his wrists tied to the headboard and my mouth full of him.

Afterword

If you're reading this, it's because you've finished Jace and Ruggiero's love story. It means the world to me that I was able to share their story with you. I can't thank you enough for believing in me, for believing in *them* enough to see it through.

Look out for future appearances in the pending sequel featuring Ruggiero's best friend, Lucky.

If you enjoyed witnessing Jace and Ruggiero's romance unfold as much as I enjoyed writing it, please consider leaving a review on Amazon, Goodreads, or another platform of your choosing. Reviews are monumental in gaining recognition as an indie author, as well as helping readers find books that itch that certain scratch.

Thank you again for reading *The Hateful Heavy Heart.* I hope it scratched that itch for you. And if not, hopefully your next read will. Happy reading!

With love,

L.M. Golder

About the Author

L.M. Golder is a twenty-something-year-old living in the good ol' Midwest with her loving husband and her two cats.

When she isn't writing, she can be found reading romance, fantasy, and historical fiction as well as watching her favorite shows on Netflix. If she's doing none of those things, she's probably buying more books to add to her ever-growing list of physical to-be-reads.

You can connect with me on:

🌐 https://www.instagram.com/lmgolderauthor

🔗 https://www.amazon.com/author/lmgolder